"Jamie Carie takes readers on a passionate, unique, unforgettable adventure. The characters will steal your heart and keep you awake nights!"
—Laura Frantz, author of *The Colonel's Lady*

"An irresistible regency chase that will tease, taunt, and steal your heart."
—Julie Lessman, award-winning author of The Daughters of Boston and Winds of Change series

"Jamie Carie captured my attention on page one. Soon she also had a strong hold on my heart. And she didn't let go even when I finished the last page. I can't wait for the next book in the series."
—Lena Nelson Dooley, author of *Maggie's Journey* and *Mary's Blessing* in the McKenna's Daughters series as well as the Will Rogers Award winning *Love Finds You in Golden, New Mexico*

"Get lost in Ireland in this rollicking adventure with a brave, headstrong heroine and a relentless yet honorable duke determined to save her from a dangerous quest. With rich characterization and an intriguing plot, Jamie Carie's *The Guardian Duke* will leave you breathless for the next installment!"
—Susan May Warren, award-winning, best-selling author of *Baroness*

"I could hardly wait to read the second novel in the Forgotten Castles series, an *The Forgiven Du* was just as thrilling as the first book. *The Guardian Duke* r with Gabriel and Alexandria and long for

and *The Forgiven Duke* made me happy and anxious by turns, on the edge of my seat to see what would happen next. The characters are so real to me! With all its suspense, mystery, and romance, *The Forgiven Duke* has left me holding my breath, waiting for the third book, to see how Gabriel and Alexandria's story ends."

—Melanie Dickerson, author of *The Merchant's Daughter*

A Duke's Promise

OTHER NOVELS BY JAMIE CARIE

The Guardian Duke (Forgotten Castles Book 1)
The Forgotten Duke (Forgotten Castles Book 2)
Pirate of My Heart
The Snowflake
Angel's Den
Love's First Light
Wind Dancer
The Duchess and the Dragon
Snow Angel

Jamie Carie

a Forgotten Castles novel

A Duke's Promise

PUBLISHING GROUP

Nashville, Tennessee

Published by B&H Publishing Group,
Nashville, Tennessee

Dewey Decimal Classification: F
Subject Heading: LOVE STORIES \ MYSTERY FICTION \
FAITH—FICTION

Information in the scientific note at the book's end
is provided by Leo Kristjánsson.

1 2 3 4 5 6 7 8 • 16 15 14 13 12

To my son Nicholas,

How to describe the joy you bring into my life? My baby (okay, okay, I'll stop calling you that!). You will be thirteen this year, and I want to stop time and just keep you at this wonderful stage. You bring so much light and laughter to our lives. God blessed you with the gift of balance—someone smart, intuitive, witty, and with good looks! And then there is your love for God. I sometimes feel I've had the least time with you since becoming published, but God has stepped in and filled your heart with a longing and love for Him, for which I am deeply thankful. Stay like that and everything else will fall into place.

I'm so happy God gave you to me!

Acknowledgments

This series would not have been possible without the help of my two Julies—Julie Gwinn at B&H Publishing and my editor, Julee Schwarzburg. Your kindness, patience, and dedication to a work of this scope has blessed me enormously and enabled me to do the best job I could. I know you join my prayer that many will be blessed by Gabriel and Alexandria's story.

An enormous thank-you and hug to Diana Lawrence, art director at B&H, for these stunning covers. You always capture the essence of my stories so well!

And to Leo Kristjánsson, a geophysicist at the University of Iceland, Reykjavík, Iceland, and an expert on Icelandic crystal. Thank you for your time and endless patience explaining the properties of Iceland spar to someone who is fascinated by physics but only has a small understanding of it. Perhaps one day I'll get to see those Icelandic pools of azure and the Helgustadir quarry. Until then, it has been my privilege to speak with you on these subjects.

Chapter One

London, England—June 1819

The silken curtains around the bed fluttered from the summer breeze that blew through the open windows of the duke's bedchamber on number 31 St. James Square. Candlelight flickered across the room, a place she had only passed by while living here with him, peeking inside, wondering at the depths of his private chambers. The light of the candles made wavy shadows against the creamy paneled walls and Alexandria, the new Duchess of St. Easton, tried to ignore Clarissa's incessant chatter as the maid helped her out of layer after layer of her wedding costume.

Alex tried to look anywhere but at the bed, and yet she couldn't tear her gaze from it—the royal blue counterpane trimmed in gold, the massive four posts of carved wood draped with dark curtains, the piles of pillows. She swallowed against the knot in her throat and turned, lifting her arms and following the nudges of the maid.

"Great heavens, Your Grace, sit down before you faint. You're as white as a ghost, you are."

Alex obeyed, relieved to sit and rest her wobbly knees. She stared in the mirror at her reflection and watched as Clarissa took out the spiderweb-thin, diamond tiara from her hair, which Gabriel's mother had given her as a wedding gift, and brushed out Alex's long, dark hair. A suspended feeling of dread and terror surrounded her.

He would come in at any moment.

He would come in and find out about everything.

The fact that she wasn't exactly sure what it was he would find didn't help at all.

Clarissa clucked and shook her head as she plucked at the delicate chemise, her last article of clothing. "I don't know why they let a bride wear white on a night like this. It only makes it worse if there's any bleeding. Saints a mercy, somebody should think of dark bedding and clothing on a night like this."

"Blood?" Alex whipped her face around toward Clarissa's animated frown. "Does one always bleed?"

Clarissa patted her shoulder with a reassuring smile. "Only the first time, Your Grace, and some girls don't bleed much even then. Don't you be frettin' now. I shouldn't have said anything seein' how nervous you are, but since I did," she shook her head in an ominous way, "just know some bleedin' is normal. It won't last long."

Had she bled before? With John that night in Iceland when he had, well, might have violated her body while she was drugged from the cup of tea he had given her? Just thinking back to the details of that night made her stomach fold inside itself and a wave of nausea flooded her throat. Alex closed her eyes and tried to remember as she had so many times since that fateful evening. She didn't remember any blood. Not on the bed or on her clothing, but she'd been so shocked, so hurt and confused that she hadn't really looked either. There may have been a little and she just hadn't seen it.

Father in heaven, help me get through this!

The sound of the door opening made her start. She turned, saw him—saw his beautiful, fierce, and beloved face—which made her heart hammer like the pounding of a horse at full gallop. Clarissa bowed, quiet for once, and crept away. Alex stood but took a step back until the backs of her knees pressed against the bench at the dressing table. She tried for a wobbly smile and failed.

Gabriel Ravenwood, the Duke of St. Easton, and now her husband, stepped out from the shadows of the room and walked toward her. Instinctively Alex reared back, her gaze locked with his. Gabriel continued toward her and when close enough gave her that smile that always made her knees turn to mush. One side of his mouth quirked up a little higher than the other, as if he knew his effect on her, his eyes intense with depths of emerald green. His steps held the stealthy grace of the animal people often compared him to—the panther. Dark, lethal, green-eyed enchantment.

She held her breath. Excitement and terror warred within her as he came right up to her and stopped, so close she could see the dark, shadowy beard that had grown across his face over the course of the day and the thick, black eyelashes that were almost too pretty on a man.

"You're not frightened, are you?" His hand came up to lift her chin so she had to look into his eyes for him to see the truth or lie in her answer.

"No." A bad lie, but she hoped he hadn't been able to hear the squeak in her voice.

His hand moved from her chin to trace along the curve of her jaw with a mere brush of his fingertips. "I like your hair this way," he murmured, taking another step closer, his fingers coursing through her hair, the weight of his hand making her head fall back, her throat exposed. "Do you have any idea how beautiful you are, Alexandria?"

She closed her eyes and shook her head, turning away. How could she be beautiful after what John had done to her? And not telling Gabriel before they married that she was quite possibly not a virgin? There wasn't anything beautiful about that.

But he didn't know all of that yet. She stood beneath his exploring fingertips on her face, trembling like a leaf about to give way and drop to the ground. With one forefinger he traced the arcs of her eyebrows, her cheeks, and then the curve of her mouth. She opened her lips to let out the rush of breath. Her head fell back in submission to his touch as his lips finally came down on hers.

Her arms crept up to wrap around his wide shoulders. Love for him, an intermingling of welling emotions, rose to her throat in an aching pulse, pushing aside her dread and fear. She wanted to laugh and weep at the same time, but mostly she wanted to give him everything, all of her.

SHE WAS FINALLY HIS.

Gabriel immersed himself in the feel of her—her petal-soft skin, her quivering lips, her lashes against his face. With his hearing gone, he reached internally for her reactions, reading vibrations from her throat and the thudding of her heart pressed against his chest. She didn't seem afraid now, not like when he'd walked into the room and seen her pale face. No, now she seemed pliant and eager to be in his arms.

When the back of her legs came up against the feather mattress, he leaned over her, kissing her more deeply, bending her back toward the blue counterpane, the heavy folds of the bed curtains creating a secret space of flickering twilight. She blinked, opened her eyes as he lifted her and laid her on the blue silken surface. Standing, he saw the questions return to her eyes.

He said nothing. There was no need for words with Alexandria much of the time. They communicated with a look, a touch, their own special body language of signs and signals and long-locked gazes. It had started with letters . . . and become so much more.

Dear God, I love her.

She scrambled underneath the counterpane and he blew out the bedside candle, flooding the room with darkness. He slid in beside her. "Come here, Alexandria."

Without sound and now little sight, the feel of her in his arms roared through him, making her seem soul-deep close to him. Fragile . . . sweet, delicate, woman . . . wife. His hands roamed over her body, branding her and making her his in truth. She tensed and, he thought, cried out, whimpering against his shoulder. He held her close, running his hand over her hair and murmuring words of comfort. He hoped the worst was over.

Afterward, he pulled her back against his stomach and sighed deeply into her hair. Within moments, a deep lethargy took over and he fell asleep.

Chapter Two

*A*lexandria? Are you crying?" Gabriel blinked awake, feeling her body shaking next to his. He sat up and turned her shoulder to search her face, the pale streaks of dawn giving enough light to make out the tear tracks on her cheeks.

She looked away, wiping at her cheeks with the backs of her hands. She shook her head as if denying it, the ivory of her skin turning rosy.

"What is it? Are you hurt?" Gabriel flung back the covers. He saw the blood, more than he'd imagined might happen on a wedding night, and bit off a dark word. "Why didn't you tell me? Are you in pain?"

She reached for the covers and pulled them to her chin, sitting up and shaking her head at him again. "I'm fine."

But she didn't seem fine. She looked like he'd done something horrible to her. Despair and some fear made him frantic. Springing from the bed he hurried to the dressing room, pulled on a dressing robe, and opened the door where his valet slept. "George, get Her Grace a hot bath in here right away. And send in her maid."

George sat up and nodded, scurrying to do his bidding.

Gabriel shut the door and padded back to where his wife sat, wide-eyed and so pale in the massive bed. He took a long breath, came around to her side of the bed, and sat beside her, taking up her hand. He leaned his head over her hand, closed his eyes, and pressed his lips against her knuckles. "I'm sorry. I didn't know it was so bad for you. Why didn't you tell me?"

He opened his eyes to read her answer, his brows rising, pleading with her to talk to him. Dismay and panic rose within him as her eyes filled with tears again, overflowing and dropping one after another down her cheeks. "Alexandria, come here." He took her into his arms, her shoulders shaking with the pent-up sobs. "It'll be better next time. I promise. I should have prepared you more . . . I didn't know you would bleed so much, but I don't think anything is wrong. We'll get you a hot bath and then call the doctor, all right? You'll feel better soon, I promise."

She only cried harder.

Gabriel pulled her away from him and searched her eyes. This was not usually the way she would respond and it made him afraid. The Alexandria he knew would brush it off and trust that it would be better the next time. But she was near hysterics. "Talk to me. Are you afraid something is wrong with you? Is it the amount of blood?"

She shook her head, then tilted it to one side and looked at him with such sadness that it wrenched his heart. She started to talk and then stopped.

Curse this deafness that came and went and left him reeling with the constant change. He wanted his wife to be able to talk to him like any wife would speak to her husband. He rose, then walked over to his desk and took up the writing paper and quill. He held the paper out, sat beside her with the ink pot, and nodded toward the quill. "Tell me."

She took a deep breath and took the delicate quill in her hand. She dipped it into the black ink and began to write in that familiar handwriting that had struck him from the first moment he had seen it in the opera house where he'd first lost his hearing. It was that handwriting that had stayed in his mind while his head exploded, that appearance of her signature he'd looked so forward to seeing arrive in the post in the months following while he struggled with this affliction God or fate had dealt him. And now, as he watched the way she wrote with quick, slashing curves to her letters, a tendril of dread filled him. Something was wrong. More than a young woman losing her virginity. Something was very wrong.

Clarissa scratched at the door along with two footmen carrying a large metal bathing tub. They set it up behind an ornamental screen where Gabriel often bathed, filled it with buckets of water, the steam rising in the air behind the screen, and bowed from the room.

"Clarissa, fetch Her Grace clothing for the day. Something loose and comfortable. We will be putting off our travel to France for a day or two. Tell the housekeeper we shall be at home all day and she can talk to Alexandria this afternoon about any meals and delaying the trip. In the meantime, call Dr. Bentley and—"

"No." Alexandria put a hand on his arm and shook her head. "I don't need a doctor."

Gabriel frowned at her, studying the entreaty in her eyes. Was she afraid to let the family doctor examine her? Bentley knew every member of the St. Easton family intimately. It was something she would have to get accustomed to, especially if she became pregnant. He meant for her to have the greatest care imaginable while she was carrying his child. But the pleading in her eyes made him sigh. "Very well. We can always call him later if the need arises."

He motioned to the maid. "After the bath is poured and you have delivered Her Grace's clothing, see that we aren't disturbed unless I ring."

"Yes, Your Grace." Clarissa bowed from the room, her usual effervescent personality subdued.

Gabriel paced the room as the bath was readied and Alexandria wrote. Finally they were left alone.

He sat back down beside her and gazed into her puffy eyes, leaning forward to kiss her lightly on her lips. He paused there, telling her with gentle movements how precious she was to him. He could feel her tears slip between their cheeks. Would she ever stop weeping? What was he to do with such silent grief?

He lifted his head and gave her what he hoped was an encouraging and sympathetic smile. She looked down at the speaking book and then, with a rattled breath, held it out. Gabriel hated the book in this moment. Ever since he lost his hearing, he was forced to use it when having more than a brief conversation. What he wouldn't give right now to hear her voice for the first time and let her confide in him instead of this carefully thought-out written text.

He shook off the despair and stared at the words. *It isn't the blood. Well, it is, but not for the reasons you think. I am greatly relieved to have bled and can't seem to stop crying about it. I'm also feeling wretched that I've hidden this from you.*

His head came up. "Hidden something from me?"

She bit her bottom lip and nodded through the tears.

You see, when I told John that I wouldn't marry him because I didn't love him and thought I might be in love with you, he panicked and did a horrible thing. He put something in a cup of tea that made me very relaxed and sleepy. When I woke in the morning, he was there in the bed, with me, without any clothing on.

Gabriel swallowed hard, shock and rage making his skin flush with heat.

I thought . . . we both thought he had taken my virginity. He said I had to marry him because I might be with child and I couldn't make our child illegitimate. He said no man would want me now, and I thought of you and thought he was right. I had no choice. But in Reykjavik when he was arranging the ceremony, I confronted him and told him that even if I was with child, I couldn't marry him. That's when he locked me in the attic of the blacksmith shop. And then you rescued me, but afterward, you left me and when I didn't see you, you avoided me and wouldn't talk to me. I wanted to tell you but I was so afraid.

For all of those first weeks here in London, I thought I might be carrying John's baby, and I didn't know how you would react to that. When you asked to marry me, I froze. I wanted to say yes because I do love you and my greatest desire was to be your wife, but I couldn't without telling you what happened. I dreaded you knowing that I might not be a virgin. I couldn't bear the thought that you might not want me any longer. Then when you said we could marry and have a honeymoon looking for my parents in Italy—I knew I had to risk it. So finding out that I truly was a virgin is so relieving, but I can't bear to keep all of this from you any longer. I'm sorry.

Gabriel's breath grew shallow as he digested her words like stones settling in his heart. She'd lied to him. She'd deceived him. Married him for a chance to keep looking for her parents. Did he even know her?

He looked at her and narrowed his eyes, the pressure behind them stinging with tears of betrayal.

"I thought you knew me, Alexandria. How could you not tell me? Not trust me? If you found yourself with child, were you planning to foist John's child on me without my knowledge?"

When she started to speak, he put up his hand and shook his head. "Have your bath. I find myself in sudden need of some fresh air."

ALEX CRIED WHILE SHE BATHED. She cried while she dressed, cried while she tried to choke down some of the hot chocolate they'd brought her, and cried while she stared out the window, wondering where Gabriel had gone and if he would ever come back.

I have ruined everything.

The thought wouldn't stop its torturous circling. She prayed, begging God to send him back to her, prayed his heart would soften toward her and he would forgive her for not telling him. She prayed for help to know what to do next. And most of all, prayed her marriage wasn't ruined forever. After three hours of wallowing in a devastated state, she stared at her tear-splotched face and red-ringed eyes in the mirror of her dressing table. Enough was enough.

She faced the fact that somewhere along the way, she had lost herself, the old Alex who was plucky and determined, bright and optimistic. Sometime along this journey she had let the fierce desire to find her missing parents change the way she thought and behaved, and it wasn't right. Until she got back to her real self, the person God created her to be, nothing would go well. It was time to speak the truth, trust God to work everything for her good, and step out into her life with faith, humility, and courage. No more feeling sorry for herself. She was going to find her husband.

With that thought predominant in her mind, she rang for Clarissa. The woman had deep worry lines between her brows as she entered the room, but Alex ignored it. "Clarissa, see that this room is tidied up, the bedding changed, the bath taken away. Have His Grace's valet come in and take care of all this strewn clothing, but first help me into my riding habit. I'll not mope around in dishabille a moment longer."

"That's the spirit." Her maid gave her an approving nod.

"Do you happen to know where His Grace has gone?" Alex knew the house gossip must have been in high form this morning, and Clarissa had a special knack for finding out what was happening and filling Alex in on every little morsel, from the scullery maid's sweet tooth to her own husband's actions and whereabouts.

"Hanson said he left on foot. Speculation is that he went to his sword master and is working out his angst with swordplay as he often does, or just taking a long walk. Of course, a long walk could take him anywhere, and with three hours gone"—she shrugged—"he might have gone to White's or one of his clubs, Your Grace. Though he hasn't gone there much of late, not since his hearing problems."

Alex was tired of being called "Your Grace" already. "Clarissa, when we're in private, you might just call me Lady Alex like you always have."

Clarissa frowned. "Heaven help us, that wouldn't be proper at all, and besides, I won't remember when to switch back and forth. Too confusing, Your Grace."

Alex sighed. "Very well. I suppose I will just have to get used to it. Now, come and help me into this riding costume. And then ring for Hanson to have the carriage brought around."

She wished she could ask Gabriel's sister to accompany her, but Jane had moved back into her own house, the need for a chaperone no longer necessary and saying it was time to take up her own life again. Alex had promised to write to her as much as she could on their honeymoon, but she would have to be careful not to divulge too much about what they were really doing. She couldn't risk the prince regent finding out they weren't really going to stay weeks in Paris, but instead were headed to Italy.

"Suck in a little more, Your Grace. This riding costume is a mite tighter up top than the dark blue."

Alex took a deep breath and then let out all the air she could and sucked in her stomach. A pretty shade of green with swansdown trimming the collar and cuffs, this riding habit had a wide neckline and with the benefit of the corset made a fetching décolleté. No sense going after Gabriel in something dowdy. It was time to remind him that she was his wife and that despite her horrible mistake—she loved him. She reached for the black hat with green ribbons and ostrich feathers while Clarissa fussed with pinning it on at just the right angle.

"There, you look lovely, Your Grace."

"Thank you, Clarissa. Pray my mission is successful."

"That I will." Clarissa eyed her. "Judge his mood now. Some folks take a while to think things through and cool down. Those types can't work things out right away."

Alex thought about that. She supposed she was the direct sort who wanted to talk about it and resolve things quickly. Of course, she was also the burying sort when it came to deep disappointments, like with her parents.

She refused to let herself be angry with them, but when she really stopped and thought about how she had grown up alone, well, there was something deep down that wasn't good at all. Someday would her anger surge up and explode like the volcanoes she'd seen in Iceland? And what of Gabriel? What would they think of her marriage and husband?

"That's good advice, Clarissa. I will tread carefully and pray the Holy Spirit will guide me in what to say and when."

Her maid nodded her approval and Alex turned to leave the duke's bedchamber. She stopped at the door, considering. "Clarissa, one more thing. Have some of my things moved in here, the things I use daily. Scatter them about if you know what I mean. I don't intend to use my bedchamber any longer."

A slow smile spread across her maid's broad face. "Yes, Your Grace. An excellent notion."

Alex smiled back. Now to find her angry husband.

Chapter Three

The heat from the oven smelled like yeast and cinnamon. A childhood pleasure, the comfort of dough and sugar and melting sweetness. Gabriel sat in the back corner of the always crowded inn's common room and inhaled the treat for which the Goose and Gridiron was famous. He hadn't indulged in this particular treat for some time, but upon charging from his bedchamber and the tearful face of his new wife, he had found himself not knowing where to go.

The usual haunts of his sword master's establishment or one of the opera houses he frequented had entered his mind, but he turned away from them as too predictable. He needed to be alone . . . to think, to let the anger that hovered frighteningly close to the side of rage cool down a few degrees before he did or said something he would regret forever. And so he found himself on Fleet Street and lured by the yeasty smells of fresh sweets from the oven.

He sipped hot tea and took a long inhale of the heavenly smelling air. If only life could be so sweet. But no, life's sweets were occasional cushions against the sharpness. Like now.

When he questioned everything. When he wasn't sure who, exactly, he had married.

He ate the rest of the doughy goodness and downed his tea in a big gulp. The crowd around him, in chairs around tables, playing cards or lounging, reading, two young men passing a pennywhistle back and forth and laughing, made clear the fact that life was sailing along despite his shock. If he looked at the whistle, humble instrument that it was, he could just make out notes of yellow scattering through the air like dandelion puff around the men. But even that didn't take the sting from his heart. He began to sort through emotion and logic with a fine poker, finding truth, God help him, and wisdom in the midst of the heartache.

He thought back to Lord John Lemon first. Gabriel had never liked the man, but he hadn't imagined John capable of doing what Alexandria claimed. To drug her? Trick her into thinking he'd taken her virginity and then threatening her with an illegitimate child as means to secure her hand in marriage? He still could hardly believe it. But why would Alexandria tell him if it wasn't true? She *had* been a virgin and hadn't had to explain anything if she didn't want to. There was no reason he could think of that she would make up such a tale, which meant it must be true.

He felt a sick lurching in his stomach imagining the scene between them. How John must have cornered her, threatened her, the look on his face and then on hers. Gabriel pressed his hand to his forehead. For the first time, God forgive him, he was almost glad he had shot the man.

He turned his thoughts to Alexandria. She'd told him about her doubts about John in her letter from Iceland. She explained that she had agreed to a marriage of convenience and was having second thoughts. She made it plain that the reason she had gotten herself in such a predicament was the importance of her goal, her sole purpose of finding her parents and hopefully finding them alive. She'd been very, very honest about that.

Gabriel took a deep breath and allowed the deeper contemplation to come to the surface—he had done a similar thing to her. For a long time he had been afraid to tell her he was deaf, a time where he had kept her at arm's length, judged her reaction without giving her a chance to have one, made assumptions out of fear . . . not so different from what she'd just confessed to.

Still.

The thought that she had waited until after their wedding night when she would know for certain, that she hadn't trusted him with the truth, that she had married him with such a secret! He leaned his head into his hands and closed his eyes.

God, it hurts. I feel tricked . . . betrayed . . . like a fool.

He opened his eyes and saw a flurry of movement near the door. He straightened, peering through the crowd. His heart skipped a beat as a familiar red cloak swirled into the common room. She lifted her hand, a pale and familiar motion, and raked off her hood, sky blue eyes narrowed and scanning the room.

Alexandria could *not* have found him here.

Gabriel found his mouth curving into fierce satisfaction despite his desire to stay angry and hurt. Her eyes locked to his. Her lips formed a grim curve, her eyes determined. She threw back a side of her cape and stalked toward him, commanding such attention that the eyes of the entire room were now upon them. There wasn't anything afraid in her as might be expected. No, she looked fearsome and as mad as a wet cat.

She came to a stop at his table and leaned a little toward him, her gaze roving his face. "So, this is where I find you, in a backstreet tavern?"

Gabriel shrugged beneath hooded eyes. "I happen to like it here."

With a regal mien she surveyed the place, seeing it for what it appeared to be on the surface, he was sure. She shot a glance back to him, genuine curiosity lighting the sparkle of humor in her eyes. "Well, there must be a good reason. Care to tell me why?"

Gabriel couldn't help his answering smile. He grasped her arm and pulled her down on the narrow bench beside him. With a nod and flick of his hand, he gestured to the serving woman to bring more rolls. "I suppose I'll have to show you."

Alexandria turned toward him and took one of his hands under the table. In a softer voice she asked, "Are you still angry?" Her eyes spoke volumes of sadness and remorse.

"Just answer me this. Why didn't you tell me before we married?" Gabriel watched her lips closely as she answered.

"I thought you wouldn't love me anymore."

"Alexandria, it wasn't your fault. John did this to you. Why would I blame you and not love you anymore?"

"But I gave him false hope. I told him I would marry him so it seems partly my fault."

Gabriel leaned closer and asked in a fierce whisper, "Do you blame your parents at all for abandoning you in that crumbling castle? Or do you think that partly your fault as well?"

She opened her mouth to speak and then paused and shut it. Her eyes turned confused.

"You have to stop taking responsibility for other people's actions. You intended to marry John when you said yes, I'm sure of it. How he reacted to you when you, with time and reflection, changed your mind was his choice. And how your parents chose to raise you was their choice. You didn't do anything wrong for them to leave you there."

Alexandria's eyes began to fill with tears. She looked away but he still read her lips. "How do you know these things so deep in my heart?"

"Because I know you. Don't ever doubt it again. Do not ever lie to me again. You can trust me with your whole heart. I vow I will not treat you as those others have."

"I'm sorry. I won't lie to you again. Please forgive me?" She pleaded with her eyes.

Gabriel leaned forward and kissed her, ignoring the attention they were still getting from the other patrons.

Alexandria leaned back and turned a rosy color as the serving woman set down a platter of hot rolls with a broad smile. She said something, which made his wife all the rosier, and then motioned to eat up.

Gabriel picked up a sticky roll. It was more than a sweet offering. It was a peace offering. He held it out to her, eyes locked, trying to say that.

She took the roll to her mouth, inhaled, and took a bite. Her face broke into a broad smile and then a laugh. "Now I understand. We have to bring some home to Clarissa."

Gabriel chuckled thinking that this was the first of many conflicts and resolutions they would have in marriage. *God, grant me strength and humility.*

As they left together, Gabriel asked, "How did you find me?" They stepped into the carriage where there was a ready supply of paper and a lap table Gabriel had ordered installed. She wrote quickly and passed it over to him.

I followed the clues, of course. Hanson saw the direction you were headed, and your valet remembered what you were wearing. You were walking so I asked a few people if they'd seen you. One shop owner on Fleet Street was particularly helpful. He saw you enter the Goose and Gridiron. It wasn't very difficult.

He didn't know whether to be proud of her sleuthing skills or alarmed that his wife was traipsing about the streets of London questioning strangers. She still had little idea of her position and how she was supposed to behave, and a trusting nature from being raised on the windswept and lonely isle of Holy Island that was innocent and charming . . . and dangerous. "Alexandria, I won't have you unescorted and speaking to strangers. We cannot forget the danger we still find ourselves in. Until that missing manuscript your parents were hired to find has been located, we have to be especially careful. The Spanish are none too pleased with me."

She took the paper back and wrote. *Of course. And I was careful. I took the carriage instead of following you on foot. Whenever I got out to speak to someone, I made sure the coachman could see me at all times, and I only spoke to women or the obvious owner of an establishment. I didn't just question anyone walking about on the streets.* She peered up at him with a little frown, exasperation in her eyes. "I'm not as inexperienced as you might think."

He thought of the ambush from the Spaniards and the weeks of torture, those rings in the wall that had nearly dislocated his wrists, his shoulders, the beatings he endured at their hands. She had no idea what these people would do to get the manuscript stolen from the British Museum that purportedly held the plans to build the world's most powerful weapon. She still didn't seem to realize the danger. How was he to make her understand?

"Alexandria, do you remember when I told you that the Spaniards who had been following you across Ireland captured me and took me to Madrid? That I couldn't come to you in Iceland for so long because of them?"

She nodded, her blue eyes wide.

"Last night. Did you notice my back? It was dark, but did you feel anything?"

She shook her head, her gaze now alarmed.

He shrugged out of his waistcoat and pulled his shirt from the back of his breeches. He scooted closer, took one of her hands in his. "Reach up and touch my back."

"What?"

"Just do it." He turned his back toward her. He couldn't hear her reaction so he waited, hearing only his heartbeat thud with worry. He jumped when her fingertips slid across his back, tracing one of the thin scars. He turned to face her.

Her eyes snapped fire. "The Spaniards did this?"

He nodded.

"I can't believe they did this to you. I want to hunt them down and . . . shoot them! What else? Tell me everything."

He certainly would not do that. He didn't want her terrified to leave the house, just have a glimpse of what they were capable of. "You needn't know all the details. Just know they meant to do anything to find you and that manuscript. We must be very, very careful. I've hired four former Hessian soldiers to act as footmen and accompany us on our journey to Italy. Promise me you'll always have me or one of those men with you when you go anywhere."

She nodded. "I promise."

The look in her eyes told him she meant it.

Chapter Four

W e've captured the Featherstones, Your Grace."

"Have you?" The dark man's lips curved into a sensual smile. "You've brought them here?"

"Yes, they are just outside, under guard in the hall."

"Excellent." He could feel the pleasure already, streaking through him like wildfire at the thought of Katherine Featherstone, the famed, beauteous treasure hunter herself. Another flash of lust, hotter still, when he thought of her daughter. All the secret portraits he'd had painted of her over the last months. Miniatures and sketches from afar. The Spanish sent soldiers after her—impatient imbeciles. He sent artists. Creative spies who watched Alexandria's every move, captured her blossoming womanhood in drawings and paintings, and reported back weekly. He'd had them framed and hung in a special room, one he visited often.

"And Alexandria? Where is she now?"

"She has just left London with her new husband, the Duke of St. Easton."

"Yes." His throat rumbled with displeasure, like a bear sensing another of his kind in his territory. That marriage had been an unexpected development, but now that the deed was done, he would just have to make the best of it. Casting a net, trapping them both, and then taking another duke's riches, his power, his wife—it would be an added pleasure. "They are headed toward France?"

"We believe so, Your Grace."

It would be over a month before they were within his reach. Plenty of time to test Ian and Katherine's characters. Plenty of time to bend Katherine to his will. "Separate the Featherstones and take them to the dungeons. They are not to see each other again. Tell them nothing."

"Yes, Your Grace." The guard bowed and turned to go.

The duke turned back to his desk and the maps spread across it. So many possibilities while the world scrambled to reorganize after Napoleon's fall. So many in need of an alliance.

He closed his eyes, his lips curving into a line of antici-pated satisfaction. If he could just get his hands on the manu-script . . . dear Augusto de Carrara . . . he could have it all. So close. Just within his grasp. He could almost taste the glory. He laughed low and dark.

And the Featherstones, all three of them, were going to make it happen.

HE STILL LOVED HER.

The fact that Gabriel had forgiven her made her giddy with relief. Today was the beginning of their long journey, and she was determined to tread carefully, convince him of her hon-esty and love. It was a new beginning for them, a fresh start, and she meant to make the most of it.

The road to Dover proved rutted and dry, the weather espe-cially warm for a June day. Their cavalcade of ten—the Duke and Duchess of St. Easton surrounded by eight guards—made an impressive scene in their matching blue livery as they passed the brick wall of Greenwich Park and then through the little village of Blackheath. They rode at a brisk pace, kicking up clouds of dust, making for the English Channel two days hence.

The summer sun shone down on the top of Alex's dark hat, causing the hair at her temples to curl with sweat. She looked over from her place high atop one of her husband's silky black mares and allowed a small smile to play across her lips. The wind blew against her hot cheeks as memories of the night before flooded through her. With nothing between them except truth, they had reveled in each other in a way she hadn't known was possible. She could even now close her eyes and feel his long eyelashes brushing against her cheeks—his caresses with his hands and his lips. She'd turned to flame in his hands, molten limbs, flickering pulse, and white heat.

Biting down on her lower lip, she studied his profile from under the brim of her hat. He was the most beautiful man . . . how had he come to love her? Why? He could have had anyone and he'd picked her. He had hid his only "affliction" as he called it for fear she wouldn't love him. How could he think such a thing? The angles of his face made her heart swell, the dark shadowy beard that covered his lower face gave him a dangerous mien. His wide shoulders, so straight and strong under that tailored coat. He wore all his clothes with effortless ease and manly grace, gifts he didn't know he possessed but that made every woman in a room stop and stare and sigh. His quiet confidence. She felt young and silly beside it. She hardly knew what to do with it. Life had turned out so suddenly splendid.

God, I feel too much for him. It's too strong. It makes me afraid.

As if sensing her regard, he shot a look over at her. His green eyes, so penetrating and intense, stole her breath away.

He knew what she was thinking . . . remembering. The corner of one side of his mouth lifted in a rakish smile against the bright sunlight behind him.

She put her hand up to angle the brim of her hat to better see that smile. His horse slowing until they were side by side, he reached out to her with his eyes, his teasing lips fading, becoming straight and serious. His eyes darkened, narrowed, blazed with love and possessive passion for her. Her mouth fell open. Her breath left her in a puff. She had to look away, blink hard to see again in a landscape that was so piercingly bright, filled with texture and color and brimming with life—like him—so bright, so beautiful.

It must be dangerous, loving this much.

The road wound through the countryside, through Shooter's Hill where the highwaymen were famed to roam. Gabriel stayed close by her side as they rode through that stretch of hills and vulnerable valleys. There were stands of trees on either side where an attacker could easily hide in wait while they, vulnerable and caution-filled, traveled through the open, sun-bathed valley. But it was the middle of a beautiful day, and not even a duke's purse lured the thieves out this day.

Hours later they rode into Ashford, having made good time and more than halfway to Dover and England's coast. Alex slid down from the sidesaddle and tied her horse up with the rest of them at the front of the inn. Gabriel came around and clasped her waist, leaning into her hair at her ear to murmur, "For someone who says she doesn't ride, you've done well today."

Alex turned in his arms and placed her hand against his heart. The light was fading and she didn't know if he would be able to read her lips so she leaned close, took off her hat, and tilted her head toward his face. "I love you."

His lips curved into a warm smile. "And I, you. My duchess."

Alex closed her eyes and reclined against his chest, nodding, agreeing to the covenant. Somehow it felt more real than their wedding vows in the opulent church, more real than any ceremony, just the two of them, under the beginnings of twilight with pretend footmen who were really trained assassins running about them, getting everything safe and in order.

She wished she could whisper words of love into his ear instead of letting the moment pass because she didn't have the speaking book, but she couldn't. She kissed the place beneath his ear instead, telling him with a whisper-touch that he meant everything to her. She hoped he understood.

THE EARLY RAYS OF THE sun streamed through the inn's lone window and across the wrinkled white bedding and his wife's face. Gabriel lay on his stomach, his hand curled under his chin, and watched her sleep. Her dark hair fanned out across her pillow, lavender-soaked tresses that felt like silk in his hands. Dark brown brows and lashes made contrasts of color against her pale face. Her lips, rosy and a little swollen from kisses, a tiny reddened area on one side of her face where his beard had rubbed against her delicate skin, showed in the morning light.

A fierce protectiveness surged through him as he thought of how young and innocent she was of the ways of the world. How she had managed thus far without him, he didn't know. She had gotten through surprisingly well so far, traveling through Ireland and picking up protectors along the way, garnering lifelong friends the way other people collected coins. In Iceland she had faltered, but when he thought of what John had done to her, his stomach twisted. She was so resilient, so easy to forgive and love again. She might be an innocent in many ways, but she had an internal strength that never wavered for very long. God must have given her that.

He leaned forward and rubbed his cheek next to hers, whispering in her ear, "Bestir yourself, beloved. The road calleth."

She turned onto her back and raised one arm above her head. Gabriel traced a line of kisses on the delicate, white skin of her inner arm. Her lips curved into a smile. Her throat vibrated with a purring sound.

He scooted closer, bracing his hands on either side of her and, with a neat turn, suspended his body over her, waiting for the moment when she opened her eyes. She laughed, reached her arms up to twine around his neck, and blinked awake, the sky blue of her eyes filled with joy.

"I have a surprise for you," he said in a deep, teasing voice.

"You do?" Her brows shot up. "What is it?"

"It's not for slugabeds," he answered with a wicked smile.

Her face was almost comical, so quickly did her brows slant together and lips pout with indignation. "I am no slugabed, Your Grace. You've simply kept me up late!"

He laughed and collapsed on top of her, rolling them to their sides. That was true enough, and as much as he wanted to continue the pattern, they had a long day ahead of them. After a quick kiss on her forehead, he turned and sprang from the bed, padding over to the chair where his clothes lay scattered across the back. He saw a flutter of movement from the corner of his eye and knew she was scurrying into her clothes, or rather trying to without the help of her maid.

Clarrisa had gone into a fit of vapors when asked to accompany them, so they left her behind with a promise from Gabriel that he would hire French maids to attend Alexandria in Paris. But there was no one but him to help her now. He chuckled, buttoning his shirt and coming over to her.

"Here now, turn around. Without Clarissa I see I shall have to play lady's maid as well as all my other responsibilities." He gave her a mock sigh as he did up the laces on her corset and fastened the hooks on the petticoat.

She thanked him with a kiss on the cheek. "When can I see my present?"

Gabriel shook his head but grinned. "After we break our fast in the common room, then you may have your present. Dress in something comfortable today. Not that stiff riding habit."

AFTER GABRIEL LEFT, ALEXANDRIA HURRIED to finish her morning routine. It was different—and embarrassing!—being married. Why, he had paraded around the room stark naked in full daylight and thought nothing of it! And what was she to do every morning on this journey, so close that he knew her every move? This would take some getting used to.

After dressing in a comfortable muslin gown in pale yellow, she sat on the bed and prayed her morning prayer, asking God to bless their day, protect them from evil, and forgive her sins. "And please give me wisdom and grace with all my dealings with my husband." It was all so new and exciting, surprising and disturbing at the same time. Her heart skipped a beat as she rushed from the room, thinking of her coming present.

After breakfast Gabriel took her hand and led her out into the sunny morning. He went to his saddlebag and pulled out a rectangular box, turned, and unclasped the buckles along the side. He opened the lid. Alex took a step closer and peered inside.

"A pistol?" Her gaze flew to his. "You're giving me a weapon?"

"Yes, a flintlock pistol. And a short sword as well. I want you to learn how to shoot and fight should the need arise. I want you prepared for anything."

She placed a hand on his upper arm. "The danger is so real as that?"

He nodded. "We will start with a quick lesson this morning and then along the road, and at every opportunity you will practice. By the time we reach Italian soil, I expect my wife to be able to hold her own if it comes down to protecting your life. After being captured by the Spanish, I know better than to underestimate our enemy . . . or overestimate my own abilities. Will you give it a try?"

Alexandria carefully lifted the shiny flintlock pistol from its velvet home. She held it pointing down and away from them. "Is it ready to fire?"

Gabriel chuckled. "Not yet. Come over here. I've had targets set up for us." He led her to the back side of the inn. A low fence clogged with weeds circled part of the yard, making a chicken coop. A few chickens milled about, pecking at the ground. "I'm not to shoot a chicken, am I?"

He gave her that disarming one-sided smile. "No chickens. Look at what is sitting on the fence rail."

She took a few steps closer. Two glass bottles and an empty tin balanced on the split rail. "Oh, I hope I don't get a chicken instead." She looked up at him, not knowing if he had read her lips or not.

"Let me show you." Gabriel took the firearm. "See this? That's the hammer. Move it back to the half-cock position." He showed her how it clicked into place and looked up at her with raised brows. She nodded. "Now, we take this paper cartridge." He took one from his pocket and tore it open with his teeth. "It has the ball and powder already measured out."

"I have to carry gunpowder on my person?"

"There is nothing to fear."

Alex was sure that wasn't entirely true. She had heard of more than one person who had mishandled gunpowder in a variety of ways to their detriment.

"Now, fill this flash pan with a little powder. That's the igniter that will later spark the shot and ball. We then pour the rest of the powder down this long barrel and push in the ball. Take out the ramrod here underneath the barrel and ram it all the way back. Put the ramrod back into place and you are ready to fire."

She nodded understanding. He handed her the primed pistol and pointed at the targets. "Pick your target, Your Grace."

She frowned at the title, noting that he called her that when he wanted her to brace up and be the duchess, but she squared her shoulders and aimed the pistol, holding it with both hands.

"There's a kick to it." He moved behind her. "Since this is your first time, I will stand behind you and support you against it." His chest came flush with her back, his legs on either side of her skirt. She bit down on her lower lip and narrowed her eyes, trying to concentrate.

The pistol was heavy, more so than she thought it would be. It shook a little in her hands as she pointed it toward one of the tall glass bottles. She squinted down the barrel, squeezed the trigger, and then let out a squeal as her body sprang back into Gabriel's. The metal ball whizzed through the air too fast to see, but she heard a satisfying clink and they both saw the bottle explode into tiny pieces.

She whirled around, his arms around her. "I did it!"

She wanted to go on and on and talk about how she had shot the bottle, but without the speaking book she would talk too fast. She was already, unconsciously, only speaking in short sentences. It came as a shock to realize that she was changing so fast and that they might never have a normal, long conversation. A stab of sadness brought shadows to her heart, quelling the joyous moment.

Lord, please heal Gabriel. We need a miracle. Show us the way to his healing.

He was grinning at her though. He spun her around and laughed. "You were wonderful. Just wonderful. A natural shot."

After several more times, she felt she had the basic movements down and could quickly load and reload the weapon. When they were finished, he showed her how to clean it and then they packed it away in the saddlebags and headed for the white cliffs of Dover.

Soon they would leave England. The next time she stepped on English soil, God willing, would her parents be beside them?

Chapter Five

 $\mathscr{G}$ abriel kept Alexandria close as they boarded the ferry on Dover's crowded quay. The sky was gray, the air crisp and cool, the water calm, but he didn't let the outward calm of the scene still the inward caution that danger could come from any direction. And a seaport, crowded with strangers, was rife with opportunities. His wife must have sensed the tension in his body. She looked up at him with wide eyes filled with concern. "What is it? Is something wrong?"

Gabriel shook his head and led her to the railing, thinking to distract her with the sights. Sprawling and enormous, Dover Castle sat on top of the white chalky cliffs that faced the sea. "Look, you can see the castle and the white cliffs so well from here. It has changed so much since the last time I saw it. It was rebuilt and improved during the war. I do believe it is the best garrisoned castle in England."

She followed the direction of his pointing finger and nodded, but when she looked back at him, her eyes told him she knew he was trying to distract her. Turning toward France, Gabriel pointed at a smudge against the horizon. "And that is Calais. See the tallest shadow against the sky? That is the watchtower. During stormy weather its light has saved many ships, leading them safely to its shore."

"How long will it take to get there?" Alexandria glanced at the passengers around them.

"A couple of hours if the sea isn't too rough. Not long."

An hour later and well into the Strait of Dover, dark clouds swept in on a fast-moving wind and the sea began to churn. The little ferry dipped up and down in the growing troughs of the sea like a piece of driftwood. Gabriel clung to the rail, sweat starting to make a trail down his back. Why hadn't he thought to bring the ginger root that had saved him from intense seasickness when the Spanish took him?

Alexandria clung to the rail, restless beside him. "Gabriel, are you ill? Is it the sea?"

He shrugged. "I have always gotten seasick but, for some reason, it is worse since I lost my hearing."

"You look gray. Should we find a place to sit down?"

He shook his head as his stomach rolled with another dip, sea water spraying droplets into his face. People were abandoning the deck. "You go with our guards down into the hold where it's warm and dry. I have to stay in the open as long as I can. It helps a little to look at the horizon."

"But it's not safe. The water could come up over the bow at any moment."

"Which is why you must go below. I know what I am doing. Now go."

Alexandria narrowed her eyes at him but obeyed, taking uneven steps toward the stairs that led down into the hold with Kurt and Eddie, two of their guards, flanking her. As soon as he saw that she was safe, he leaned over the edge of the ship and emptied the contents of his stomach, then collapsed at the base of the rail, clinging to it. How had he forgotten how truly miserable this was?

A man came over, knelt down, and shouted something over the wind, but Gabriel couldn't read his lips. The man grabbed his arm and tried to help him up. As soon as Gabriel stood, a piercing sound, high and loud, shot through his head. Gabriel covered his ears with his hands and sank back to the slippery deck. Dizziness swamped him.

He barely managed to lean over, the ship rising on a swell, to vomit again. The man who had been trying to help him slid away, terror filling his eyes. Gabriel ground his teeth but the screeching noise continued. Panic filled him. It felt as if his brain would burst. "Oh God, I've just found her. Don't let me die now."

He prayed the prayer aloud but the familiar vibrations from his throat felt different . . . sounded different. Had he just heard his own voice?

Hope, despite the misery, filled him until his eyes brimmed with tears. He let out a croaking laugh, the tone just on the edge of his consciousness. It was like the last time, as if he were underwater and barely able to make it out, but it was there—sound. He tried to stand again. He had to get to Alexandria. He had to hear her voice before it went away.

He glanced around. No one was left on top. Another great dip of the ship and a gray wall of water crashed across the deck. Gabriel stumbled and clung to the rail with all his might. He would not get swept over and drown. Not now!

As soon as the water slid away, he leapt from the railing and crawled as fast as his legs would take him to the stairs. The ship climbed another trough of water as he climbed up the deck. He only had a few precious minutes before they crested and then plunged down the other side. If he didn't make it down into the hold before then, he would be swept away.

The ship teetered for a moment, time slowing as water roared around him, and balanced for a heart-stopping moment on the top of the wave.

He wasn't going to make it.

His throat worked in despair. Suddenly a head popped up from the stairs. It was Eddie, a big, burly man with black hair, a thick black beard, intelligent eyes, and good with a sword. Gabriel had liked him immediately when interviewing for guards after receiving the letter from the prince regent that the Spaniards were none too happy about the ship Gabriel had sunk. Eight guards they had ended up with—four his and four the regent's. Gabriel would have to figure out how to get rid of the regent's guards in Paris, if he even made it to Paris.

"Eddie, help!"

Eddie sprang from the stairwell and charged toward him with leaping strides. He grasped hold of Gabriel's hand and dragged him toward the stairs. The ship was plunging down, down into the depths of a trough. At the top of the stairs, Gabriel let go of the man's big hand, turned so his feet dangled in the hole, dropped down, and scrambled down the stairs. They were both breathing heavy and soaking wet but they'd made it.

The seasick feeling faded against the pounding of his blood. He collapsed at the bottom of the stairs. Eddie hauled him up with a big grin and slapped him on the shoulder. "Come along, Your Grace. Your wife is worried sick."

Gabriel heard the words fading in and out but mostly as a deep rumbling that if he concentrated hard enough, he could make out. They made their way through the crowd in the long room to where Alexandria stood on tiptoe, peering over a man's shoulder with intense relief and tears in her eyes. As soon as he was close, she rushed to meet him and threw her arms around his neck.

"I can't believe you stayed up there. What a stupid, stubborn, brain-feathered . . . dukelike thing to do. Thinking you can outwit a storm. I thought I'd lost you." She reared back and seemed to be considering striking him across the face. "Don't ever do that to me again."

"Brain-feathered?" He cracked a smile. And then a chuckle. And then a full-blown laugh. He'd never been so glad to hear a setting down in all his life. Her voice, still foggy but with growing clarity, was exactly as he had imagined it would be. Clear, feminine, sweet—well, angry now, but it would be sweet when her temper cooled—and just a note of the northern clime's accent from her home on Holy Island in Northumberland. His shepherdess wife . . .

Oh, God, I'm afraid to tell her. What if it didn't last? What if it only lasted as long as they were on this ship, a place that stirred something in his ears and head and somehow made him sick and helped him at the same time?

"Are you laughing at me? At my fears?" A vein in her temple throbbed but Gabriel couldn't help it. He was just so happy, sick still, a little dizzy though that was getting better, but happy. He pulled her away from the gawking crowd toward the back wall of the room and then spoke over the roaring of the storm into her ear. "Alexandria, I can hear you."

She reared back. "What? How is that possible?"

"I'm not sure. I think it has to do with seasickness and vertigo. I heard a loud, piercing sound out there and then something happened. I started to hear the storm and my voice. I don't know how long it will last. The time before, when I was traveling to Holy Island to fetch you, it only lasted a few weeks.

It may only last minutes this time or months or . . . God willing, forever. Don't get too hopeful yet, you understand? Just talk to me, beloved."

Her blue eyes filled with tears as he spoke. She shook her head. "What do I say? I don't know what to say!" Her eyes were big and confused and hopeful, so hopeful.

"I want to hear you laugh."

"But I feel like crying."

Gabriel let out a bark of laughter at that, and then seeing her smile around her tears, he laughed louder and harder. Alexandria clung to his arm and let out a choked laugh, and then another. In a moment they were both laughing and clinging to each other. Bells, musical bells, with drops of color bursting through the air around them. Red and yellow, bright lights of color that faded almost as soon as he saw them bathed the corner of the hold.

He had begun seeing colors with music and certain sounds such as the clanging of swords shortly after losing his hearing. It was something that brought him great solace, a gift from God that helped him cope, but now he could hear and still see the colors. Was such a miracle possible?

The people closest around them were looking at them in differing degrees of confusion and disapproval, but Gabriel barely noticed. He wanted to sing or dance or play the pianoforte. He wanted to shout praise and thanksgiving and hold his wife and make her laugh. He wanted to hear all her sounds and hold them tight to remember, in case this was a window of time, a short gift. In case it didn't last.

A dip of motion caused the ship to tip in the other direction. Water flooded into the hold. Some of the passengers screamed, some shouted directions, waving their arms and gesturing for the crowd to move to the other end of the rectangular hold. They held to each other, many praying aloud, others cursing, and some looking ready to faint from fear.

But a strange calm enfolded Gabriel. The God who made these waves, made everything they could see, smell, touch, taste, and hear, He was in control and knew the fate of each of them. He was a God of miracles who gave and took as He saw fit. Why shouldn't He ask to be their everything? It was the only reason they existed.

Chapter Six

Calais, France

The passengers cheered as the ferry docked in the quay at Calais, all happy to have arrived safely to shore. *Calais, France*. Alexandria liked the sound of the words and knowing that Gabriel could hear her say them made them all the sweeter.

She gripped his arm, looking about the shoreline, seeing the watchtower in the distance Gabriel had spoken of. *"Es-tu allé en France souvent?"*

"You speak French?" Her husband's green eyes glowed with surprise.

"Enough to get along, I hope. I had no one to speak it to, so I'm not sure how correct it is. Mostly I just read books written in French and taught it to myself that way."

Angry concern flashed across his face. "Your parents left you alone too often. As to your question, I have been to France on several occasions. Most recently to Paris just after the revolution. The city was so much different than in decades past. I hope it has improved so you can catch a glimpse of its former glory."

"I am looking forward to seeing it, but I just want to get to Italy. It feels like we are wasting time."

Gabriel lowered his voice. "Do not speak too loudly of our plans. There may be listening ears. We must go to Paris first and spend a few days appearing to enjoy ourselves. The regent must be convinced that we are only on our honeymoon trip." Gabriel looked around with a darting gaze at the crowd dispersing from the ship, causing a chill to run down Alex's back. She felt better knowing that Eddie and Kurt were right next to them.

"We will stop at the Crow and Rooster for food, a carriage, and horses. It will be a bit slower than horseback, but the journey is long and we will need the shelter."

Alex nodded, walking quickly beside him and trying to keep up with his long stride. They would waste no time staying in the pretty city of Calais. "How long will it take to reach Paris?"

"Something in the nature of six days, depending on the roads and any number of unforeseen circumstances."

Alex was content to let her husband lead them. He seemed to know the town and what best to do. A few streets later they finally came to the inn. Kurt swept the door open for them and they stepped inside.

The room was crowded and smoky, both from pipe smoke and the blackened fireplace on the far side of the room. Alex wrinkled her nose. People in various states of traveling dress, from the fashionable riding habits and uniforms to a young lad wearing naught but rags and accompanied by his haggard-looking mother, milled about the noisy room.

"*Une salle!*" A room! A man shouted next to her.

"*Partagerez-vous, hein?*" The innkeeper asked that he share.

Alex strained to pick up more of the conversations around her, but they were talking so fast. It became a soft blur and she gave up.

She observed Gabriel. He was having a hard time hearing as well. The room must be too loud and muddled. He had said he had to concentrate especially well in such circumstances, that it was as if he were underwater. When it came their turn, she started to speak to the innkeeper and ask about a coach, but Gabriel stopped her with a hand on her shoulder. "A duchess does not haggle, Your Grace. Let Kurt and Eddie find out what they can. You come with me. I've arranged a private room for our dinner."

How he had managed that when they only just arrived she couldn't imagine, but she wasn't surprised. Her husband knew how to travel with every comfort. Alexandria followed Gabriel up a narrow stairway to a small landing where they were greeted by a young maid. She bobbed a curtsy at each of them and then gestured that they follow her. At the end of a hall, she opened a door and stepped aside for them to pass. "Dinner to be served shortly, Your Graces." She looked up at Alex with an awed smile.

"Thank you." Alex nodded at her, still unused to such reverent treatment.

When the maid left, Alex turned toward Gabriel with a perplexed smile. "However did you manage all of this?"

He came closer and rested his hands on her waist. "I sent one of the guards ahead." He quirked one dark brow. "With a heavy purse."

"Should we spend so much on comforts? It feels wrong somehow."

He reached up and plucked the pins that held her hat in place from her hair, tossing them onto the nearby table. "Would you rather dine below with the masses? I had thought a quiet place, when we can manage it, will help our journey become less tedious." He swept off her hat, sailing it through the air to land on the table beside the pins. "Besides, I cannot hear your voice down there. And for as long as this hearing spell lasts, I want to hear everything."

Of course he would want that. She needed to learn that things, oh so many things, were different now. His hands settled on her waist again. She looked up at him like she had trained herself to always do when she spoke. "Yes, of course, I am sorry I didn't think of that."

He leaned forward and kissed her forehead. "Don't be. Now, come and sit at the table and I will pour you a cup of tea."

"Shouldn't the duchess do that?" Alex grinned at him, her humor returning.

"By all means." He swept out an arm toward a simple wooden table that had been set with dishes and a tea service and watched her as she maneuvered her skirts around the narrow space.

After they were seated, Alex poured the tea. "What would you like to talk about, Your Grace?"

He leaned back in his chair, stretched out his legs, and looked at her with hooded eyes. "Anything you desire, beloved."

She peered down, the endearment sending heat into her cheeks. "Well, my favorite color is green and I dislike oysters. I feed them under the table to Latimere when he is around."

Dear Latimere, she had wanted to bring her enormous Great Pyrenees with them on this journey, but it wasn't practical. She missed him already.

"Hmmm." She thought for more things Gabriel might not know about her. "My favorite game is chess." She laughed and sat back in her chair when his brows rose in surprise at that. "Henry taught me. You wouldn't know it to look at him, but he is an admirable chess player."

"Ah, Henry, your butler. Now that doesn't surprise me," Gabriel mumbled.

Alex laughed. "Oh, you met him, didn't you? In Holy Island when you came to fetch me. Henry and Ann were more like grandparents than servants to me. Were they terribly stubborn?"

"Impossibly so."

"Yes, well, now you know why I didn't tell them where I was going. They would have tried to talk me out of following my parents to Ireland for certain. But you found me out. Was it the coachman?"

"His wife, actually. She and all the townspeople of Lindisfarne seemed to know your nature very well, and they all thought you had gone off to find your parents. But Ireland is a large island and the coachman's wife gave us the right direction."

Alex gave a mock sigh and placed her chin in her hands. "I knew it was a mistake. But I had to have transportation, and I didn't think traveling alone on horseback a very wise course of action."

Gabriel coughed into a curled fist. "Thank God for some modicum of common sense."

Alex hooted a laugh. "You must admit, I kept you guessing." She peered up at him from under her lashes with teasing flirtation. "I stayed one step ahead of you and your stalwart secretary, Meade, for months."

Gabriel reached out and grasped her hand, sudden heat in his eyes. "It may have been a game to you, but you had no idea the danger . . . I thank God that He protected you."

Alex was saved from having to come up with an answer by a knock on the door. She sprang up to answer it, not wanting to admit that she might have been just a little rash . . . stupidly, naively brave . . . certainly lucky. Blessed to have gotten this far on this quest to find her parents.

The maid came in accompanied by two other footmen with covered trays, bowls, and more dishes. Alex sat back down while they arranged the table, her heart beating a little faster every time she looked into her husband's deep green eyes.

When they left, he cocked one side of his mouth up in that smile. "May I serve you, Your Grace?"

She nodded, butterflies fluttering in her stomach while he put portions of roasted duck floating in cream sauce, asparagus, baguettes shiny with butter, and a bowl of *soupe à l'oignon gratinée*, the most delicious onion soup she had ever tasted. She drank tea while he served himself.

"Why is your favorite color green?" he asked after a few moments of silence.

She hadn't really ever had a favorite color until seeing his eyes. But she couldn't tell him that, could she? "Hmm." She fiddled with her spoon and dipped it repeatedly into the soup bowl. Why did it feel so strange to say it? Why not just blurt it out? "You have a very, um, particular shade of green eyes. Has no one told you? I think you could impale a person with that gaze alone."

She took a breath, plunging on when he remained silent. "At the masquerade, the first time I saw you . . . you were wearing that black demimask, and Montague had said you were famous for your green eyes. That's when I knew it was you I had danced with. That's when I found my favorite color."

She had been looking him straight in the eyes while saying that part, but now she stared down at her plate.

"Alexandria."

"Yes?" She stabbed at a piece of asparagus and pushed it around the plate.

"Alexandria, look at me."

She hesitated, then obeyed.

"That is the loveliest thing anyone has ever said to me. Thank you."

Her smile wobbled but she managed it. "You're very welcome."

"Now, tell me *everything* that occurred in Iceland."

GABRIEL WATCHED HIS WIFE RECOUNT the last five months. She spoke softly, especially when talking about John, and he would have to lean in to make it out. She noticed immediately and spoke louder, against the small pops of the fire and from the beauty of her lips. He found himself reading them along with hearing her words, a habit now and one he wasn't entirely sure he would ever give up, even if his hearing remained as good as it was now or improved.

A knock at the door turned their attention. Gabriel rose to answer it.

"The carriage is ready, Your Grace." Kurt, a tall, blond man of few words and one of Gabriel's hired guards, informed him.

"Very good. Ready the men. We will be down in five minutes."

Kurt bowed and turned to go. Gabriel turned back to Alexandria with a sigh. "It seems that our repast is at its end. We can make it to the next town yet today if we make haste."

Alexandria pinned her hat back on and curtsied with a teasing smile. "Ready when you are, Your Grace."

Ah, if only they had a little more time he would really kiss her, but he settled for a peck on her lips and then swept the door wide.

They made their way to the outdoors where two horses were being hitched to a rickety-looking carriage. "Is this the best conveyance to be had?" Gabriel asked Kurt.

"The *only* conveyance to be had, Your Grace."

"Very well." He took Alexandria's arm to lead her to the carriage, hoping it would stay in one piece for this stretch of the journey.

A sudden commotion at the door of the inn made him turn around. A shot of unease tingled down his spine. There, standing behind a spindly pillar, was a man. Someone was hiding, watching them. His gaze swept the rest of the yard and then darted toward Kurt with an intense look. Understanding lit Kurt's eyes. With a slight nod, Kurt moved closer to Alexandria, covering her back.

Eddie came from around the back of the carriage and locked eyes with Gabriel, who gave a slight jerk of his head toward the man behind the pillar. Eddie nodded and moved to guard Gabriel's back.

The Spanish? Had they found them?

Gabriel turned and scanned the inn, the horses tied to the hitching rails, the trees and yard and around the corners of neighboring buildings. Another man appeared suspicious, his clothing of the lower class but a weighty sword at his belt. He stared at Gabriel.

Something was not right. It was as if the man knew him.

There was no time to warn the other guards of this second man before a shot was fired.

Chapter Seven

A blast of sound and smoke surrounded them. Alex screamed, her body pulsing with shock, and spun around, searching for the source of the pistol fire. Gabriel took her arm in a tight grip and pulled her toward the horses. The jerk on her arm caused her to stumble, lose her balance, and nearly fall to the ground, but Gabriel hauled her up and half carried her away from the inn.

Men rushed from all sides of the inn, their guards and strangers, some taking cover and others taking aim toward the shooter. They made a swarming cover for Gabriel and Alex.

When they reached the horses, Gabriel's hands moved lightning swift as he jerked the harness off the biggest one.

"What are you doing? What's happening?" Alex yelled.

"I am getting you out of here!" Gabriel took hold of her waist and threw her up onto the horse. "The carriage will be useless. We'll have to ride."

Alex swung her leg over, grasped hold of the reins with both hands, and sat up. Gabriel swung up behind her, taking the reins and placing one arm around her waist. Out of the corner of her eye, she saw one of their guards fall to the ground. Oh no! If only she had her pistol loaded!

Gabriel's body bucked against hers. For a moment the terror that he'd been shot filled her chest with pounding fear, but then he kicked the sides of the mare and she realized he was using his body to command the horse to run. The horse obeyed, wheeling around with a loud whinny. Off they shot, straying from the road, racing through the gardens and lawns of shops and houses.

A shout from behind them sounded through the air. Alex looked over her shoulder. A man on a horse was coming after them. Gabriel was at her back, a protective shield. What if he was shot?

"Give me your pistol!" she shouted at him.

"You've had two lessons and neither of them was while galloping on a horse. You'll only hurt someone."

"Well, we have to do something!" More shouts. What were they saying? She didn't recognize the language. She looked back again. "There are two men and they're gaining on us!"

Gabriel turned to glance behind them. "Take the reins. Don't let her slow down. Ride her toward places with cover. Understand?"

Alex nodded and grasped hold of the reins. Gabriel clenched his thighs tight to the horse's side and pulled out his pistol. She tried to zigzag the horse, but she was clumsy and the poor beast seemed to be getting confused. She saw a stand of trees up ahead, gritted her teeth, and took a firm grip on the reins. "Come on now. Let's make for those trees. You can do it," she encouraged low over the horse's ears.

Gabriel turned and Alex jerked as the firearm discharged, creating a cloud of smoke and then dissipating. They raced through it.

"Got one."

She heard the deep purr of satisfaction from Gabriel's voice. They were almost to the trees.

A sudden, unseen dip in the land caused Alex to fly up from her seat. She came back down with a shriek, feeling herself sliding to one side. "Help!" She was going to fall off. The ground loomed in front of her.

Gabriel clasped her around the waist and hauled her back against his chest. Her back slammed into his stomach. Her breath left her in a whoosh. The firearm flew from his hand and landed on the road behind them.

"The pistol!"

"It's gone." He groaned in her ear. "Give me the reins."

Alex felt sick. What had she done?

Over hedges and around corners they fled to the outskirts of town. The other horseman grew farther and farther behind until he was gone, but Gabriel didn't let the horse rest. Every time the poor beast started to slow, he commanded her to pick up the pace again. She was lathered and panting by the time they came to a deserted-looking road along the shoreline of France.

Finally he let the mare slow to a trot and then to a walk. Alex turned and peered behind them. "Is he still coming after us?"

"I think we've lost him for now. But they will continue to come. They will not give up until they have that manuscript."

Alex shivered hearing those words.

The manuscript.

The dreaded, highly sought-after manuscript from Sir Hans Sloane's collection. The author of the manuscript, Augusto de Carrara, had been a weapons expert back in the 1600s, and he had lived in Florence and the marble caves of

Carrara. Hence Gabriel and her reasoning that they would find her parents in Italy.

And that letter, the plea from her mother for help that Mr. Planta at the British Museum had shown Gabriel. Alex wondered for the hundredth time—had her parents any idea of the danger when they accepted such a quest? King Ferdinand of Spain was desperate to get his hands on it as well as their own prince regent, George IV. They had heard that France's reinstalled king, Louis XVIII, was interested too, and now these men were chasing them. Who were they? Would she always be hunted until the manuscript was found? She wished it had never existed.

"But we have to go back for our guards. One of them was shot, I'm sure of it."

"They'll find us. I will not take you back into danger."

"But how will they find us? Are we even on the road to Paris?"

"This is not the route I had intended we take, but it will do. Kurt and Eddie won't be far behind us, I daresay, and the regent's guards are better lost to us, though I don't wish them dead."

"The regent's guards? Do you mean that the regent sent those men with us?"

"Yes, I hadn't meant to trouble you with it, but some of our guards are straight from the royal palace. Kurt and Eddie are my men, along with John Henry and Sir Walter. The other four are from the regent's retinue. I knew George would watch us, but I didn't know he planned to be so obvious in his spying. We will need to devise a way to detain them in Paris when we slink away to Italy. I haven't thought of how yet. This enemy, whoever he is, might have helped our cause."

Although Alex could see the logic in his thinking, she wouldn't wish harm to any of their guards. "Who is this enemy?"

"I caught a glimpse of them and they had the olive skin of the Mediterranean people. Perhaps the Spanish have found us again, I'm not sure. We cannot take any chances with them."

A sudden idea came to Alex. "What about a signal? Is there something we could do to signal our whereabouts to the guards? Something that an enemy wouldn't recognize?"

Gabriel remained silent for a moment. "A signal fire or shot would attract too much attention. Something like Tomas's flag, do you mean?"

Tomas was the boy in Iceland Alex had found trapped by a fallen beam in the church belfry. After his rescue the whole of Reykjavik had become her friends. "Yes, like a flag or a note left somewhere." She shrugged. "Or perhaps they will find us unaided. I do hope they bring our baggage. We have nothing but the clothes on our backs. What shall we do about that?"

"I have coin enough for lodgings and food, but you're right, I have important papers, travel documents, and letters." He paused. "It would not bode well to have those fall into the wrong hands."

"I hadn't thought of that. If someone learns we are going to Italy . . . that would be very bad, wouldn't it?"

"Very bad, indeed." Gabriel sighed into her hair and squeezed her around the waist. "We shall put our trust in God, and for now, head to Boulogne-sur-Mer and a place to rest this horse."

THE ROAD TO BOULOGNE-SUR-MER FOLLOWED the winding coastline with sea breezes and long rays of afternoon sunshine lighting their way. Gabriel couldn't relax though. His body hummed with protective energy. They were too much in the open with little sandy beaches and low scrub to their right side and more sparse grasses and bushes to their left. Not at all suitable for taking cover. If he were alone, he would circle back and look for his guards, but that was too risky. Better to install his bride in a guarded room in a Boulogne-sur-Mer inn, purchase new weapons, and search for news by himself. Of course, his wife would balk at that idea. He knew her well enough to know she would sneak out and follow him if he didn't make sure she couldn't.

A small smile played at his lips. He admired her for it and had known the kind of woman he had taken to wife, but the thought of her in the clutches of the Spanish king made his smile turn grim. He would do anything to keep her from such a fate, even if it caused her to hate him for a time afterward.

"Look, I see the town!" Alexandria perked up in front of him and pointed toward a dark silhouette against the blue sky. "We've made good time, haven't we?"

She turned her head and he looked down into her happy eyes. "That we have. Riding at a headlong speed for half the journey tends to shorten the time."

Alexandria patted the side of the mare. "Poor thing. We nearly ran her to ground. She deserves a long rest and a very good meal of oats, don't you think?"

"Aye. That she does." He kissed her temple and dug his heels lightly into the mare's sides. "Let us see if we can hurry her toward that end, shall we?"

Alexandria gasped. "That hardly seems fair."

"She'll be all right. We need to get off this road."

"And find some food."

He shook his head and smiled. "You're always hungry."

"I am not! You shouldn't say such things to a lady."

"How about a duchess?"

"Especially not to a duchess!"

They both laughed.

A few minutes later they were trotting into the town. Signs of the destruction from the French Revolution lay all around them. Gabriel pointed to a pile of stone and rubble on the top of a hill. "Look. The remains of Basilica of Notre-Dame de Boulogne. It was a cathedral that housed a famous statue called Our Lady of the Sea. They say the statue was discovered in a boat floating in the harbor. After it was taken to the cathedral, miracles began to occur."

"Where is it now?"

"I believe they burned it. The war destroyed many cathedrals and great works of art." They came into the city and rode past the rubble in silence.

They soon turned into a long lane bordered by rows of shops and inns, the light making square panes of yellow on the cobbled street. A blackbird crouched over something dead, pecking at it with a shiny, black beak. Chickens roamed another corner, mindless of the people milling about. A plump, white chicken squawked with a flurry of feathers in protest of sharing the road and then went on pecking in another spot as if nothing had happened. Alexandria laughed at it, a sound he would never tire of hearing.

"There. That looks respectable enough." Gabriel pointed out his lodging of choice, a neat little timbered building with fresh paint and quieter than some of the others. "Come, let's get settled."

"Will we stay long and wait to see if the guards catch up to us?"

"I will give them one day. If they do not appear soon, we'll have to see about hiring some men and continuing on to Paris without them. They will make contact in Paris, I'm certain. Both Kurt and Eddie know the address where I have planned for us to stay."

"But how will they find us here?" Alexandria looked up with anxious eyes. "Wait. I have it. We should make a big fuss that the Duke and Duchess of St. Easton are here so word will spread. That way our guards might hear of it."

"And so might our enemies." Gabriel shook his head. "Too dangerous."

"But surely no one is here waiting for us. You said this is not the route you planned to take. And we lost the men following us. What danger can there be?"

Her logic made a certain amount of sense but still, Gabriel was loathe to make their presence known. He was also not relishing the idea of being on the open road without Kurt and Eddie. "All right, but be careful."

"Of course." Alexandria grinned, eyes twinkling at him. "I always am."

Chapter Eight

Boulogne-sur-Mer, France

And I'll be needing three goose-down pillows, a hot bath before bed, and a maid to assist me." Alexandria turned her head toward Gabriel and winked, mouthing the words, *Montague taught me my theatrical skills.*

Gabriel wanted to chuckle at the mental image of that, but instead he gave the innkeeper—a thin, elderly man who appeared half perplexed and half afraid of his wife—an even stare. She didn't appear to need his help making a spectacle that the Duke and Duchess of St. Easton had arrived, so he just glared at people in that haughty aristocratic way so common among his set.

"And see that our horse has extra oats. And that someone brushes her down good and proper. His Grace and I were robbed of our other horse and the poor thing is quite worn out."

"Yes, Your Grace. Anything else?"

"Yes, we will have our supper at eight o'clock sharp. Prepare your best table." Alexandria tapped her fingers against the table they were standing beside. "I would like to be shown to our room now, to freshen up."

"Yes, Your Grace." The old fellow turned to a spritely looking girl of about fourteen and directed her. "Take their lordships—"

"The Duke and Duchess of St. Easton!" Alexandria snapped with huge eyes at the insult. "Or 'their graces' at the very least."

The old fellow gave a long sigh and corrected himself. Gabriel choked back a bark of laughter. Alexandria must have heard him because she turned her head and glared at him, which made Gabriel want to laugh all the more. His wife was utterly . . . fearless. He wanted to kiss her square on the mouth, right here in front of everyone, and see if that cracked her facade.

They were led upstairs to a small, sparsely furnished room, the girl backing out with low curtsies. As soon as she shut the door, Alexandria spun around with bright eyes and a little smile. "I think it worked, don't you?"

"That they know the Duke and Duchess of St. Easton has arrived?" Gabriel chuckled and came over to her. He took gentle hold of her chin and lifted it so her merry eyes were locked to his. "Yes, I think so. I didn't know you were such a great actress."

"Well, I can't take all the credit. Montague and even Baylor were good teachers at times when they escorted me across Ireland. One time Montague pretended to be interested in Mistress Tinsdale in Killyleagh. She was quite taken with him, even baked him a pie." A look of confused wonderment crossed her eyes. "Now that I consider it, perhaps he was court-ing her in truth."

Her gaze snapped back to Gabriel's, her lips moving so fast that if he couldn't still hear her, he would not be able to read them. "At any rate, I had to pretend to be a *boy*! Can you imagine? I was terrified, but we did learn a clue that led us to the manuscript's author, Augusto de Carrara. What do you suppose he wrote in that manuscript that has half of Europe slavering over it like starving dogs? What kind of weapon could he have invented, do you think?"

She finally paused and took a much-needed breath. Gabriel gave her that second and then dipped his head, pressing his lips ever so lightly against hers. "Whatever it is, it is not near the treasure that I hold." He pressed a little harder, cutting off her next words. A soft sigh escaped her and then she was kissing him back.

Her eyes softened, indistinct when he broke them apart. She blinked slowly. "Your fortune . . . do you mean?"

He pulled her closer, kissing her temple. "No, beloved. The treasure that I'm holding in my arms."

"Oh."

It was such a soft, feminine sound. And he heard it. Profound thankfulness spread through his whole being. *Thank You, God.* He wouldn't have been able to hear that yesterday, not even a few hours ago.

His hearing was getting better.

There was a catch in his throat as he leaned down and gave her one more kiss, holding her close for a long moment. Then he sighed and pulled back. "Come, my duchess. We have our supper downstairs. With your fire-breathing antics, I doubt it will be late."

They made their way back down to the common room. The stage had arrived and several new people spilled through the door, demanding food and beds for the night. Gabriel sat with his back to the wall, facing the crowd and watching for any suspicious persons. There were four women of various ages, two children who appeared to be brother and sister, and three men. With the people already eating, it made for a crowded and noisy room.

Gabriel was glad they were in a more secluded spot where he could watch everyone as they ate the roasted chicken, creamed peas, and loaves of crusty bread. Nothing seemed out of the ordinary until another man entered the room.

A man wearing Gabriel's pistol on his belt.

ALEX JERKED HER GAZE TOWARD her husband as she felt his whole body stiffen. "What is it?" she hissed, hoping he could hear it. She kept her head down and glanced around the room from beneath lowered lashes, her stomach quivering.

Gabriel put his hand over hers under the table. "See that man who just came in? The thin fellow with the black hat pulled low over his eyes?"

Alex saw the man he referred to and nodded.

"Look at his pistol."

Alex sucked in a breath. "That's yours, isn't it? It is the only one I've ever seen with a pearl handle. Do you think he is with the men that were after us?"

"Could be. Or he might have found it on the road. He doesn't look Spanish at any rate."

"We need to find out and get your pistol back."

"Yes, we do."

Just then the man caught Alexandria staring and looked right at her. She lowered her head, taking a bite of peas.

"Just behave as usual." Gabriel continued to eat. "When he leaves, I will follow him, find out his business, and take my pistol back. It was my father's and I find I desire to have it back."

"I'm going with you." Alex slid a piercing look over at him.

"It's too dangerous. Stay in the room."

"That is exactly why I am going with you. You might need me."

"Alexandria," Gabriel said in a warning tone. "Don't test me on this. We are unarmed."

"And you want me to hide here in a room?" Alex gritted her teeth. "What if there are others? I will be safer with you." She didn't mention that she was really more afraid for him going alone. But the fact that she might be afraid to be left alone would perhaps help her cause more. It wasn't a lie . . . exactly. "There. Look, he's leaving." She started to scoot her chair back from the table, but Gabriel placed a hand on her thigh, locking her to her seat.

"Wait."

She kept her head down and waited.

"Very well," he said in a low hiss as he removed his hand. "I haven't time to see you safely to the room. Just stay behind me and don't make a sound."

"Yes, of course." Alex nodded. "You won't even know I'm there." She stood and followed his lead to the door. Once outside, she glanced up and down the dark street. "There." She nudged Gabriel's back. "He's just up ahead."

Gabriel started after the man, Alex just behind him. After a little while, their target turned a corner and went down another street. Gabriel picked up his pace until they came to the corner and then stopped and peered around it.

"He is heading into a livery stable. Probably for a horse. Be very quiet now."

They eased around the corner of a dark shop, hugging the buildings, and went about halfway down the street. They stopped at the edge of an open stable door. Alex inhaled to whisper that she could hear voices, but Gabriel shook his head and put a finger to his lips. He reached for her hand, curling his warm grasp around hers. They pressed against the building, listening intently.

"I got this here fancy pistol, see? I'd like to trade it for that big bay over yonder." A voice said from the far side of the stable.

"Bring it into the light." Another deeper voice demanded.

A few moments of silence and then the second voice accused. "Where did the likes of you get something as high falutin' as this pretty piece, I'd like to know?"

"'Twas my grandfather's. He died a little while back and left it to me."

"This pistol hadn't even been invented in your grand-father's day," the second man scoffed. "It sure is a beauty though . . . I think I'll make a trade—"

"You will do no such thing. This man is a thief and that gun belongs to me." Gabriel stood away from the wall and then strode around it.

Alex gripped her hands together, glee and terror at what they were walking into filling her.

She followed him inside and stood next to him, chin up and out, trying to look like Gabriel's mother when she gave someone the cut direct. Both men paled and shrank back at the sight of them. It seemed to be working.

"Now see here," the livery owner said. "I want no part of stolen goods, my lord."

"It is the Duke and Duchess of St. Easton whom you address," Gabriel said in succinct staccato. "Hand over my pistol. My initials are engraved on the handle. S. E. Now. If . . . you . . . please."

The livery owner held up his hands. "I never touched it, Your Grace. Forgive me."

The other man had eyes as big as saucers. "I didn't steal it. It was lying in the road. I swear it! I didn't steal nothin'."

Gabriel walked over, wrenched the pistol from the man's hand, and then took a firm grasp on his shoulder. "Let's just see about that, shall we? You are coming with me." He fixed the livery man with a stare. "We will need your best two horses early tomorrow morning." He reached in a pocket and took out a large coin, flipping it through the air toward the livery owner. "You have such a thing, do you not?"

"Oh yes." He bowed. "First thing tomorrow. A fine stallion for you and that nice bay for your lady wife. I shall look forward to it."

Alex followed Gabriel, who was hauling the other man by the shoulder, to the dark side street. Gabriel backed the man to the side of a shop and leaned into his face. She held her breath as he began to speak.

"Where did you find this pistol?"

"On the road!" The man gasped around Gabriel's fingers closing in on his throat.

"Where, exactly, on the road?"

"It was in-in the grass, just layin' there. The sun caught the handle. I saw it and rode over and picked it up. I swear on my mother's grave."

"Were you traveling alone?"

"Yes, come up from sellin' some grain in Calais."

"Did you see anything unusual happening in Calais? Anything of interest?"

The man's eyes shuttered. "No."

Gabriel started to twist his collar more tightly. Alex shot forward. "Your Grace, please." She nudged Gabriel away and faced the man. "Hello, I'm Alexandria Feath–er . . . St. Easton and we could really use your help."

"My help?" The man straightened his collar away from his throat and stared at her with distrust in his eyes and high color on his thin cheekbones.

"Are you a farmer?"

He looked down and flushed. "Of a kind."

"What kind?"

"Well, my brother, Reginald, he's the farmer. Likes to keep to 'imself, Reginald does. Don't like people much, so I go in and trade when necessary."

"I see. So you handle the selling and transporting of the goods. You must travel a great deal."

The man shrugged, shook his head a little, warming up to her. "That's why I needed that pistol so badly. To trade it. My horse is lame, too much of a load on 'em last time and he's played out for a while. If I don't get me a good horse, that grain sitting in my brother's barn will rot."

Alex raised her brows. "But what of the profits from your sales? Surely your brother would want you to take some of the profits for a horse."

The man hung his head and said nothing.

"Did something bad happen? Are there no profits?" Alex placed her hand lightly on his arm.

The man shrugged again. "I ain't supposed to tell," he muttered to his shoes.

"Well, you can tell me," Alex said in a straightforward, almost offended way.

The man's gaze darted toward Gabriel, who was watching the scene with hooded eyes. Alex drew his attention back to her. "Sir, what is your name?"

"Jean Duvall."

"Well, Mr. Duvall. I think we might help one another. You need a horse and we need a good man to help us."

"Alexandria . . ." Gabriel's voice was a soft yet deadly purr coming from her right shoulder. Alex shooed him away with a backward hand motion.

"You see," she continued, "we had a misfortunate encounter in Calais that caused us to lose our guards. We are not sure if they have taken the more direct route to Paris . . . but we are in a great hurry and cannot tarry here long to see if they will find us. We need someone to go back to Calais, search them out, and deliver a message. When you return with our guards, you will have your horse."

"Alexandria." The word was more of a hiss now. Alex turned toward her husband and shot her own daggers with her eyes.

"How will I know these guards?" the man asked.

"We will give you a description of them and the St. Easton livery they are wearing. You will take the pistol with you to prove to them you are with us. You could even confirm their identities by asking them who the pistol belongs to."

"Well, that sounds easy enough." He slid his hands into his pockets and hunched forward.

"There is just one thing I need to know before I can trust you with such a journey."

"Yes, ma'am." The man seemed eager now, almost desperate to please her.

"What has become of your profits? Perhaps we can help with that as well."

Jean hung his head and looked off to one side. He tapped the toe of his boot and cleared his throat. "It ain't a tale fit for a lady's ears."

Alex bit her lower lip. "Would you tell it to my husband?"

Jean shot a glance at the duke and flushed.

Alex turned a little toward Gabriel and raised her brows. "I think perhaps it is time to retire to the inn, Your Grace. Perhaps you and Mr. Duvall could finish our business in the common room while I retire?"

Oh, dear. She'd never ordered him about before and the look on her husband's face was quite priceless after that statement.

Quite priceless, indeed.

Chapter Nine

It was a common enough tale, Gabriel reflected as he sat back in his chair, eyeing the man his wife had hired. Hired! He'd watched the entire scene with his own eyes, and he still didn't know how she'd won Duvall's loyalty in so short a space. But won it, she had. The man was spilling his story and begging for the job, promising to find his guards at any cost.

"So you see, Your Grace, we've gots to pay off Pimminy every month, and by the time we done that, there ain't hardly enough left over to feed ourselves."

"And you owe Pimminy because you both courted his daughter and you ruined her." Gabriel shook his head. "Why not just marry the chit?"

"Oh, Pimminy won't have neither of us and we don't want her now, anyhow. She tricked us good, she did. Playing up to me and then doing the same to my brother when my back was turned. I think she's still up to her old tricks but no one is talking."

"How much longer must you make this restitution?"

"Another year at least! He said three years ought to do it, but he'll find his reasons to keep fleecing us if he can."

"What would happen if you just stopped paying him?"

Duvall paled to a sickly white, his eyes wide with fear. "He'll kill us. He's got money, men, powerful connections, Your Grace. He could arrange some accident and no one would question him."

"I daresay you have a powerful connection now too," Gabriel drawled out, tapping his fingers against the scarred wood of the table.

The man's mouth dropped open. "You would go against Pimminy?"

"No promises, but I will look into it." The last thing he needed was to get embroiled in French politics and anyway, they were wasting precious time. On the other hand, Alexandria would demand to know what this man's story was and want to help. It was one of the many things he loved about her, but it could be maddening at the same time.

Duvall bowed from his seated position. "Bless you, Your Grace. I would kiss the hem of your coat if'n you'll allow me."

"That will not be necessary." Gabriel shook his head. The realization of how Alexandria had won this man's allegiance, all their allegiance, was suddenly crystal clear. She cared about people. Genuinely cared. His show of concern for Duvall's circumstances was inspiring the same thing. They may be able to trust him after all.

"All right, Duvall, I've decided to hire you." He took the pistol out of his belt and slowly slid it across the table. "Keep this hidden until you think you've found my guards. They will be wearing blue-and-gold uniforms. Two of the men are the leaders, Lieutenant Kurt von Struben and Lieutenant Eddie Stonebridge. I am a fair hand at sketching so I will draw you pictures of them. You should either encounter them on the road between here and Calais, or they might be taking the other road from Calais to Paris. Keep going until you find them." Gabriel took out some coins and passed them over. "Traveling expenses."

"Merci." Duvall nodded.

"Travel fast and talk to no one unnecessarily. When you suspect you have found my guards, show Kurt or Eddie the pistol. If you've found the right men, they will recognize it. Then give them the note and tell them where we are. When you return, with them I hope, you will have your horse. Do you think you can manage all of that?"

"Yes, Your Grace. But might I ask a question?"

"Certainly."

"How did you get yourselves separated from your guards?"

The man wasn't an idiot, which was good, but Gabriel didn't want to tell him more than necessary.

"We were put upon by thieves. During the skirmish I took one of the horses and spirited my wife away from the scene. We are traveling to Paris for our honeymoon and her safety is, of course, my utmost concern. I would rather not take her back to look for my guards myself and am hoping they are just behind us. We will wait until midday tomorrow, but if I haven't heard from you by then, I will assume my men are still in Calais or on the other road and we will strike out for Paris in a carriage. Tell the men to follow this road and catch up to us as soon as may be."

"I will find them, Your Grace."

"Very good. I will see you here at first light with the letter ready." Gabriel stood and narrowed his eyes at the man. "Don't think to cross me, Duvall. I will have no patience for failure in this matter, do you understand?"

The man nodded and wiped the sheen of sweat from his forehead with a sleeve.

"Good. Sleep well. You're going to need your rest."

GABRIEL MADE HIS WAY UP to their room, opening the door with a slight squeak. A candle burned near the bedside table and his wife, his sweet, impossibly naive and yet wise-beyond-her-years wife, lay curled on her side, fast asleep. It had been a long day. Was it only this morning that they had traveled to Calais? That he'd heard the water crash and break over the ship? That he'd first heard her laugh? It seemed weeks ago.

Gabriel moved toward her around the side of the bed and knelt, his face inches from Alexandria's. He leaned closer, closed his eyes, and listened for the sound of her breath. He could smell the lavender in her hair, but he couldn't make out her breath.

It didn't matter. *God, it doesn't matter. I'm so happy. So . . . thankful. Even if it only lasts this day. Thank You.*

His eyes fluttered open, his gaze roving her face, so peaceful in sleep. He took in his side of the bed and was a little afraid to sleep. What if he woke up to silence? What if it only did last this one day? Despite his claim, he knew that deep in his heart he wished for his affliction to be over. Deep, deep in the part of his heart where he rarely probed, he hoped he'd learned all the lessons from it God had wanted him to learn. That was what afflictions were for, weren't they? And he was a changed man—he was so changed—there was no denying that.

But had he changed enough?

The memory of clutching Duvall's collar just an hour ago made him pause. It hadn't taken very long to feel like a strong, capable man again—a duke used to immediate respect and deference, a peer of the realm, power humming through his veins. He pictured his face over Duvall's, stern and demanding and . . . conceited. His stomach started to tremble and his throat tightened. Who was that lofty man with pride riding high on his cheekbones? He'd been broken, humbled, brought to his very knees, hadn't he?

Yes, by God's judgment, by God's truth, by God's love. Gabriel knew some of him had been changed. Much of him. *Oh, God! I want to be like You, I do. But it is costing me everything! Down to my last sinew and breath. I honestly don't know if I can do it.*

He clenched his eyes and took shaky breaths—repentant, sorrowful, humble, broken clay. He didn't list his sins; he didn't have to. With the scales from his eyes, he saw them as God saw them. He just crouched on the floor beside the bed, his head in his hands, his heart an open book.

After several moments, a deep peace came over him. He breathed long breaths, felt the muscles in his face relax, felt the pressure at the bridge of his nose loosen and fall away. Following a strange instinct that felt like someone calling him to movement, he leaned his head to one side, stretching out his neck, and then to the other. He took another long breath, his head floating up and feeling strangely light. Something popped, a soft pop and yet it bordered on pain in his left ear. Fear assailed him.

What are you doing? You are being ridiculous.

Do you think this will help things?

You might be making it worse.

The darts of doubt were so strong. His heart started thumping with the effort to combat them. Scripture from Ephesians shot through his memory.

"Put on the whole armour of God, that ye may be able to stand against the wiles of the devil. For we wrestle not against flesh and blood, but against principalities, against powers, against the rulers of the darkness of this world, against spiritual wickedness in high places. Wherefore take unto you the whole armour of God, that ye may be able

to withstand in the evil day, and having done all, to stand. Stand therefore, having your loins girt about with truth, and having on the breastplate of righteousness; And your feet shod with the preparation of the gospel of peace; Above all, taking the shield of faith, wherewith ye shall be able to quench all the fiery darts of the wicked. And take the helmet of salvation, and the sword of the Spirit, which is the word of God."

Gabriel imagined the shield of faith, imagined holding it against the thoughts and seeing them ricochet away. He breathed deep and pushed away the doubt, concentrating on God's peace and love that he had felt only moments ago.

But now it felt like he was trying to make something happen. Now it felt forced—in his own strength, not in God's. Where did it go? What had happened?

Frustration hummed through his veins. He wanted that peace back, that feeling that something, something healing and wonderful, was happening deep in his ear and nose cavities. But it was gone. Was his hearing?

He looked back at Alexandria, traced the curve of her cheek with his gaze and then, very gently so as not to awaken her, the side of his finger. The fact that she would love him either way struck him again. How thankful he was to have found her. How blessed he was to know he'd married a person who loved the real him, faults and all, and not some version set out for good company. His head dropped and he closed his eyes again. His thoughts turned toward Italy and her parents.

Dear Lord, help me keep her safe. I fear we are walking in the shadows of darkness and soon it will be dark all around us. Your light is our only survival.

ALEX WOKE WITH A START and turned over. Where was she? It was so dark. She took several long breaths and recognized

Gabriel beside her, remembered that they were married now, that they were in France. She reached out and touched him, his back. The lines of scars brought her fully awake.

She'd had a dream, a bad dream, the worst dream ever. A man, his face dark and shrouded, screamed at her parents.

"Tell me where you've hidden the manuscript."

Her father, stripped of his shirt, yelled out as a long, braided whip lashed across his back.

Her mother screamed, manacled to the wall by her wrists, her lovely face grimacing in pain.

The nightmare had seemed so real. Was it even now happening?

Alex clutched the thin blanket to her neck, fear chilling her skin and raising goose bumps on her arms. Had she been alone, at home, waking from a bad dream she would have leapt from the bed, gone down to the banked fire in the kitchen, and made something hot to drink. She would have then taken that hot tea and wandered about, outside the castle, picking her way across the pebbled beach near the soothing sounds of the water until the dark mood lifted from her.

She wanted to do that now.

Gabriel was sound asleep and softly snoring. She didn't want to wake him. What would he think? Sniveling over a dream. She was too used to taking care of herself to consider for very long that he might hold her, comfort her, even pray with her. The thought that she should try for that came strong, but it would be too embarrassing! What if he only chided her for waking him up?

She shook her head at that. It would only take a few moments to go down and at least see if anyone was awake and if she could get some warm milk or tea. Just a few moments outside would do, feeling the wind in her hair and smelling the salt-laden air, the seabirds, the fish and mossy smells. It made her ache with a longing for home.

With fluid movements she turned to the edge of the feather mattress and swung her legs around. Before the bed could move much, she lifted the blanket and slid out, landing on her feet with a soft thump. She waited, standing there in the dark room, listening for his breathing pattern to change. It did not. Her mouth curved into a smile.

Feeling like her old self, the one who knew how to sneak around Henry and Ann and the other villagers on Holy Island, she bit her lower lip and crept to her red cape and shoes.

As she swung it around her shoulders, she nearly laughed. She could almost feel the sea breeze against her hair. Oh, how she missed it. She hadn't realized how much until this very second.

The door was easy to slip through. With light-footed steps she went down to the cold, dark common room. She wrinkled her nose. It smelled like spilled spirits and stale tobacco. She raced on tiptoe to the back where the kitchen should be. Sure enough there was a banked fire. With a little raking from the poker, she soon had enough of a blaze to boil water.

Rummaging through the cupboards she found what she really wanted—coffee and a cheese cloth to strain it with. The process took only moments, but her heart raced every time she glanced over her shoulder at the door. It would be dawn in an hour or so, according to the clock on the mantel, and she would have to hurry to have her moment by the sea.

Finally the wonderful-smelling drink was ready. Alex found a sugar bowl and stirred in a couple of pinches. Then, with her big cup in hand, she left by the back door. The night air blew her hair, long and loose, from her face. She lifted her face to the thin moon and closed her eyes. It felt like freedom

beating in her chest. Not that Gabriel kept her locked inside
. . . well, not locked exactly, just so comfortably ensconced in
every luxury and proper societal protocol that she had forgotten
what this kind of freedom felt like.

It felt like home.

The clinging effects of the dream sloughed off like an old
skin as she ran down the street toward the shore. Her heart
pounded and her hair flew behind her like a dark flag, whipping in the stiff coastal breeze. She ran faster, free and flying
and not afraid anymore. Her face broke into a grin.

If she hurried, she would get to see the glory of first light.

Chapter Ten

*G*abriel woke with the first rays of morning light tinge-ing the room with a rosy glow. He sat up and rubbed his hand over his face. The letter. He had to quickly write that letter for his meeting with Duvall. He slipped from the bed, thinking not to wake his wife, and quietly pulled on his trou-sers. Turning, he glanced toward the bed. He stopped, frowned, and walked over to the rumpled blankets. "Alexandria?" He glanced around the room. She was not there, not anywhere.

He came fully awake in an instant. Where could she have gone? She had fallen asleep early. Perhaps she was already dressed and down breaking her fast. His brows came together. He rather hoped she would have thought to wake him and go down to breakfast together, but she did have an independent streak that was bone deep, probably from having to practically raise herself on that lonely island.

Gabriel had to admit that when he had gone there to fetch her, there was a barren beauty to the place that struck him to the core. He was glad he'd visited her home, that crumbling edifice of a castle, and seen how she was living. It helped him understand her now.

Still, he would have to teach her. A woman didn't go down to breakfast alone, especially a new wife and a duchess.

He walked over to the little desk in the room and took out paper and quill. After a few lines he explained the situation to Kurt and Eddie, sanded the ink, folded it, and poured some wax from the lone candle in the room onto the fold. With his signet ring he pressed the wax and held until it was cool. That and the pistol should give them proof enough that his messenger was genuine.

He rose and strode down the stairs to find Duvall and his wife.

ALEX STOOD, PALMS OUT, EYES closed, the sea air blowing her hair about her shoulders, her face tilted toward the morning shafts of light through the clouds. She stood on the beach—rough sand between her toes, her shoes cast aside far behind her—and prayed for her parents.

The dream had faded but her worry had not. *Dear Father in heaven, dear glorious One from on high, please help me get to them and soon. Please keep them safe until I can find them.*

She didn't know what else to pray. She had asked so many times. So much time had gone by and still she hadn't found them. She had clues, she had hope, but the path felt darker, more dangerous than just the Spanish after them. There was something else, some dark evil that dogged at their heels. She could feel it, and Gabriel could too. She could tell by the tightness of his shoulders, the strain around his mouth, and the panther gleam in his green eyes. He was looking for it and it was growing nearer . . . stronger. Almost palpable at times.

Why?

What had her parents gotten themselves into?

"Alexandria. Thank God."

She whirled around to see her husband plowing toward her. The look in his eyes, that look she had just been thinking of, was now directed straight at her. She took an involuntary step back.

He came to her and crushed her into his arms, his head pressing down on the top of hers. His breath was rough and raspy in her ear. "Dear God, I thought they'd captured you. Alexandria . . ." He splayed both hands along the sides of her face, raised her head, and stared into her eyes with such a look . . . such a pained and terrified and relieved look. Oh! What had she done? Tears pricked Alex's eyes.

"I'm sorry. I had a bad dream."

"You had a bad dream?" He grasped her by the shoulders in a tight hold, his brows drawn together. "Were you walking in your sleep?"

"No . . . I—" It sounded silly now, silly and foolish what she had done. She took a quivering breath. "In the past . . . when I was home, I always made a cup of hot tea and walked the beach to shake off a bad dream. I didn't think."

"No, you did not think. You often don't think before you act. This is not Holy Island, Alexandria. This is France. And we are in danger, you know this."

Alex nodded, head down. "I'm sorry," she said in a voice so soft, she didn't know if he had heard her. She bit down on her quivering lower lip as a fat tear fell to the ground and landed on the tip of Gabriel's shoe.

Gabriel made a growling groan and hauled her into his arms again. "Don't cry. I was just . . . afraid. I've never known such fear. When I walked down to the common room and only Duvall was there, my heart stopped. No one had seen you leave.

No one knew anything. It was as if you had . . . vanished. My mind went mad with imaginings."

He shook his head and breathed heavily into her hair. "It's not your fault. You're not used to having to be so careful. You have to stay close to me. Very close on this journey. Does it feel constraining?"

She nodded against his white shirtfront smelling of starch and him. "It feels different."

"It feels good to me." His caress against her back changed, became something more intimate and loving. He nuzzled her ear. "I like having you close. We are on our honeymoon, after all."

Her fist curled against his chest, catching some of the fine lawn of his shirt. "You'll tire of me after a while."

He caught her chin and looked at her lips. "You really believe that?"

She shook her head and then nodded.

"Alexandria, if you keep things hidden deep in your heart they can take root, both good things and bad things as we've both discovered in this last year. Let's agree to get them into the open, into the light where they can be exposed for what they really are. Tell me what is deep in your heart."

Tears clouded her vision. She wasn't sure why she had said that, something to do with absent parents probably, but she was sure there was a wall around her heart and that even in loving Gabriel so much, she had kept parts of herself safely behind that wall. She wanted to shrink back behind it now. She wanted to turn tail and run. But when she looked deep into his eyes and saw only love, so much love for her . . .

She gulped down her tears and raised her chin. "I wonder if we shall tire of each other being so close every moment."

A flash of pain like a thrust from a knife emerged and then the green of Gabriel's eyes hardened to sparkling emeralds. "I see."

Oh, he didn't see at all. But it was too hard! She couldn't tell him her greatest fear was that she would give him everything—her heart and soul . . . her love—and then he would leave too. That someday he would pat her on the head, give her a peck on the cheek, and go off to his own interests and adventures without her. How could she bear it if he did that? Just the thought of it now made her sick with worry. She already loved him too much.

Yes, you already love him too much. Some distance would be good.

She *believed* the voice. Whether it came from her own mind or from some other place, it felt safer, more comfortable to believe it.

"We should go back to the inn. Perhaps you would like a little privacy to freshen up in our room while I deal with Duvall." His throat moved as he swallowed hard. "I left them in rather a hurry."

"Of course," Alex said in a small voice.

"I have a matter to look into and then, if we have not seen the guards by noon, we will continue to Paris."

His curt words cut like a dagger to her core—retaliation to her words. She had wounded him, but the way to repair the damage seemed impossible now. The wall was up and the warning flags around her heart were whipping in the wind.

God, is this marriage? This dance of emotion and expectation and cold, stark fear? It was harder than she'd thought it would be.

"I'll just get my shoes," she murmured and disentangled her arms from his.

WITH DUVALL SENT OFF TO find the guards and Alexandria having her time away from him, Gabriel decided to write Mr. Pimminy a letter before seeing about the horses for Alexandria and his travel to Paris. He asked for paper and quill and set to work.

12 June 1819
From the office of the Duke of St. Easton, His Grace,
Gabriel Ravenwood
Dear Mr. Pimminy,
It has come to my attention that my friends, the Duvall brothers, have had some issue with you and your daughter. While I can only imagine the depths of your suffering over her lost virtue, I am certain we can find a more satisfactory means of restitution than fleecing the Duvalls of all their profits. I have proposed to Jean Duvall that he offer his hand in marriage, which of course would restore her reputation and give her the grace of a home and children that she deserves. She will, of course, come with a large dowry so Mr. Duvall can restore his fortune and keep her in all that is decent and comfortable. If the woman protests to such a match, then let us consider the matter closed and you will have no more dealings of any kind with the Duvalls.
I am now traveling to Paris. Let us hope that if your name comes up during my attendance at court, it is in a positive light.
Best regards,
St. Easton

After placing his seal on the fold and sending the letter off with a boy to the posting house, he sat back and rubbed the bridge of his nose, hoping he hadn't just set more thugs upon their heels. He looked up as Alexandria came around the corner. She paused, clinging to the corner with one hand and gazed at him, chagrin in her eyes.

"Why have I consigned myself to the bedchamber?" Her brows rose.

"I believe you wanted some time away from me." Gabriel quirked a brow back at her.

"It's terribly boring up there."

She seemed so miserable that he decided to save her pride somewhat. "I was just going to pick out our horses."

She brightened immediately. "Oh?"

He gave her that one-sided smile. "It's not a very glamorous task, picking out horses, but if you don't mind bearing my company, you might come along."

"I-I don't mind your company." She bit down on her lower lip.

"Come here, Alexandria." Gabriel stood and pulled out the chair next to his, then seated himself close beside her and poured her a cup of hot chocolate from the ready pot. He spread strawberry jam, knowing that was her favorite, on a slice of fresh bread and put it on a little plate for her. He leaned close to her ear and murmured, "Why don't you eat some breakfast? I know you must be hungry, and I'll tell you about Duvall's scandalous tale."

Her eyes widened with excitement. "You will? Is it very awful?"

"Awful enough." He sat back in his chair and took a sip of his coffee.

Alexandria leaned over and gave him a kiss on the cheek. "I'm sorry."

He was surprised he could hear such quiet words. The dull roaring of yesterday was even less today. And she had whispered in his left ear, the one that had that strange pop occur the night before. Something was happening.

He took her hand and raised it to his lips, looking down through his lashes at her.

She took a flustered inhale.

"As am I. It may take us a little while to learn how to get on with each other in this marriage. We must be patient with one another."

"I do believe you're right." Her forehead puckered. "Are you always right, Gabriel?"

"Undoubtedly." He kept his face serious.

"It might become rather tedious, you know." The teasing tone and flirtatious smile on his wife's face made a streak of desire race through his blood. The urge to carry her up the stairs and ravish her that instant made him feel like a schoolboy. He gave her the half smile instead.

"A cross you shall have to bear, I suppose."

Alexandria nodded, a giggle escaping. "Quite a heavy one, I assure you, being married to someone so wise and knowledgeable. So talented and handsome . . . so very dukelike."

"Eat your breakfast, Your Grace."

She took a big bite of jam, leaving sticky red on the corners of her mouth, and he just couldn't help himself. He leaned over and kissed it away.

Alexandria gasped. "There are people behind us!"

He shrugged. "We are newly wedded. They will understand."

She seemed to consider that for a moment and then held out her bread. Her voice turned soft and teasing again. "Would you like some?"

He shook his head, an infinitesimal movement. She was incorrigible. The thought of her doing to him what he had just done . . . He took a long breath and looked toward the stairs.

"Perhaps we have time for a little nap before we see the horses." His gaze darted back to hers.

"But I'm not—oh." A tinge of pink rose to her face. "That can be done in the daytime?" Her wide eyes made him softly chuckle.

"Oh yes. That can be done anytime."

"Oh." She took a big bite of bread. "Do hurry and tell me Duvall's story then. I have always eaten my meals rather quickly."

"SO SORRY FOR THE DELAY, Your Grace."

Kurt and Eddie, along with the other guards, swung down from their steeds and came forward to crowd around Gabriel and Alexandria just outside the livery stable. They had just purchased their horses and were leading them outside, Gabriel dreading the long road to Paris without his guards but not wanting to lose any more time. Thankfully, he wouldn't have to.

"Excellent." Gabriel grasped his man's shoulder. "Duvall found you, then." He glanced over and saw Duvall with a big grin on his face off to one side of the group.

"Yes. We fought off the enemy but stayed the night in Calais, attending the two of our men who were injured. This morning we tracked you to the road here to Boulogne-sur-Mer. Duvall met us about halfway with the message."

Gabriel's gaze swept over the cavalcade, seeing one of the regent's guards was missing as well as one of his own—Sir Walter Robbins. "How are the injured?"

Eddie spoke up with a half-cocked grin beneath his beard. "They'll be right as rain in a fortnight, Your Grace. Sir Walter got nicked in the thigh with a lead ball and the regent's man, Williamson, was hit in the arm. We set them up real nice in a tucked-away inn with the promise of a physician checking on them daily. They are awaiting your orders of where to go once they are able to ride."

"Very good. Send word to them to go back to London. I do not need men who are not up to their best. We shall hire more in Paris should the need seem apparent." Gabriel paused in thought. Down to three of the king's guards. How to get rid of the others without alerting the regent that they planned to spend only a few days in Paris instead of the months he'd hinted at?

"And the enemy? Did you discover who they are?"

Kurt shook his blond head, blue eyes narrowing. "Not Spaniards, as we suspected. Two escaped and two were killed." He flexed his fingers and curled them into a fist. "I did get some information from one of them before he breathed his last."

Gabriel let out a grim chuckle. Kurt von Struben, a German Hessian soldier in years past, could be quite ruthless when he needed to be. "And what, pray tell, did he reveal?" Out of the corner of his eye, Gabriel saw Alexandria stretch out her neck to hear every word.

Kurt glanced at the other guards. He took a step closer and lowered his voice. "He spoke in Italian. My Italian is deplorable, forgive me, but something like, *ils continueront à venir pour elle.*"

"They will keep coming for her?" Gabriel's heart dropped at the threatening words. He glanced at Alexandria. The Italians wanted Alexandria too?

"Me?" she asked in a quiet voice, her eyes huge in her face.

"I asked who is coming for her," Kurt murmured in a harsh tone. He shook his head, eyes downcast. "It was too late." Kurt reached into his coat and pulled out a smudged paper. "We found this in his pocket."

Gabriel studied the Italian words and frowned. His Italian was about as good as Kurt's. But two of them jumped out at him. Two words he recognized:

Featherstone and the *Carbonari.*

God help them, were the Carbonari involved in this too? He thought back to everything he had ever heard about the Italian Carbonari. Secret revolutionary extremists. From all accounts they wanted a constitutional monarchy or a republic after Napoleon had been defeated and the Papal States reinstated. They must have heard of the manuscript and the plans. They, too, had reason to need a powerful weapon.

Gabriel set his mouth in a grim line and shoved the note in his coat pocket. No need to alarm anyone, least of all Alexandria. "Gentlemen, to Paris." He lifted his arm in a gesture of solidarity.

While the guards turned to mount their horses, he murmured to Alexandria that he would just be a moment, went over to Duvall, and clapped him on the shoulder. "Good work, Duvall. I have already paid the liveryman for a good horse for you."

"Many thanks, Your Grace. You'll be helpin' more than you know."

"As to helping, I've sent Pimminy a letter. I don't imagine you will be bothered by him again, but if he proves imprudent, write to the Duke of St. Easton in Paris. I will be checking the post there frequently."

Duvall's little eyes grew round. "I don't know what to say." He knelt on one knee, grasped Gabriel's hand, and kissed his ring. "Your Grace, God be with you. You are the greatest of men, you—"

"Yes, yes, no need for all that. Get up."

"If there is anything I can ever do for you—"

"You can tell me the whereabouts of my pistol." Gabriel raised his brows.

"Oh yes!" He pointed at Kurt, who had mounted a tall gelding. "I gave it him, Your Grace."

"There is one other thing," Gabriel said in a low voice, looking back into Duvall's eyes.

"Yes?"

"Don't breathe a word of this to anyone, not my name or anything that occurred. Not even to your brother. Do you understand?"

"Oh yes! Not even my brother." Duvall nodded vigorously.

"Good. Well, farewell, Duvall."

"Godspeed, Your Grace." Duvall turned and hurried into the livery stable.

Gabriel went back over to Alexandria, who was mounted and ready. She lowered her face toward him and smiled as he approached. "You handled him very well," she said for his ears alone.

Gabriel shrugged and gave her a half smile. "You might have taught me a thing or two."

"Really?" Her blue eyes sparkled with mirth. "What a singular notion. I do believe I'm quite overcome with shock."

"Now you're sounding like a duchess."

His wife hooted. "Well, don't depend on that to last very long."

Gabriel mounted his horse and came up alongside her. He reached for her hand and kissed the back of it. "Excellent. I'm afraid I would miss my hoyden shepherdess."

Alexandria swallowed hard and cast her gaze at the men, all of whom were watching the scene with interest. She tugged her hand away, her face filling with a becoming pink. "Shall we travel to Paris now? I am looking forward to seeing the sights of such a famed city."

Gabriel chuckled. "Yes, my dear. Five days and we will be in *La Ville-Lumière,* The City of Light."

And in five days they would begin their deceit, throwing off the regent, the French, the Spanish, and now the Carbonari. How had they gotten this deep into the mires of this mystery?

Chapter Eleven

Paris, France

The clatter of the horses' hooves echoed across the cobbled street of Saint-Honorè as they swept into one of the largest cities in the world—Paris, France. Evidence of the revolution could still be seen in the scarred and fallen houses and shops and the abandoned streets with traces of rotten decay in the air. They trotted past graveyards spotted with mounds of recently disturbed earth. Farther on, people milled the streets in odd forms of dress, men in long coats that reached their ankles and women in short, scanty skirts. Alex pressed her hand against the glass of the coach window and took it all in, feeling sad somehow . . . bereft . . . as if death hovered ever near in this place.

"It will get better," Gabriel spoke near her ear from beside her.

He could still hear her. A week now and he still could hear—a fact that made her heart swell with hope. She sat up and looked at him. "It will?" She couldn't fathom how it could but she hoped he was right.

"I think so." He gestured to the other side of the carriage and ahead to the east, where they were traveling toward the center of the city. "It won't be the same as before the revolution, but it is coming back. The Tuileries Gardens are still intact, I'm told."

"The people look so poor and wretched."

"They have good reason. They are not much better off than before the revolution. The monarchy is back in control, though with limited power." He shook his head. "I am afraid all the bloodshed was for naught. They do not have the republic they so desperately wanted."

"I'm glad we will not be staying very long."

"As to that, we need to plan." Gabriel lowered his voice. There was no one else inside the carriage, all of their guards riding on horseback either before or behind them, but there was a coachman on his perch in front of the carriage and one could never be sure how much he could hear. "I have made arrangements to rent a house at Place Vendôme, a square near the Tuileries and in the best part of the city."

"How long will we stay?"

"I am hoping only a few days, a week at most. We will get settled in, attend the opera, the theatre, visit the Louvre." He picked up her hand and kissed the back of it, a smile in his voice. "I will buy you a wedding gift from the famous jewelry store at Palais Royal that will set the tongues wagging with rumors that we are in Paris, and then we will be seen at popular cafés like Tortoni and Legac's."

Alex made a sound of distress. "It sounds like we will be in the city for some time."

"I know, *ma chérie*." He looked back out the window at the passing city. "We must be seen enjoying ourselves as newly wedded tourists or the regent will not be convinced by the reports from these guards he has chained about our necks. And there will be others watching us, as you know. We must be very convincing."

Alex leaned back against the leather seat and chewed on her lower lip, her mind whirling. The way Gabriel talked they would be several days in Paris, and that was just too long. Her parents needed her. She could feel it—they were running out of time.

She sat up and grasped Gabriel's upper arm. "Wait. I've just had an idea. What if the guards see what they expect to see, but it is really a ruse?"

Gabriel leaned close and rubbed his thumb against her cheek. His brows pulled together and that half-cocked smile played around his lips. "What do you mean?"

"What if we hire impersonators? A man and a woman who look like us? They could stay in our house, dress in our clothes, and go out, very carefully of course, with their hats pulled low and the woman veiled. They could use umbrellas and mostly leave the house at night, just enough to be seen upon occasion." She leaned toward him, warming to the idea. "They could even invent rumors for staying inside the house. An illness or . . ." She smiled up at him with a teasing tone in her voice, "newly wedded reasons."

Gabriel chuckled. "You're serious."

"It could work! We could leave all the sooner, and by the time they discovered our deception, we would be well on our way to Italy with none the wiser where we have gone. By the time they get word back to the regent"—she paused and peered at him with all the hope she felt—"we may have found my parents."

Gabriel gazed into her eyes for a long moment and then drew closer and kissed her. By the time he backed away, her head was spiraling with that warm, dizzying sensation that was familiar from his kisses. "Does that mean you approve?"

"That means, dear wife, that sometimes I forget I've married a sleuth."

"And you approve of the idea?"

"I do believe it might work. I can't believe I didn't think of it myself."

"Well, you can't think of everything yourself. I have to be able to come up with some of the ideas in this marriage."

"I am quite certain that will not be a problem for you." Gabriel chuckled again. "And I know someone who will help us find our counterparts."

"Acquaintances of yours?"

Gabriel nodded. "An old hunting friend. Eccentric fellow. I think you'll like him."

"When can we meet with him?"

"I will send a note around as soon as we get settled."

"Sounds perfect." Alex nodded and sank back against the seat again, squeezing her hands together with a silent prayer.

"YOUR GRACE, IT IS SO good to see you again!" Rory Beauffremont shouted. The middle-aged man had shocking white hair and bushy black brows over intense dark eyes, dressed in the full dress uniform of buff-colored breeches, white stockings, shirt and cravat, and a deep blue coat complete with golden epaulettes, medals, and tassels—just as Gabriel had described him.

He bellowed the greeting, arms extended wide in welcome. "Do come in and introduce this exquisite creature at your side." He didn't wait for the introduction, just came forward, grasped Alex's hand in a painful grip, and bowed low over it, turning out one muscular leg with an elegant flair. Alex suppressed her desire to laugh and shot Gabriel an amused glance instead.

"Don't tell me, don't tell me, let me guess." He came up for air and stood studying her for a long moment. "Great heavens, you've finally got yourself a bride."

Alex's eyes widened but she refrained from saying anything. Gabriel chuckled and clapped the man on the arm. "It's true, my dear fellow. Can you believe it?"

"I daresay I can, looking at her. Such a tender age. Are you taking her on the grand tour?"

Gabriel shrugged. "A honeymoon of sorts." He turned to Alex. "Alexandria, may I present Lord Rory Beauffremont." He turned back to his friend. "Rory, meet Alexandria Ravenwood, the Duchess of St. Easton."

"I shall have to ring for my wife." Rory gestured for them to follow him farther into the room. "She will want to meet her straight away."

"By all means."

They settled in the elegant drawing room while Rory instructed his hovering servants. Upon returning he flung out his coattails and sat across from them. "It has been such a long time, Your Grace. Tell me all the news from London."

"I'm sure you have heard of Queen Charlotte's passing."

"Yes, yes. The regent running things now? As misbegotten as this place is with Louis back on the throne, I'd not be in a hurry to return under that hand in control."

"Yes, well, he's manageable. Barely."

Rory turned his intense eyes upon Alex, making her want to shrink back but she didn't. "Forgive me, ma chérie. Politics are so boring, are they not? How are you enjoying Paris?"

"I find it very . . ." She wasn't sure what to say. It seemed as if the people were either the walking dead or pretending hard not to be. There was an edge here that made her uneasy, as if the grim reaper still hovered nearby. "Interesting."

"We've only just arrived, Rory." Gabriel cut in. "She has yet to see the glory of Paris, only the road to it."

"Ah yes." His eyes turned downcast. "The city is in dishabille, is it not? But we will rise again, like a phoenix from the ashes. Mark my word, Paris will be back in her glory someday soon. Come, you must see the Théâtre des Variétés. It is back in operation and so delightful. And Beauvilliers, the most celebrated restaurant. You must take her there. People from all corners of the world come to Paris for the food."

"Who is going to Beauvilliers? You know it's my favorite, Rory!" A very thin woman with curled white hair to match her husband's entered the room. When her small eyes spotted Gabriel, she squealed like a schoolgirl. "St. Easton. What a delightful surprise!" She swept into a low curtsy and then glanced at Alex.

Gabriel stood and went over to her, drawing her over to Alex's chair. Alex didn't know whether to stand or not but decided she had better. The woman was tall enough without her remaining seated and towering over her. "Countess, allow me to present my wife, the Duchess of St. Easton, Alexandria Ravenwood. And this is Lady Alice Beauffremont, Rory's better half."

Alex smiled and gave a small curtsy as Rory boomed with laughter. The countess curtsied back, just low enough to show deference.

A sudden commotion at the door to the salon made them all turn. Alex choked back a laugh as a small piglet, complete with ribbons bobbing around its ears, waddled into the room.

"Ah, Stella, come here my pet." The pig obeyed much as a dog would and, to Alex's further astonishment, nestled in the countess's skirts. The woman picked her up and shrugged at Alex. "Dogs make me sneeze."

"She is very adorable."

"Yes, and clean, would you believe it? I found her under my carriage wheel, one little leg caught, but she is right as rain now. Aren't you, my darling?"

Alex shot Gabriel a look full of laughter as the countess rubbed her thin nose against the pig's wide snout.

"Do sit down," Rory boomed. "Refreshments are here, I see."

They all sat back down and had tea and scones. Alex found the flaky pastries so good she could hardly keep from eating more than two. The countess on the other hand only nibbled on one and then fed the rest, bit by bit, to her pig.

"Rory, I have to admit that we've come for another reason other than a visit."

"Not surprised. You always were up to something or another. What's it this time, St. Easton?"

"Yes, well, the regent has been keeping a rather close eye on us and given orders that we only travel to Paris and back. He has even appointed some of the Royal Guards to travel with us. As I'm sure you can imagine, I am straining at this leash."

"Hmm." Rory rubbed his chin. "Yes, I can imagine."

"I would like to take Alexandria on a more extended tour of Europe, but to do so we must convince the regent's guards that I am still in Paris." Gabriel nodded toward Alex. "My lovely wife had the idea of hiring impersonators to act as us for a few weeks. People who look something like us from a distance, you see. They could appear in public, dark places such as the theatre or the opera upon occasion and during the daytime carefully shrouded with hats and scarves and the like."

"Why, that's an excellent notion. Your Grace is so clever." The countess smiled at Alex.

"Please, call me Alexandria." The fact that this older, elegant woman was deferring to her with lofty titles made Alex feel more than a little uncomfortable.

"And you must call me Alice then." She resumed feeding Stella, who was grunting on her lap for another bite of pastry.

"It just might work." Rory nodded with a thoughtful look in his eyes. "We'll need actors, of course. A couple who could really capture your gestures and speech."

"What of Annabelle Riesling, dear? You know her rather well, I think." There was an edge to Alice's voice and her smile seemed to turn brittle. "She does have about the same figure as Alexandria, does she not?"

Rory turned red around the neck. "Isn't she a blonde, my dear?"

His wife waved that away. "Hair can be dyed. If the price is right, I'm quite sure she would do just about anything."

"What of Lord Ashbury for St. Easton?" Rory hurried out. "He is about the right height and has that jet black hair. In need of some blunt too, after that last bout with the gaming tables at Palais Royal."

"There are others, of course." The countess pursed her lips. "We shall have to interview several to find the perfect pair."

"A sound plan," Gabriel interjected. "Might I put upon both of you to do the interviews? Alexandria and I must distance ourselves from any contact with them, keeping our identity and our business anonymous, of course, until the candidates have been chosen."

"What a delightful mission, St. Easton."

"Yes, it says much of your trust in us, but I must ask—" Rory paused with drawn brows—"why is George putting such a leash about the two of you, of all people? Don't seem right."

Gabriel shook his head. "That is something you would do well not to inquire about, nor to speculate to anyone about. Trust me when I say, the less you know the better, for your own safety."

"Top secret, eh?"

Gabriel looked from Rory to Alice. "And somewhat dangerous. I can tell you that much. Should you agree to help us, be on guard. Aside from the regent's guards watching us, we have been followed by others."

The countess shivered, eyes turning bright. "Oh, we haven't had something so delightfully adventurous in some time, St. Easton. How delicious."

"Yes, this should be entertaining." Rory winked at Alex. "I have a feeling our new duchess is full of surprises."

Alex swallowed hard and smiled. If they only knew just how much that sentiment was true, she was quite certain, duchess or not, she would be shown the door.

Chapter Twelve

"Come, beloved, today we are tourists."

Gabriel reached over and stroked the inside of Alexandria's arm, which was flung up over her head. She turned over, away from him, and kicked out in her sleep, causing Gabriel to release a soft grunt.

"Now that was unfair." He leaned over her and whispered into her ear, "I thought you said you weren't a slugabed."

"Perhaps I'm becoming one," came her drowsy response. "What time is it?"

Gabriel kissed her cheek and sprang out of bed. "Time to see Paris. I have a surprise for you."

Alexandria turned over and squinted up at him. "A surprise? Another weapon? I'm not sure I like surprises. Tell me."

"Certainly not. Hurry." He cracked a smile and tugged on the thick coverlet. "This surprise you will like, I am certain. I will meet you below the stairs in one half an hour."

He padded across the bedchamber in a dressing robe and crossed to an adjoining room, which they were using as a dressing chamber, calling for the valet who came with the house on Vendôme Square to attend him.

He planned to give the Beauffremonts a couple of days to arrange the impersonators and in that time make an obligatory call at Louis XVIII's newly restored court to introduce his new wife. But before making their official presence known, he wanted to show Alexandria the various sights of Paris, starting with an afternoon on Boulevard du Temple, then dinner at the famous restaurant Beauvilliers, and then a special treat at night at the Tivoli Gardens. The guards would accompany them, but he hoped they wouldn't need them. Just one day to spend enjoying her first encounter with Paris without danger breathing down their necks. Perhaps they should go in some sort of disguise.

At that thought he rang for Kurt and Eddie to meet with him while he was being shaved.

"I've decided to only take four of the guards with us on our outings today. You two and two of the regent's guards— you may choose which ones. Don't wear the St. Easton livery for this day. I would like us to remain as unnoticeable as possible. Dress as commoners, heavily armed commoners, you understand?"

"Yes, Your Grace." They turned to obey.

Edward, one of the many servants who had come with the house and the man acting as his valet, bowed and waited for his instructions.

"Send word to my wife's maid to dress her modestly in a simple day dress. Nothing that would draw undue attention."

"Yes, Your Grace." Edward gave Gabriel's cravat one last tug and then bowed and hurried from the room.

Gabriel took his own advice, removed his pearl-handled pistol from the armoire drawer, and hid it, along with a short sword and a knife, on his person. He turned from the mirror, satisfied with his image, and then paused.

Bending on one knee, he dipped his head and closed his eyes. *Protect us, Father. Give us this day to see Your glorious creation. Help our plans come to fruition so we might find Alexandria's parents and give them strength in their situation, whatever it might be. Keep them alive. Thank You for my continued healing.* He took a long breath and then stood, hoping Alexandria could lay aside her burden and enjoy the day.

An hour later they were in a rented carriage and traveling down Rue de Rivoli toward the Boulevard du Temple, their guards following a short distance behind on horseback.

"This part of the city is still magnificent, even with the damage from the revolution."

Gabriel patted her hand and smiled. "Just wait."

A few minutes later they turned onto Boulevard du Temple. Alexandria sat up straighter and leaned out the side of the open carriage to see the busy, tree-lined boulevard. "Oh, look. Is it a fair?"

"The largest fair you will likely ever see." Gabriel directed the driver to pull the carriage to the side of the road and helped her out.

They walked along the crowded street passing booths selling all manner of treats—cake, gingerbread, ices, and lemonade. Gabriel bought two ices and led Alexandria back to the center, where a group of people had congregated. "Come, let's see if we can get a bit closer."

They squeezed in, shoulder to shoulder with Parisians dressed in their most fashionable clothing to see and be seen.

"Can you see it?"

Alexandria stretched on her tiptoes. "It's a bear! What is he doing?"

The bear wore a colorful, conical hat and a linked chain around his neck, which his owner held tight to on one end.

With his other hand, he held a stick up above the bear and sang at the top of his voice while the bear bounced up and down on his powerful legs.

"He's dancing . . . or attempting to," Gabriel said with a laugh.

"Oh, it seems cruel."

"I doubt he enjoys dancing but he looks well fed. Come, look over there." Gabriel pointed to another act. A man balancing high above the street on a wire.

They hurried over and stood with a silent crowd, half holding their collective breath as the lithe form, dressed as a Harlequin, made his slow progress across the wire. Gabriel grinned at Alexandria's slack-jawed face. When the man reached the other side, the crowd clapped and cheered. He bowed and then climbed down like a monkey skirting down a tree.

Alexandria let out a big breath. "I'm so glad he made it without falling!"

Gabriel steered her well away from a bullfight that was blocking the other end of the street. "Come. There is one more thing to show you before our dinner at Beauvilliers."

Back to the center of the street, Gabriel pointed to another group of people. "It's just over here, I believe."

They walked to the circle and edged their way to a place where Alexandria could see. Two jugglers balanced spinning plates and tossed colored balls back and forth to each other while a man on stilts walked comically among them, trying to disrupt their play.

Alexandria clasped her hands together. She squealed with delight as a monkey came from nowhere and snatched the balls away, juggling them himself. "Oh, Gabriel, I've never seen so many things! Paris is amazing."

He leaned over and gave her a peck on the cheek, feeling happier than he had in days. He glanced around and saw the guards hovering inconspicuously around them, they, too, seeming to enjoy the show. This is what life would be like after they found her parents. This normalcy and lack of constant caution. This joy on his wife's face in the simple pleasures of life. He was tempted to risk the regent's wrath, tie up his guards, and run away to Italy this night. But he couldn't. They had to be patient and do this the right way.

Lord, if only we had wings to fly to Italy. It would be ever so much faster.

NIGHT DAWNED LIKE A FLAME against the horizon—reds and orange, the last blazing yellow of the sun, a flaming sunset that sank behind the trees and buildings with the cityscape in black forms wavering, shadows of last light. The summer air had grown crisp. Alex pulled the lap robe in the open carriage closer against her waist and sighed. What a day! What an amazing day Gabriel had shown her. And yet, there was more he had whispered into her ear as they left the restaurant.

The food of Beauvilliers had been like nothing she'd ever tasted. Was it any wonder people came from around the world to sample it? Sauces so rich the meat had melted in her mouth. Potatoes simmered in cheeses and butter, milks and curds, and bread so light it tasted like snowflakes on her tongue. Rich wines and richer desserts. The choices seemed endless.

She had walked to the carriage happier than she'd ever felt in her life. A duchess's life could be grand indeed.

Alex stared over at her husband's profile. She still couldn't believe he was hers. In all her imaginings of suitors, she had never dreamed of this, him. High cheekbones, barely saved from being called sharp, those penetrating green eyes that were impossible to look away from, his signature short black hair. Those lips . . . such perfectly formed lips.

She smiled.

"What are you thinking?" Gabriel shot her a look, brows raised, eyes full of mischievous heat.

Heat rose to her face. She shook her head. How to tell him that she was happy he was hers? *How to say, you are so beautiful you take my breath away.* She let him reach and grasp her hand instead.

"It has been such a wonderful day, the best day. Thank you." She smiled at him and had to look away, tears pricking her eyes.

"There is one thing more." Gabriel chuckled soft and deep. "To be honest, it is a rumor and I am not sure we shall even see it. But if we are lucky . . ."

"Yes?" Alex moved closer, grasping his upper arm.

"Well, it is something I have always wanted to see."

She couldn't imagine what that could be. Hadn't he seen just about everything? Done almost all known to modern man? "What is it? I can't bear the suspense."

He pressed his warm hand against the one on his arm. "My greatest surprise. You have liked them thus far this day, have you not?"

Alex nodded up at him. "I liked them very much."

"Just a few more minutes then." He leaned over and kissed her. "Perhaps I can keep you occupied while you wait."

Alex closed her eyes and gave herself up to his lips moving over hers under the twinkling Paris stars. She had to learn to let go . . . to trust. She had to *choose* to trust both her husband and God.

They clattered down the cobbled street of Paris in the growing twilight in intimate silence, their bodies pressed close to each other's side, their hands clasped, the buildings passing in shadowy glimpses of this time and place. They turned down a street still busy with the traffic of sightseers and adventurers. Alex let her mind loosen, let all thought of the harrows to come drop away and felt each moment of anticipation for what was to come.

Sudden fireworks burst into the sky. The horses shied away but their coachman pushed them toward it. Another blast, and then more sparks falling from high in the sky and illuminating the darkness with lights dripping down like glittering diamonds.

Alex gasped. "What is it?"

He smiled, his face alight with laughter and the bursting colored lights above. "It is true then. She's here."

"Who?"

"Her name is Sophie Blanchard. She is a balloonist for the king. Look!" He motioned up and Alex saw for the first time a giant balloon of multicolors hovering in the air over the square where they were stopping. She shook her head in wonderment, unable to comprehend it. People surged the square, pointing and gazing up.

"Who is she? What is she doing?"

"She's flying," Gabriel said with a soft smile.

Another explosion of light and color lit up the sky. Alex pressed her curled hand to her chest and watched, spellbound. What world had she stepped into?

What world would tomorrow hold?

When she'd prayed, begged God for adventure and purpose, all those growing-up years on Holy Island, she hadn't known God would answer her like this. She had not known what she asked for. She took hold of Gabriel's hand and squeezed it.

"Do you like it?" The sparks of light in the bright night sky reflected in his eyes.

She nodded. "I wish I could go up in one of those balloons. Can you imagine the view?"

Gabriel seemed thoughtful. "I am glad to hear you say that."

"Why?"

"Because I think I've just received an answer to a recent prayer."

"What do you mean?"

He whispered into her ear, "A faster, much faster, way to Italy." He returned his attention to the sky and the giant balloon.

"You mean in the balloon?" Alex's head jerked up. "Is it possible? Is it very dangerous?"

"Now you're afraid." Gabriel chuckled.

"Not afraid." Alex bristled. "Just cautious. I should like to know more about it and talk to this Sophie Blanchard."

"Exactly my plan. We shall meet with her tomorrow if at all possible." He squeezed her hand, a small smile playing around his lips. "You would really do it? Most women wouldn't and a great deal of the men I know too, I suspect."

"If it is reasonably safe . . . and faster. I would do it for them."

Gabriel put his arm around her shoulders and hugged her close to his side. "I've married a true adventurer."

Alex shrugged. "There is little help for it, I'm afraid."

They watched the balloon, a colorful sphere of slow-moving grace, float through the air in companionable silence. Alex imagined herself in the wicker basket where Sophie stood, hanging on to one of the lines and waving down at them, with a mix of excitement and fear.

Was it possible? Could they really fly all the way to Italy?

Chapter Thirteen

The café where they had arranged to meet Sophie Blanchard was just down the street from their rented house. They entered the crowded room where elegantly clad Parisians, sitting or standing in chatting groups, drank rich, strong coffee or decadent chocolate from delicate cups. The smells of the place alone made Alex want to close her eyes and just stand about and inhale, but the people were too interesting to close her eyes for even a moment. She scanned the crowd instead, looking for the famous aeronaut.

They had received a note this morning that Mrs. Blanchard would be happy to meet them at noon to discuss her balloon. "Do you see her?" Alex asked Gabriel. "I didn't get a good look at her last night—it was so dark. Would you recognize her?"

"Her note said she would be wearing a red hat. That should narrow things down."

Alex turned toward the other side of the room and craned her neck to better see. There, against a far wall, was a seated woman in a red hat, though she was hard to see she was so small. Alex nudged Gabriel in the side with her elbow. "There. Is that her?"

"Let's go and see, shall we?"

Alex clasped Gabriel's arm while he traversed the crowd. "Madame Blanchard?" he asked toward the woman's back.

She turned and looked up at them. Her face was small and serious with wide-set eyes, a thin nose, and a pointed little chin. "I am Sophie Blanchard." She glanced from Gabriel to Alex, intelligence sparking her brown eyes. "You must be the Duke and Duchess of St. Easton." She rose, a lithe move that was compact in its gracefulness, and curtsied. "I am happy to make your acquaintance."

Alex found herself hard pressed not to stare in fascination. She was no bigger than a twelve-year-old girl, but her eyes spoke of a much older person. They had seen things, the other side of things perhaps, which gave her an otherworldly air.

They sat on either side of her and ordered their coffee. Madame Blanchard kept her hands folded in her lap while she spoke. "You attended the exhibition last evening?"

"Yes." Gabriel took a sip and nodded. "It was most astonishing. How long have you been an aeronaut?"

"My husband introduced me to it. He died ten years ago, fell from a balloon, but I have continued on. It has become my sole occupation now."

The spark of fire blazed in her eyes and her chin raised a notch as she said it, and Alex knew exactly how she felt. Women were hard pressed to be included in the affairs of men, and while investigating and treasure hunting were rare, women who flew in balloons were by far fewer. There was a spine of steel in this Madame Blanchard and Alex felt it like a kindred spirit.

"I admire your talent, Madame Blanchard. And your bravery," Alex said.

"I thank you, Your Grace. People consider me a rather strange curiosity, I suppose, but it is what I was born to do."

Alex liked the sound of that. She smiled at the small woman. "I understand exactly what you mean."

Madame Blanchard raised her brows, not breaking eye contact for a moment. "You do? I confess I have not in my acquaintance very many who do. What, if I may be so bold to ask, makes you believe me? Most think I am a little mad."

Alex shook her head. "Not I. I suppose I can attribute my notions of such things to my parents. They are famed treasure hunters and we have never lived a conventional life. They travel around the world on hired missions. My father is the steadfast one and takes care of all the details while my mother—" She paused, grasping for a way to explain her. "My mother is attuned to that which most people never bother to stop and look for."

Alex narrowed her eyes, unable to put it into the right words. "She sees things. She knows a person, not their personality so much although sometimes that comes with it. She sees inside to their spirit, I think."

"That sounds rare indeed." Madame Blanchard leaned in, interest lighting her eyes. "And more frightening than ballooning."

"She is never frightened by it that I know of. She just sees it but has little judgment toward people, not categorizing them and their foibles as either good or evil. Mostly she accepts people as they are, like someone who sees the full picture of a person at first glance but sees the beauty within. It's very hard to describe, but she spoke of it a few times when she was home on Holy Island. You see, my parents are missing and I have decided I must find them."

Madame Blanchard looked from Alex to Gabriel and back again. "Is that why you have asked to meet with me, Your Graces? I can see you have more interest than a few questions about my balloon. You have something more in mind, do you not?"

Alex considered her husband. It was time to lay out the plan they had stayed awake until the deep hours of the night working on.

"We do indeed, Madame Blanchard. My wife's parents were last seen in Italy. We fear, if they are still alive, that they are in grave danger and we have need to travel there as soon as possible. The trip by carriage would take weeks . . . but by air? I would like to know how long such a trip would take and if it is even possible."

He paused and raised his brows. "We are prepared to pay well. You could retire if you wish or buy any number of balloons on what I am willing to pay you, but—" He looked down at his clasped hands on the elegant table. "I'll not put my wife in undue danger. I need to know . . . is it possible for the three of us to travel by balloon to Italy and cross the Alps?"

Madame Blanchard's eyes lit with a feverish gleam. "It is possible. I have dreamed of such a thing."

"What is the longest journey you have ever attempted?" Gabriel asked.

"I have traveled from Rome to Naples. I have been over fourteen hours in the air." She paused and counted on her small hands. "At sixty or so miles per day, taking shifts for sleeping and staying in the air without landing . . ." She shrugged as if talking about a carriage ride. "Of course that is only if the weather cooperates, but it is possible that we could cross the Alps and make northern Italy in eight days."

"Eight days!" Alex looked at Gabriel. "That's amazing. We have to try."

"Yes, but what are the risks? Leave nothing out, Madame Blanchard."

She fiddled with her crossed fingers and tilted her head back before speaking again, the hint of desperation in her eyes, and Alex suspected she was battling with Gabriel's promise of wealth against the very real danger—and telling them the truth. Alex reached over and grasped her nervous hands.

"I'm not afraid. Tell us."

"The winds. That is the first worry. They gust in patterns that are hard to predict from the ground. The steering—it is almost nonexistent. You know ships? They use the currents with sails and various instruments to go in the direction they want to go." She shook her head. "With wind, it is not so predictable. A balloon becomes its toy, and while I can manage the height with the degree of hydrogen I employ, if the wind changes its mind, there is no steerage that we have discovered to overcome it. Blowing off course can cause delays, and well"—her eyes turned grave—"most difficult landing places."

Gabriel nodded, his eyes thoughtful. Alex leaned in, desperate. "But you've done it before, haven't you?"

Madame Blanchard nodded. "Sometimes the wind favors me. Sometimes I have been able to guide my balloon enough by maneuvering the lines and the ballasts, but I am light and one person. Three of us?" She shrugged. "You asked the danger, but I do not know all of them on a trip of that length. I have never attempted anything so far." She turned to Alex. "If we are successful it would get you to your parents faster, Your Grace, but are you willing to risk your life for it?"

Alex regarded Gabriel. His eyes were shuttered—a little tired, a little worried, determined, but most of all, acquiescent. She saw in those green depths a willingness to let her decide, a willingness to do whatever it took for her to find her parents and peace.

The look brought a sting of tears to her eyes. The full knowledge of what she asked of him penetrating deep into her heart. Was she being selfish? Should she just let go of this mission and make a life, a beautiful life, with this man?

She swallowed hard around the knot in her throat and found that she couldn't give up. It just wasn't within her to quit. The hard truth was—she was willing to risk both their lives to find them.

With a deep breath, she turned toward Madame Blanchard and shared a glance with a woman who seemed to know exactly what she was feeling. "When can we leave?"

Madame Blanchard reached out her frail-looking hand and grasped Alex's hand in a tight grip. "I am at your beckoning."

"You must call me Alexandria." Her lips curved into a determined line, that feeling of purpose filling and spreading from her heart to her eyes.

Madame Blanchard matched her gaze. "And I am Sophie." She laughed, a louder, fuller sound than seemed possible from someone so slight.

Alex lifted her coffee cup. "To adventure."

Sophie clinked her cup against it and to Gabriel's quickly raised cup. "And to your mother," Sophie added with wide, blinking eyes and a look of similar determination that took up her whole face. "I find myself eager to meet her."

A LIGHT RAIN FELL AS they traveled by closed carriage back to their rented house. The footman opened the door when they arrived and held up the popular green umbrella that was all the rage in Paris to cover Alexandria as she alighted to the cobbled street. Another footman hurried forward with another umbrella to cover Gabriel, which he mostly ignored, letting the brim of his hat shield his face and eyes hooded with deep thought.

Was he making a mistake? They could be injured, or worse, killed. Worse yet, Alexandria could be killed and he could live. Would he be able to ever forgive himself if something like that happened?

And yet their speed might mean the difference between life or death for her parents. And if they kept their plan a secret, made their escape from Paris at night flying high above the city? It would be as if they had just vanished . . . disappeared into thin air. What better way to foil the regent and anyone else trailing them. No one would ever catch up to them by horse or carriage.

He looked ahead at his wife hurrying through the rain, running up the steps to the front door. He saw the vulnerable spot at the back of her neck, that place he liked to kiss and inhale the combined scent of her hair and skin. His stomach twisted with the thought of that delicate neck broken in a fall, a great fall from the sky. It was his job to protect her—not put her in more danger. He took a shuddering breath.

Lord, I need a sign. I can't make this decision without clear guidance from You.

They hurried into the entrance, shook off their rain-spattered wraps, and handed them to the hired butler.

"You have callers, Your Grace." He bowed and indicated the silver salon done in shades of silver, blue, and gray.

Gabriel's spine stiffened, instantly on guard. "Who is it, Belvedere?"

The man held out a calling card that Gabriel read from over Alexandria's shoulder. The Count Beauffremont. Good. Hopefully he had found actors to impersonate them.

Alex shot a look over her shoulder at Gabriel that said she was thinking the same thing. She unpinned her hat and tidied her hair and then took Gabriel's waiting arm.

"Rory, Countess," Gabriel greeted them, his gaze scanning the room and seeing two other people, each with their backs to them at the windows looking out at the rain. "So good of you to come so soon." He quirked a brow at Rory, indicating the strangers with a jerk of his head. Rory grinned back.

All was silent for a moment and then Alexandria laughed. "Gabriel." She still held to his arm and now looked up with sparkling eyes full of mischief. "I do believe that man over there has your exact posture."

The man in question turned around and bowed a small, confident bow.

"Oh! He does look a bit like you." Alexandria squeezed his upper arm.

"And the woman?" Gabriel drawled out, squashing the surge of ridiculous jealousy at her excitement with the man.

They held their breath as a woman with Alexandria's height and hair color turned and curtsied. She smiled at Gabriel. "She is very pretty," Alexandria murmured.

"Not nearly as pretty as you, my dear," Gabriel whispered toward her ear. Rory and the countess came forward.

"Close enough, wouldn't you say?" Rory boomed. "This here is Mademoiselle Annabelle Riesling." The woman curtsied, her chin cocked to one side, and peered at Alexandria with interest.

Alexandria inclined her head in return and smiled at the woman.

"And this is Lord Ashbury, from the Ashburys of Derbyshire but more recently the hills of Susquehanna, Pennsylvania. An American now and the devil of a crack shot. Not a bad impersonator either." Rory laughed. "Do Napoleon, Lord Ashbury, do!"

Lord Ashbury grew shorter and stouter of chest before their eyes. With one hand he whipped his bangs into a side sweep, narrowed his eyes, and pursed his lips. "I have no need of the pope. I will crown myself." He turned and bellowed. "Josephine, my life, my love. Come assist me with my crown."

They all laughed. Gabriel had to admit that he was good. "So these are the actors. Excellent. Please be seated everyone. Rory, come now, what have you told them?"

They all settled in the seating area of the wide salon while Rory talked in his usual loud voice that made it very easy for Gabriel to hear.

"I only explained that they should be hired to impersonate the two of you for a few weeks while you fly the coop and go on a more . . . extensive honeymoon, shall we say?"

Gabriel seated himself across from the actors and looked from one to the other. "There is no doubt you will be well compensated for your trouble, but there is some chance of danger. I feel I must warn you of that before you agree."

"What, exactly, can you tell us of this danger?" Lord Ashbury asked. "And the reason for the deception? I confess that a couple of your rank needing to skulk away from Paris has my curiosity aroused."

"It is of a delicate nature and involves my wife's parents. They are the ones we fear are in great danger if not found. We are going after them with the clues we have at hand, but there are those who wish to find them as badly as we do, and they have been pursuing us. You may be followed. We need you to mimic us enough in public, from a distance or in dimly lit places such as the theatre, to keep those watching us believing that we are simply enjoying a honeymoon in Paris. The longer you can accomplish that the better and . . . the better rewarded you will be."

"Would they try to capture us?" Mademoiselle Riesling asked, not appearing especially afraid.

"They might." Gabriel leaned forward. "You will have guards around you to protect you, but only three of them can know you are actors. The other guards will have to be fooled. It will be no easy task, I assure you."

Lord Ashbury cast a quelling glance at Annabelle Riesling. "We have discussed it and are certain we can accommodate your wishes, Your Grace. There is just one thing. We will need at least a day in your constant company to pick up your mannerisms and voice. Two days would be better."

Gabriel looked at Annabelle Riesling, who nodded intently. For whatever reason, she needed this opportunity as badly as Lord Ashbury did. "You may have the rest of this day and tomorrow. Tomorrow evening, as soon as it is dark, we must depart."

"Might we know where you are going?" Annabelle asked, her blue eyes close to the color of Alexandria's, wide and innocent.

"It would be better if you didn't know that, don't you think?" Alexandria inserted with a small frown.

The young woman flushed. "Yes, of course, Your Grace."

"Very well." Gabriel rose and bowed to the countess and Rory. "I thank you, dear friends. You have made good choices. I do believe this just might work."

Chapter Fourteen

*A*lex chafed at having Annabelle Riesling follow her every move throughout the rest of the day. The woman watched her constantly, and while Alex understood the need behind it, it still gave her a start when she glimpsed Annabelle copying the angle of her chin when she spoke, repeating one of Alex's phrases in a near-silent whisper, or mimicking the way Alex's hand cupped her cheek as she sat at the dining room table. Alex had to admit that the position really didn't look very duchess like. She should stop propping her elbows on the table like a child.

Later they rode through the city, seeing more of the sights of Paris—Gabriel and Alex in the front of the open vehicle with their impersonators in the back. They rode through the Tuileries Gardens and Palace of Versailles, still imposing and royal but with signs of the destruction that wreaked havoc on the city not so long ago.

"Gabriel, you mentioned visiting the king? Will we present ourselves to Louis XVIII?"

"I have reconsidered. I have learned that King Louis has little sway on France's government. He is a constitutional king, probably straining at the bit, but with little power and a lapful of his own problems. I think he is the least of our worries, and if he hears we are in Paris, he may want us to visit regularly."

Alex lowered her voice, talking straight ahead. "Yes, that could become a problem. But France is said to be one of the countries looking for the manuscript. Do you think that is true?"

"Perhaps France thinks to offer some of its new coffers in return for something so valuable. I suspect they—if there is a *they*—are waiting for someone else to find the manuscript and then they'll swoop in with an offer worthy of the half the Louvre. Napoleon has made France rich with stolen treasures from around the world, especially from the art of northern Italy. His armies gutted churches, abbeys, and monasteries." He made a soft sound in his throat. "The palaces and museums of France are glutted with Europe's booty. Louis isn't too smart, but he must know he has the upper hand in the reward arena. We've not seen the French coming after us yet, not in the flesh anyway, but we've seen many who can be bought. I am guessing that if they care about the manuscript at all, this will be their game to win."

"Should we not pretend to be among those capable of being bought?"

Gabriel chuckled. "I do appreciate the way your mind works. Would that you were not discovered to be the Featherstone's child, their only child and heir, yes, that would be a worthy plan." He shrugged. "As it is, we had best stick to our original plan."

Alex cast a glance back at their new friends, who seemed happily chatting among themselves, and gave them a benign smile. "Should you like to practice my smile, Annabelle? I'm sure it is very easy."

Annabelle nodded. "You come across the young innocent very well, Your Grace. It is an act I am accustomed to."

Alex smirked. "Appearances can be deceiving."

Annabelle laughed. "A fact I know only too well." She cast a wry glance at Lord Ashbury. "Have you not found that to be the case with many of the illustrious members of Parisian society, my lord?"

"Oh, indeed. People of all society, I have found, are seldom exactly as they first appear."

Gabriel turned his head, brow furrowed. "Will a day be enough then? To do us justice?"

"Oh yes, Your Grace." He tipped his hat just as Gabriel would do and made a line with his mouth, both annoyed and with a tinge of haughtiness, just as Gabriel often looked. Alex couldn't help her laugh.

Lord Ashbury continued. "People rarely care to take the time and attention to look beyond the obvious first impression. It is quite easy to make an impression of any kind if one studies upon it and practices."

"I do think you are right." Gabriel turned back toward the matched bays. "It is too bad, and yet, it serves our purposes perfectly."

DINNER THAT EVENING WAS MUCH the same. Alex didn't know whether to laugh or be annoyed that every time she reached for her fork or her glass to take a sip, Annabelle copied her movements.

"Tomorrow, if it pleases Your Graces, we should perhaps do a test run." Lord Ashbury drew her attention away toward himself. He, too, had studied well and was holding his head just as Gabriel did when communicating a veiled order.

Alex smiled, charmed despite herself. "What do you have in mind, *Your Grace?*" She teased with a shake of her perfectly coiffed head. The French maids could do wonders with her appearance, she had discovered.

"A short outing. Annabelle can be veiled and I will wear a wide brimmed hat worn low. We'll tell the guards we trust, Kurt and Eddie wasn't it? And the other one you mentioned."

"John Henry," Gabriel said.

"Yes, John Henry. We'll tell them the nature of the outing and see how they cooperate, keeping the regent's guards at a farther distance as we've discussed." He paused, looking at Gabriel. "You understand that we shall have to manage each occasion as it comes and make quick decisions."

"I realize the extent of the endeavor. I have given it a great deal of thought and planning." Gabriel inclined his head, seeming half annoyed by Lord Ashbury's confidence.

"Good. I want you to know . . . even though Annabelle and I are in need of the generous funds Count Beauffremont has expounded on so well, we are a wily team and not untalented. I do believe we can keep people believing the two of you are in residence for some time." He smiled and lifted his glass.

"That is exactly what I hoped for." Gabriel also raised his glass. "Mademoiselle? Lord Ashbury? Should we come through this with our lives intact, I promise you we shall count you as friends, very well-rewarded friends."

They all smiled and laughed a little.

Alex rose and motioned for Annabelle to follow. "Let's leave them to their port, shall we? Or whatever men do when we retire to the other room." She laughed and gave Gabriel a long, promising look. "Let them wonder what we do while we are away."

Annabelle gave her a nod and rose. "Indeed, Your Grace. We have much to talk about."

"Oh, indeed, Annabelle. I still have much to teach you, I think."

HE WOKE TO HER SCENT.

Lavender and mint—in her hair, her skin—that smell that melded her special tonics and hair rinses with the lush sweetness that was unique to Alexandria. He nestled closer, brushed the dark strands of lustrous hair away, and inhaled at the point where her neck met her shoulder.

He brushed a string of kisses along the column of her neck up toward her ear, a grin beginning at the corners of his mouth as he pressed closer. He loved the way she sank into the feather mattress, the slack and sweetly vulnerable curve of her arm, her leg, her hip . . . *I love her . . . oh, God, don't let me lead her wrong.*

He closed his eyes and nuzzled against the silken skin of her neck, pulling her back into his stomach, feeling the life beat of her heart against his hand—*bum, bum, bum*—a slow and steady beat like nothing when she was awake. She was caught and precious, this moment, with predawn glowing on her skin, a sweet precursor to the glory of her flashing eyes and smiling lips when she was awake, in broad daylight, in her full glory. An image bearer of God.

Please don't take her from me. I am her guardian yet. And You . . . ours.

"Tonight we fly, beloved," he murmured against her shoulder, then kissed her ear. "Are you ready?"

She turned to her back, tangling the bedding around their legs and elbowing him in the stomach. He groaned out a laugh.

"I'm ready," her sleepy, smiling voice said toward his chest. "What are we ready for now?"

Her easy . . . sweet acquiescence brought a pang to his heart.

"To find your parents?"

She inhaled, rose up, and pushed against his chest. She blinked awake in a moment. "Tonight! The balloon!"

Gabriel couldn't help his smile. Her hair was wild, long tangles around her shoulders and back. Her eyes lit with determination. It was a look he'd seen often and he would see again and again over the course of their years together. With a deep chuckle he leaned down toward her. "Are you certain you want to do this? It's not too late to hire fast horses."

Alexandria swung toward him, a fierce move that had him rearing back. "Quite sure." She sat up onto her knees. "There is danger everywhere. We have to try. If we find ourselves unable to manage the balloon, we can always land it and hire a coach and team, can we not? It is such an opportunity . . . and dropped into our laps. It must be God's provision, don't you think?"

Gabriel sighed and threw his arm over his eyes. "God's provision or a rash idea, I haven't decided which. If you get hurt . . ."

Alex touched his arm. "We won't borrow trouble. Let's give it a try. Please?"

Gabriel lifted his arm and peered up at her hopeful, pleading face.

"Oh, very well."

"And you'll stop worrying?"

"I can't promise that."

"But you will try?" Her brows rose over big blue eyes.

"I will try."

She flung herself over him with a kiss, making the surrender worthwhile.

ALEX PEEKED AROUND THE HEAVY satin curtain in the drawing room, breath held as Annabelle and Lord Ashbury entered the shiny black carriage. Annabelle was dressed in Alex's green watered-silk gown, which fit perfectly. A darker green hat with a netted veil covered the upper half of her face, her lower half looking remarkably like Alex's.

Lord Ashbury looked very fine in Gabriel's dove-gray waistcoat and dark breeches. His beaver hat was pulled low over his eyes. Lord Ashbury stood back patiently, the picture of an elegant gentleman, while a footman opened the door. Then Ashbury put his hand at the small of Annabelle's back to help guide her into the carriage, just as Gabriel would have done. They were doing everything perfectly so far.

Alex surveyed the servants' wooden actions and the guards' faces. Kurt stayed the closest with Eddie not far behind. The regent's guards were mounted, and aside from the occasional glance at the Duke and Duchess of St. Easton, they kept their gazes roving the street and any persons passing by.

"How are they doing?"

Alex started and turned toward Gabriel, who approached her at a brisk pace. "Everything seems to be going well so far. When do we leave to follow them?"

"Soon." Gabriel looked at her and grimaced as she came from behind the folds of the drapery in a maid's costume of a faded black dress, wide ruffled apron, and mop cap. He didn't look much better in his soot-covered chimney sweep's rags. But it was certain no one would recognize the Duke of St. Easton in that garb. "You look positively ghastly, Gabriel." Alex giggled.

He gazed down at his shirt and made a motion to dust off some of the grime. "I do, don't I?" He smiled widely with startling white teeth against a blackened face. He looked up at her, his smile turning lascivious. "You, on the other hand, appear positively delicious. Come here so I might find something for you to scrub."

"La, Your Grace, I have no time to dally." She turned back to the window and peeked out. "They are leaving. We must hurry!"

"Come along, then."

Gabriel took her arm and they made for the back entry. A shabby closed carriage awaited them with a wizened-looking driver who kept reaching for a flask in his coat pocket. Within moments they were trotting down the street after their impersonators.

"Oh, this is exciting!" Alex leaned over him to peer out the wavy glass. "There they are. Going into the café."

"If they can have a cup of coffee without—" Gabriel stopped and moved closer to the window.

"What is it?"

He didn't say anything for a long moment while Alex's gaze searched the street. He pointed and she saw it, saw them, rather.

"Oh no! Not now." She bit down on her lower lip and looked up at her husband. "It's the Spaniards, isn't it?"

Chapter Fifteen

hey're following them inside! What should we do?"

Gabriel reached for the carriage door handle. "Let's cause a distraction, shall we?" He leapt to the ground and turned to take her hand. "Follow my lead."

Alex clung to Gabriel's back like a shadow, head down and hiding behind him, but she couldn't help but peep up through her lashes at the Spaniards, their uniforms and swinging swords from their belts giving them away, as she and Gabriel strode toward the door of the café.

Gabriel had taken on a hunched mien and a scuffling kind of walk that was unrecognizable as the duke. With his slicked-back hair, black-smeared face, and filthy clothing . . . and her, a dusty-looking maid who kept her head down—no one paid them any mind at all. Within moments they were right behind the three soldiers.

Just as one of the men reached for the café door, Gabriel plowed into the man closest with a heavy heave of his shoulder and a quick, silent cuff to the chin. He then spun around, dropping that soldier to the ground, and knocked another man aside the head with a powerful blow.

Alex flailed her arms and stepped backward to avoid the second man falling into her as he staggered and swayed. The man at the door was trying to run inside!

Alex yelped and pointed but it was unnecessary. Gabriel came up behind him and swiped his feet out from under him. He pulled a sword and held it to the man's neck, who was gasping for air and groaning.

It happened so fast that even she wasn't sure how Gabriel had managed to splay them all out, unconscious and deathly still, on the cobblestones so quickly.

"Hurry now." Gabriel grasped her upper arm and hauled her into the café. If anyone noticed what had occurred, they didn't act upon it. Once inside, Gabriel took on his hunched posture with slow and scuffling footsteps, Alex right behind him. They edged around the crowd of diners toward their guards and the impersonators.

Gabriel leaned back and whispered into Alex's ear, "Get the actors out of here, back in their carriage. I'll alert Kurt and Eddie and follow behind with the guards."

Alex nodded and shimmied through the crowded tables toward the couple. She caught Annabelle's attention, whose eyes sparked with curiosity. Alex motioned with her eyes and her head toward the door. When she was near enough to the pair, she sank into a curtsy and whispered down into Lord Ashbury's ear, "You've been followed. The duke has dispatched them but we must hurry. They could awake at any time."

Lord Ashbury nodded, reached into his pocket, tossed some coins on the table, and stood. Annabelle stood too, her hand grasping Lord Ashbury's arm. Alex stood aside for them to pass and then, shadowlike again, followed them out the door and to their waiting carriage. As they passed, they saw the inert bodies, a crowd of onlookers gathered around them.

"What happened?" Lord Ashbury hissed as soon as the carriage door shut with the three of them inside.

"The Spaniards." Alex pressed her dark gloved hand to her chest and shook her head, thinking of the torture, the horrible things they had done to Gabriel just months ago. "You must be very careful. The duke foiled King Ferdinand's attempts to capture me in Reykjavik . . . in Iceland."

She raised her brows at them. "My husband . . . he, ah, burned their ship in the harbor and the entire crew was killed, including the Spanish spies who had been following me for months in Ireland. King Ferdinand is most unhappy about that, as you can imagine. He demanded the regent turn us over to him but, thanks be to God, the regent demurred. The Spanish are very determined, not only to find my parents' whereabouts, but to punish the duke."

She rubbed her hands together as if to warm the chill down her spine. "You have passed your first test with flying colors, I'm afraid." Alex gave them a grim smile. "They certainly thought you were the Duke and Duchess of St. Easton."

"I'm not afraid." Annabelle lifted her chin and gave Alex a piercing stare. "If we were captured by anyone, it would soon be discovered that we are impersonators and not really you. They would have to let us go."

Alex nodded to one side. "Unless they think you know where we are. You would have to have reason to be dressed like us and living in our house. They would see through our game, I think, and even . . ." she leaned forward, "possibly go to great lengths to discover what you know about us and our whereabouts." She let that sink in, Lord Ashbury turning a tinge of gray but Annabelle retaining a stubborn turn to her mouth. "But you are both talented, as we've seen today and as long as you keep an eye out for danger and your heads about you, I think you will manage."

Alex smiled with a shrug. "We are leaving all the guards with you to help protect you and our guards know of our ruse. Kurt and Eddie will do their best to see you remain safe. But the danger is very real and right on your heels. This is the reason the purse is very large, is it not?"

Lord Ashbury sat up straighter. "We'll manage, Your Grace. You may count on that. I'm not a bad hand with a sword and Annabelle has her talents."

"Yes, well, I think the duke will do something with those soldiers, but there might be others. And there is the French. We haven't seen them come after us bodily as the Spanish, but remain on guard in that area as well. If you are invited to the palace, we think it best to invent reasons not to see the king. He has never met the duke personally, and certainly would not know me, so you may have to go and try to pull it off if you must, but it would be better to stay as hidden as possible."

"We understand completely, Your Grace. And any couple on their honeymoon may be expected to spend long hours only in each other's company."

Lord Ashbury gave Annabelle a look that was exactly as Gabriel looked at her when he was thinking of such things. And Annabelle, before Alex's very eyes, changed, turned her chin toward him, and shot him an equally intense expression of shared passion that made Alex's breath still inside her.

Was that how her response to her husband appeared? Eyes lit with desire and love, a softening to her frame that seemed to strain toward him, a deeper resonance to her breath? Alex released a single burst of laughter. Were they so obvious?

"You are very lucky, Your Grace, to have found your other half." Annabelle sank back into the cushion of the seat, her face both sad and thoughtful. Alex wondered what had happened to make the sad sheen in her eyes turn to water just before she looked away and out the window.

"I am blessed." She reached over and put her hand on top of Annabelle's. Alex wished they were alone, not with Lord Ashbury's eyes upon them, so she could ask for Annabelle's confidence, but Alex thought better of it. It was better to maintain some distance from these two.

They pulled up to the rented house and all got out. Alex scanned the area for any sign of Gabriel. She took a deep breath, seeing their old carriage clattering down the street toward them. He was on his way.

She waited, half hidden by a large bush near the entrance, until the carriage shuddered to a stop. The door was flung wide and her husband appeared, more disheveled than even when she'd left him. She wanted to rush to him but was wary of watchful eyes. It wouldn't do to cause a scene for the neighbors to remark upon. Instead, she hung back until he was close enough to hear her low voice. "Gabriel."

He turned and saw her, motioning with his head that she should follow to the back of the house. She hurried to obey, her steps a brisk walk around the house. She turned the corner and he stood waiting and took her into his arms. "Gabriel." She pressed herself into his chest, her face in the crook of his neck and shoulder. "You're not hurt."

"No."

She gave him a wry smile, wiping some of the soot from his cheek with her thumb. "I'll be glad to be away from here. It feels like a different sort of danger."

"I will be glad to get you safely away as well."

Alex buried her face in his shoulder again and nodded. She didn't say she thought they were walking right into that different danger. It wouldn't do to worry him more than he already was.

Gabriel took her by the shoulders and held her away from him, staring down into her eyes with those piercing green orbs. "We have much to do to prepare. I've had instructions from Sophie."

"What do we need to do?"

"She has given me a list of supplies to gather up. Dress warmly and bring blankets. The atmosphere will thin the farther up we go and it will get cold, especially at night. Pack light but bring some nice dresses, court clothing. We may have need of our status as the Duke and Duchess of St. Easton. And Alexandria . . ."

She smiled up at him, the beginnings of another adventure never failing to fire her blood. "Yes?"

His slow smile back sent a thrill through her. "I have a promise for you."

"A promise?"

"We *are* going to find your parents. I will not stop until it is accomplished."

Tears sprang to her eyes as she pressed her lips together and nodded. "Yes. We will. I believe we will."

Chapter Sixteen

Malaspina Castle, Massa, Italy

The door screeched open on rusty hinges. The guard shoved Ian Featherstone to the floor of one of the many dungeons in Malaspina Castle. Pain radiated from his shoulder and a grunt escaped. He realized he had barely missed being flung to the center of the cold, stone room where iron spikes, with tips so sharp they would run a man through like a pincushion, protruded from the floor. Above the rusted spikes was a trap door that led to a bedchamber above. It was rumored that in centuries past, an evil marchioness dispatched her lovers from that place to fall to a gruesome death.

And there were other rumors of this place, whispered into his ear in Italian, which he unfortunately understood all too well, by one guard with eyes wide with glazed glee. Rumors of unrequited lovers, a young daughter of the ancestry who refused to obey her father and relinquish her lover, held in one of the many towers in Malaspina Castle. The father, cruel beast that he was, had her chained to a dog representing fidelity and a boar for her rebellion. They weren't fed and died together, the wild boar devouring them all perhaps, or possibly the dog fighting the boar, protecting the young woman as long as he could until he, too, turned wild and turned on her for food.

Ian shrugged away from the floor, stood, and dusted himself off, trying to shake the evil, the dread, the stories and the words they kept whispering to him. He cradled his head in his arms and then sank back to the floor, his legs too weak and shaky to hold him up, the words swirling like the demons of this place always around him.

"Your wife, she is very beautiful, yes? We have seen all of her," a dark jailer had chuckled, leaning in and chucking him in a mock-friendly manner on the chin.

"She cries out for you to save her," another had laughed in his face. *"Your name, she said it over and over, begging. Ian, please Ian. But we do not listen. We take from her. We take everything."*

Ian had never wanted to run a blade through someone's throat as badly as he did at that moment.

God, help me endure. His breath rasped harsh through his nose, and like so many days since coming here, he prayed for sanity. *God, help me endure.*

If there was ever a time in his life where he had rejected God, even ignored Him or thought he didn't need Him—he regretted it now, deeply. Now all he did was pray. Pray that they lied, that their evil words were no more than whispers from the pit of hell. He prayed that his beloved Kate was alive yet, somewhere in this hellish place . . . And his daughter, what had become of Alexandria? Did someone have her too? Had they all been captured because of a missing manuscript? What could possibly be so important? So valuable?

They'd traveled the world on the hunt for riches and answers to puzzles and oddly momentous discoveries, making themselves rich beyond their imaginations, but never had they been so attacked from every side, so haunted and hunted while on a mission. What could it be?

Curse Augusto de Carrara! Ian balled his hands into fists, his jaw clenched, teeth aching. Curse him and his invention, whatever it was that seemingly everyone on the face of the earth wanted to get their hands on. *Curse me for letting my wife talk me into this business of treasure hunting so long ago.* He'd known it would someday come to something like this . . . deep inside he had known it would come to a bad end. He'd felt it in his bones, but how to deny her? He had never denied her anything.

She wouldn't have married you, a man of little fortune and less ambition, had she not known you would give anything to have her. She wouldn't have endured it—sheepherder and fisherman at heart that you are . . . with nothing but a nominal title and a crumbling medieval castle . . . that's all you ever were before she came along.

It wasn't entirely true, that fiery dart, but there was some truth in it. She would have married him—in body anyway— she'd had to marry, and quickly. He turned his face toward the wall and covered his eyes with one hand, remembering the stillborn baby boy, white and bloody and lying so very still on their bedding.

The child that wasn't his.

A child who had no father that Katherine was ever willing to name. He hadn't cared. He would have loved the boy. He would have made him his son and given him his own name—Featherstone and the Featherstone motto—*Valens et Volens*—"Willing and Able." It described him perfectly and Alexandria too. But not Katherine.

She'd sworn two things to him on their wedding day. One, that she would never have another child. And two, that she would bind herself to his side no matter what might come. He'd agreed, taking what he could get of the fantastic intensity and beauty she embodied. He breathed out a groan and buried his face in his hands.

They had started out in quiet domesticity—restoring the castle little by little, building up the animal herds and their pens, trading with the locals for a little better life. But it hadn't taken Katherine long to find another way, a more exciting way to live. He could see her now looking out over the beach on Holy Island, out across the wide expanse of sea with meaning and adventure in her eyes. She would turn to him and smile that smile, her eyes blazing with conviction.

No, it hadn't taken her very long to find the spark of something bigger . . . grander . . . echoing of heavenly voiced things, things too grand for him to contemplate. She'd insisted, pointing toward a dangerous yet alluring path, that he accompany her. He'd known then. She wouldn't have left him if he had tried to tie her to his life, no—worse. She would have let him drown her in the ordinary if he'd insisted, and how could he ask that of her? It would have killed her to be nothing more than a wife, a mother, a lady of obscurity living a simplistic life. So he'd given her whatever she wanted.

That was the truth.

And now they would both suffer and possibly even die for it. And their daughter . . . the daughter they were never meant to have?

Ian lay down on the stone of the cell and sobbed, his shoulders rocking against the harsh, cold floor, making him shiver from head to toe.

"Alexandria, my darling girl, I am so sorry . . ."

Paris, France

THE STARS TWINKLED WITH BRIGHT intensity, the moon a golden orb overhead in the Parisian sky, the breeze light and fine. Gabriel helped Alexandria out of the carriage at the western edge of the Tuileries Gardens where Sophie waited near the octagonal lake with her balloon.

Gabriel reached back inside for their bags, handed a lighter one to Alexandria, and then signaled to the hired driver to move along. Casting his gaze around the perimeter, he searched for signs of anyone following them. No one he could see at this late hour of two o'clock in the morning. He chuckled. Even though the sky was so bright, they just might hasten away with no one the wiser.

"Let's hurry." He nodded in the direction of the balloon. It wasn't a time to take any chances.

His wife gave a little squeak of excitement gazing up at the huge balloon. "It's much bigger than the one we saw her in before. And so beautiful. I can't believe we are about to fly!"

Gabriel smiled over at her. She was right; it was a beautiful sight—striped red and gold on the top, like an umbrella, then rows of blue with pictures of animals and symbols in gold, then a wide gold band around the middle of the balloon, with an elegant scroll of gold-leaf pattern, and finally blue with white swirls resembling rolling clouds.

There was a wide mouth at the bottom of the balloon, above the basket done in gold with lines running to the basket, or gondola as some called it, to halfway up the balloon on all sides. The gondola was quite large, shaped like a wide boat. As they neared, he saw that one side was covered with an awning of sorts, making a sheltered section for sleeping.

Sophie's head was just visible from the top of the basket, bobbing around, her hands coming up to tug this rope or adjust that line. Alexandria called to her when they were close enough.

"Sophie, we have arrived. Is everything in order?"

Sophie climbed up a ladder, spun around with quick little movements and a flurry of white petticoats, and then shimmied down the other side to the ground. She curtsied, her eyes wide and intense. "All appears to be in order, Your Graces."

"Are you all right, Sophie? You look nervous," Alexandria asked.

Indeed, Sophie did look pale, like a white-faced doll. Gabriel wondered yet again if this was such a good idea.

"I have never made a journey of this length, so there is some hesitation." Sophie's hands squeezed together and her fingers fiddled. "This is the largest balloon I could find in so short a time. I hope it will do."

"It looks perfect." Gabriel motioned to their bags. "How would you like the weight distributed?"

"Oh yes. Follow me." She climbed back up the ladder, which was longer than the basket and trailed on the ground, and hopped over the edge to the inside.

Alexandria lifted up her skirts and followed after her, as agile as any girl used to climbing trees and hiking across craggy beaches. Gabriel handed the bags and supplies up to the two women and scrambled after them.

"Here. Let me show you around." Sophie pushed back the canvas awning and revealed three sleeping cots with pillows, a bag of food stores, blankets, and clothing. Another area revealed supplies including a good deal of iron filings and sulfuric acid, should they need to make more hydrogen, which

Sophie assured them they would only need in an emergency. On the other side of the gondola, against the perimeter in neat rows were twenty or so large bags of sand.

"When we need to ascend, we throw out the appropriate number of bags, and when we need to descend, we let out a little hydrogen. The key is catching the proper air currents, those blowing in the direction we want to go, do you see?"

"I'm guessing it won't be as easy as it sounds," Gabriel murmured.

"Well, yes." Sophie shrugged her slight shoulders and pressed her lips into a tight line. "Not easy, perhaps, but possible."

"I shall pray for fair winds." Alex put a hand on Sophie's shoulder.

Sophie stared up at the bright sky. "It is a perfect night to begin."

"Excellent. What can we do to help?"

"If you could loosen the ropes holding down the balloon on one side, Your Grace, and I will do likewise on the other side, we can time it so we can hurry up the ladder as the balloon begins to ascend."

Alex clasped her hands together in excitement. "I'll do it."

"No." Gabriel shook his head. Then seeing the crestfallen look on her face, he hurried to add, "Perhaps the next time. Let's get some experience first, shall we?"

"But how will I get experience if you won't let me try?"

Sophie smiled a very small smile but remained silent, watching them. "There are four ropes. Perhaps Alexandria can untie the first one, for experience, and then climb safely back into the gondola before we untie the other three?"

"Excellent compromise, Sophie, thank you." Gabriel winked at Alexandria. "Go on then."

Alexandria hurried over the side and ran to one of the lines. It was tied to a large metal spike secured into the ground. Gabriel watched her struggle with dislodging the spike but waited in silence, knowing she wanted to accomplish the task on her own.

"I've got it!" She turned with the rope in her hand and ran back to the ladder, throwing the heavy rope into the basket and then tumbling over the edge to land on the floor of the basket with a *humph*. Gabriel chuckled and helped her up.

When he faced the ladder he stopped, seeing a group of dark-clad men coming toward them. His eyes narrowed. Were they enemies or just late-night revelers who noticed the balloon? He didn't want to find out.

"Hurry, Sophie. Let us get up and away before they come too close."

They both scrambled out of the basket and ran to the ropes. Gabriel had one of them undone first, then ran over and tossed the end up to Alexandria, who caught it with a panicked face. "They're almost here." She clung to the basket's edge, the balloon tilting to one side as it started to rise.

He turned and ran to the final rope, passing by Sophie who had the third one. "Get inside. I will get the last one."

The spike was deep in the soil. He looked up to see the group of five men almost upon them. They didn't look like the Spanish, or like the Carbonari, just Parisians out late and most certainly deep in their cups. One of them shouted, "Hey, we want a ride!"

Another laughed heartily and pulled out a pistol. "Bet we could stop them with this!"

Wonderful.

Drunken fools with weapons. Gabriel felt the spike give and pulled it free. The balloon immediately started shooting up into the air. With great running leaps he made it to the dangling ladder and grasped hold. Alexandria shrieked from above as he clung to one of the lower rungs.

"Gabriel!" Alexandria held out her hand but he couldn't reach it.

With a mighty heave he brought his feet onto the bottom rung, clinging for dear life to the rope ladder as the balloon drifted higher into the sky. He took a couple of steps up and then felt a mighty jerk.

Two men had grasped hold of the tail of the rope, dangling much lower than the ladder. One of them started climbing it. Gabriel watched in suspended horror as the man was swept off the ground and into the air, right beneath him.

With a groan of frustration and gritted teeth, Gabriel clawed and climbed up the swaying ladder. Alexandria grasped hold of his shoulder as soon as it was within reach and helped pull him up and over the side to land in the basket. He looked down at the man, who was laughing and climbing with the agility of a tree monkey up the rope.

The other men were laughing too, whooping and cheering him from the ground. Gabriel swallowed hard. He could just make out the shiny pistol, still in one of their hands.

"Sophie, do you have a knife? Quickly!"

A knife was thrust into his hand. Gabriel leaned over and began sawing on the rope.

"No you don't! Now don't you be doing that!" One of the onlookers bellowed.

Gabriel kept sawing, praying the one with the pistol wouldn't shoot it. They weren't far enough away yet and the balloon was a huge target.

The rope started to unravel against the edge of the knife. With all his strength he sawed harder. "Climb down and jump and you won't be hurt," Gabriel shouted down at the man. "I've almost got it! I don't want to hurt you. Climb down!"

Eyes suddenly wide with fear, the man looked down and then back up at Gabriel. "I'll break my neck. Let me in!"

"It's too late. The rope will break at any moment. Climb down and you won't have much of a fall. Look! We're coming over the lake now."

The stranger finally obeyed, shimmying down the rope. They had drifted on the wind enough to be over the octagonal lake. The man let go, dropping about ten feet into the water with a big splash. Gabriel closed his eyes, then opened them. The man's friends were fishing him out, and he gave a great sigh.

"I hope he can swim," he muttered.

Alexandria burst out with laughter and Sophie's eyes filled with mirth.

Without the added weight, the balloon shot up over the trees and into the night sky.

Their journey of flight had begun.

Chapter Seventeen

Malaspina Castle, Massa, Italy

The long, stone corridors and narrow stairways echoed with their footsteps. The air was damp and chilly, causing Katherine Featherstone to shiver and pull her cape tighter around her slim shoulders as the guard led her from her cell in the dungeons up to the living quarters of the family.

She didn't know why she had been summoned, nor if Ian would be there. She had only seen her husband twice since their capture, twice stared into those pained gray eyes, her gaze roving his hollow cheeks and sable hair that had more silver than she'd remembered. They didn't tell her anything. She only knew that any change would be welcome after the haunting solitude of these last weeks.

A great creaking of a door sounded above them, and then they were on a landing with the sunlight streaming in. The brightness of the light blinded Katherine for a moment, her hand rushing to shield her eyes. The guard took her by the upper arm in none too gentle a grip and led her out into the courtyard.

Enclosed by bastioned walls with gun ports, they passed the medieval keep section of the castle, used as a prison before Napoleon had taken it over but looking empty now. Birds gathered around an old, leaky fountain. Statues with missing body parts stood as if forgotten, frozen wounded left from the recent days of violence. But the plants thrived in the ancient courtyard, lush and green, smelling ripe of summertime. Katherine held her skirts away from the thick bushes that had overgrown onto the pathway, following her guard through the gardens to the residential palace.

Another door was swept open, this time on perfectly oiled hinges, and she was beckoned into a large, high-ceilinged entry. She paused to catch her breath, gazing at the grandeur of the fresco work on the ceiling and walls, shaky, her knees wanting to buckle from the long walk, so weak from the weeks of little food, fresh air, and exercise.

"Questo senso." This way, the guard barked out with a jerk of his head.

Katherine inclined her head and then raised her brows, saying in perfect Italian, *"Conduca il senso." Lead the way.* Adding under her breath, "Loathsome cur."

"Eh?" He grasped her arm again, hard.

She jerked her arm away to no avail. "I said don't put your hands on me. I can walk!" She jerked away again. This time he abruptly let go and she stumbled, almost falling backward.

She scowled at him. He grinned back, his attention moving from her face to the bodice of her dress, the same dress she had been wearing since their capture. Not a bad dress in its day—a rich burgundy silk the color of rusty blood. Now, it hung about her like little more than pieced-together rags. She didn't bother to cover the gaping collar that sagged with a great tear on one side. No, she took a step toward him and thrust out her chin.

"You'd best keep your thoughts better concealed, Renaldo. The duke will cut off your most prized possession should he hear of this."

Renaldo's eyes narrowed but he jerked away from her and didn't touch her again.

Katherine took another long breath and followed the man who brought her the once-daily food and water. He had threatened her many times before, but her hints that the son of Annabella d'Luca, the Duchess of Massa and Princess of Carrara, had his own plans for Katherine, had bought her some measure of protection.

The fact that she had only met Francis II of Massa one time, just after they'd been captured, and that he inspected her with more interest in his eyes than the whereabouts of the manuscript didn't matter. Renaldo only had to believe her reasoning behind such a claim, and he had.

They passed elegant apartments filled with thick carpets, plush furnishings, paintings and sculptures from the great masters of the Renaissance, their wide doorways open to display the power and wealth of the house of the Dukes of d'Luca. They turned a corner and strode down another interior hall, darker without the tall mullioned windows that graced most of the palace.

Katherine reached out with an instinct so finely tuned it was second nature and breathed deep in concentration. A cold breath of air kissed her cheek and then passed by with a stirring gust. She could almost hear a woman's wicked laugh. Katherine turned her head to look behind her but saw nothing, no one.

"Nasty ghost," she murmured.

A few moments later Renaldo came to a sudden stop in front of her. She stopped, her pulse quickening. Would they torture her? Or tell her horror stories of torturing Ian again? She couldn't let her mind dwell on those tales, not knowing if they were true or not. She'd had to remain steadfast in her answers.

No. They did not know where the manuscript was at.

No. They had not found it.

Yes, they had searched for it in Florence and found nothing.

She did not tell them that they had begun to search the marble caves in Carrara and had high hopes of finding the cave home of the author of the manuscript, Augusto de Carrara. And she certainly didn't tell them they had discovered that Augusto had built his machine of Icelandic crystal and Carrara marble.

They had already searched the crystal quarries in Iceland and ran into a nasty accident for which Katherine refused to take responsibility. She hadn't asked the woman to follow them around while they explored the quarries. She'd tried to convince her to leave them alone in their work. Stubborn fool.

Katherine shook her head, shaking off the thoughts, and waited while Renaldo announced their presence.

"They will see you now." The beefy guard stepped away from the doorway so she could enter.

Her chin went up a notch. She took a deep breath and stepped into what appeared to be a throne room. There were two massive chairs on a raised dais, and sitting upon them were the Duchess of Massa and her son. So, Katherine would see Franco again, after all. No wonder Renaldo had looked afraid.

She stepped up to the edge of the platform and sank into a low, graceful curtsy. She rose and studied the mother, an elderly woman who must be above seventy with white hair and fine wrinkles like spiderwebs across her face. Her eyes were sharp . . . and unkind.

Katherine's gaze darted to the son, Franco d'Luca, who would soon inherit his mother's many titles. A good-looking man with dark hair and classic Italian features of a straight nose, finely shaped, sensual mouth, and dark, thickly lashed eyes. He was very handsome in fact, but the ruthlessness in those eyes made Katherine swallow hard and disguise her shiver by taking another step forward.

"Since you will not talk," the high-pitched, nasal voice of the duchess intoned, "we have decided on a different method of finding the manuscript."

"So, you believe me that we do not know where it is?"

The duchess leaned forward, clasping long, bony fingers covered in glittering rings. "I believe your husband. *He* would have broken under the duress of the tales we've been telling him about your torture."

So they had been playing the same game with Ian. Katherine hoped that meant he was still alive.

"What do you have in mind?" Katherine raised her brows, her chin up and tilted a little to one side.

Franco chuckled, a dark and low sound that sent a shiver crawling down her spine. "You speak as if you have some bargaining power."

"Don't I? If I do not fear death, then you have no power over me."

He laughed again, his eyes turning appreciative and hungry. "You see, Mother. She is as I have said and would have made a very good duchess."

"Alas, your current duchess is in excellent health." The old woman cackled at her own joke.

Katherine remained quiet and watchful.

"Perhaps you do not fear death for yourself, Lady Featherstone, but what of your lovely daughter?" He manifested a slow, menacing smile.

Katherine's heart leapt to her throat. "You have her?"

"Not yet. But soon. Very soon."

"What do you want?" Katherine took another step closer and narrowed her eyes.

"I want that manuscript. And I will have it. We have decided to let you and your husband go free to continue your search for it." He steepled his hands under his chin and raised black brows over darkly glowing eyes. "And when you have found it, you will bring it to me . . . in return for your daughter. Nothing else will purchase her life."

"Agreed." Katherine stared hard into his eyes. "But if you are not successful in capturing her, we keep the manuscript."

The duchess cursed her in Italian while Franco's eyebrows drew down in a wicked-looking *V* over his eyes. "Don't doubt that I will have her, Lady Featherstone. We have been watching her for months, and she is even now on her way to Italy and into my very hands."

"You lie! You are full of lies." Katherine balled her hands into fists, her breathing fast and rasping from her nose.

Franco smiled again, a confident gleam in his eyes. "She is right now aboard a hydrogen balloon with the famous aeronaut Sophie Blanchard. They are planning to fly over the Alps to rescue you all the sooner. How could I possibly think to make something so astonishing up out of thin air? Doesn't that sound like something *your* daughter would do?"

A wave of weakness washed over Katherine, causing her knees to shake beneath the elegant rags of her dress. "Don't hurt her. We will find that manuscript if it exists, but if I learn you have kept her down in that dungeon or tortured her . . . you will never see it. Besides, she doesn't know any more than we do, I'm certain."

"You don't have much faith in her abilities, do you? Perhaps she does know something you and your husband do not." He leaned forward. "I will find out what she knows but never fear, Lady Featherstone, my plans of how to extract such information are leaning in . . . other directions. She *is* very beautiful, you know."

A picture of the last time she saw Alexandria—dirty bare feet, straggly hair that refused to stay pinned up, clothing thrown on that she hadn't taken the time to match, and a wee lamb tucked under one arm—rose in Katherine's mind's eye. An adventurous hoyden who never listened to the words of wisdom Katherine had upon occasion tried to instill into her—that was her daughter. But a beautiful woman? Could it be possible she had turned into such in the year they had been gone?

Her eyes pricked with tears at the thought of missing such a transformation. Where had Franco heard such things? Still, the chill from his suggestions of how to convince her to talk made her feel sick. "She is too young." Katherine's words came out as a murmur.

The duke laughed. "You must have forgotten her recent birthdays. By all accounts, she is a ravishing young woman of twenty-one years."

Twenty-one years. Ann, their housekeeper, had been haranguing Katherine to take Alexandria to London for a proper season for years now—but there had never been time. There was always another treasure hunt demanding her attention. And besides, the thought of London, seeing *him* again, the man who had taken her innocence. She couldn't.

She looked at Franco and felt she might vomit. He would do that to Alexandria, take her virginity and possibly get her with child. History would repeat itself. Bile rose to her throat as she imagined it and him . . . imagined him doing those things to her.

"I might consider that you take her place. A more . . . experienced woman has her talents."

The full meaning of the threats slammed into her. She swallowed hard. "I have to see my husband."

He laughed. "To ask permission?"

"Yes." And to see that he was really alive. "I must speak with him in private."

Franco shrugged. "That can be arranged. You will have to make plans to find the manuscript. I will even be so generous as to rent you both a house in Carrara while you search. Of course, you will be summoned for our other arrangement from time to time."

"Enough, Franco. Conduct this business at another time," the duchess barked. "I have no stomach for the details of your liaisons."

Katherine stared at the duchess dead in the eye. "Such a fine man you've raised, Your Grace. You must be so proud."

"Watch your tongue, Lady Featherstone. I would have no difficulty having it cut out."

Katherine clamped her lips together, knowing when to draw back.

"Take her to the Salone d' Luca," Franco directed the hovering Renaldo. "And have Lord Featherstone brought around. I am eager to begin this business."

Katherine turned away without looking at him. That's how she would manage it if he used her as his threats implied.

She just wouldn't look at him.

Paris, France

"EVERYTHING IS GETTING SO SMALL!" Alexandria pointed down to the moonlit view of Paris as the balloon rose higher and higher into the sky.

Gabriel glanced over at Sophie, who had cracked a smile, and then down at the city. The houses and buildings seemed like dark boxes; the trees, clumps of shadowy smudges; and the Seine River, a narrow, glittering, moving body that snaked across the expanse.

His stomach did a little flip when he looked down for very long. Funny, he'd never thought himself afraid of heights, but he felt the distinct queasiness when he got too close to the edge and glanced down, or even watching Alexandria's obvious lack of fear as she clung to one rope and leaned over the edge. He swallowed hard and turned his head away.

"Alexandria, please. Do not lean over so."

Her gaze swung to his in surprise. "Does it make you nervous? Why, I'm perfectly safe." She grinned and leaned further out of the balloon. "It hardly feels like we are moving at all. It feels more like floating."

"Alexandria," Gabriel growled.

"We are moving at the same speed as the wind so you will not feel the wind. We could light a candle and it wouldn't even flicker." Sophie maneuvered the apparatus that controlled the amount of hydrogen released into the balloon. "It will get colder though as we ascend. You might want to put on your cloak and gloves."

Alexandria nodded and dove into their clothing stores on the covered side of the balloon. Gabriel gave a great sigh. Thank God she was away from that edge, for the moment anyway.

He stared up at the stars and wondered, equations springing to his mind, how far away they were. The stars seemed to shine brighter the closer they became. He didn't feel bad when he looked up. He felt . . . peaceful.

A sudden spark of color in his peripheral vision made him inhale sharply. He turned toward it but it disappeared. Then another spark, closer, a golden bronze color. It dipped and then disappeared. He swallowed, noticing a faint ringing in his ears. That wasn't good. He looked down and his stomach rolled.

Mistake, that. Mustn't look down.

When he gazed back up into the sky, the horizon was covered in long lines of color—undulating, hauntingly beautiful colors so soft yet pure he forgot to breathe. "The auroras," he whispered.

"What did you say?" Alexandria came up to his side and peered up at him, a softness in her eyes that always spoke of her love.

"I thought I saw colors." He pointed. "Over there. And I remembered reading about the auroras. But those are in the north. You might have seen them in Iceland, but we are too far south so it is impossible." Gabriel shook his head. "I must have imagined it."

"I should like to see that someday. I didn't look for them in Iceland. Perhaps I missed them."

There was a soft longing in her voice that made it harder to hear her. Gabriel fought the urge to panic, but the clogged feeling in his ears seemed to be growing worse. Perhaps it was the atmospheric change. When he had traveled north to Holy Island to meet Alexandria for the first time, his hearing had improved. Aboard ships his hearing had either improved or worsened. The air was thinner the higher they went, so what that might do to his hearing suddenly became a startling possibility.

He might lose it again.

He took a deep breath. *God, I trust You. Help me manage whatever is to come. I choose to put my faith in You. In Your love for me. I choose faith.*

He hadn't worried about his hearing in weeks and he didn't want to borrow trouble now. He especially did not want to worry Alexandria. And he couldn't tell her about the colors. Something so astounding and unbelievable as that would worry her for certain. "Perhaps we will visit your friends in Iceland someday."

Alexandria clasped his upper arm with one hand and leaned into his side. "I should like that very much. And we must visit Baylor in Ireland. And Montague." Her voice turned wistful. "I have made so many wonderful friends on this journey."

Gabriel leaned down and kissed her temple. "As have I." He fought the urge to take her into his arms, longing for a real honeymoon, on a warm beach perhaps, instead of a quest with his new wife.

Alexandria motioned Sophie over and included her in their reflections. "And now we have you. A world-famous aeronaut to call friend. I have a feeling after this journey we will be friends for life."

"Yes, for life." A thoughtful yet sad expression crossed Sophie's face.

Perhaps she was thinking of her husband's short life—falling in a balloon accident several years ago. She'd continued his passion, never remarried, never had children, Gabriel knew that much.

He gave her stiff back a pat. "We are fortunate indeed."

Gabriel saw another flash of color. He turned toward it, saying nothing but not afraid. A deep, restful calm filled him as he watched a pale pink twist ever so slowly around a shot of cerulean blue. It somehow comforted him, even though in the back of his mind he knew something was wrong—wrong with his mind perhaps, and growing worse the farther up into the heavens they went.

He let go of all the book knowledge and the possibilities and striving reasoning, felt it all slip away into the ink of night. He practiced his faith, like a muscle little used, let go and enjoyed the color show. Let the future come. Let God's will be done.

The three of them stared out at the dark countryside, leaving Paris behind, following where the wind blew them.

Praying God would blow them over the Alps and all the way to Italy, Alexandria's parents, and blessed reconciliation.

Chapter Eighteen

Malaspina Castle, Massa, Italy

$\mathcal{J}$an sprawled onto the thick carpet with a head-jarring thud. The guards, two of them this time, mock bowed and turned on their heels toward the door. He stayed down a moment, trying to get his breath back, and then slowly rose to his knees, looking around the opulent room full of life-sized portraits of the family d'Luca.

"Katherine."

She rose and rushed toward him, kneeling beside him and taking his face into her hands. Her gaze washed over him, her face turning sad, regret heavy in her blue eyes. "What have they done to you?" She looked thinner too but still had that steel in her eyes. Still strong.

"The same thing they've done to you, I imagine." He stood and held out his hand to help her up, his tone grim. "What's happened? Why are they leaving us alone together?"

Her eyes shuttered, as if a curtain had been pulled. She shrugged. "I haven't puzzled it all out yet. Their plans are not good. But perhaps there is something we can work with."

A shaft of unease filled his chest. Whenever Katherine got that calculating look in her eyes, it boded ill. They often ended up in places and positions he'd never imagined himself in. "Tell me everything you know."

She took a step away and turned toward the fireplace, staring into the flames. "They told me they were torturing you." She shivered and shook her head. "They didn't hurt me physically, just torturous lies I refused to believe." She spun around to face him, her chin jutting out in that familiar way that made him ache for her. "I suspect they did the same to you?"

"Yes." He looked down at his worn boots, seeing them for a moment back on Holy Island, in the pasture, sheep manure on one toe and how he'd worried he would have to wash it off before going home, often forgetting. Those had been the first days of his marriage. "I believed them too much, I'm sure. I told them everything I know."

"Good thing that isn't much." Her voice sounded hard, but he knew the reasons behind it and only shrugged, agreeing.

"Franco says he will have Alexandria soon within his grasp."

His head flew up. "What? Have they gone to Holy Island for her?"

Katherine laughed, another harsh sound, pained and hollow. "Alexandria isn't on Holy Island. I suspect she left months ago. Searching for us."

"Where is she now?"

"He says she is in an air balloon, heading this way."

"That is preposterous. You believe him?"

"Yes, I think I do." Katherine came close and took his hands. She stared down at them, a sigh escaping. "You know I've felt it. She is coming for us. To rescue us."

"Your intuitions aren't always right." The words flew out of his mouth, but another part of him knew they usually were exactly right or pointed to some truth.

"It's our daughter. There is no one but you I feel more connected to."

Ian took a deep breath. "A balloon. It's so dangerous. What did Franco say? What does he want with her?"

Her face crumbled. She brought his hands to her face, a shudder going through her body.

Panic rose to his throat. "Tell me."

"He wants to use her as a bargaining tool. We are to go free, but only to continue our search of the marble quarries in Carrara. He says he will keep her here . . . *keep* her. If we find the manuscript, we can trade it for her life." Fear pooled in her eyes. "If we don't, she will die. And while he is holding her—" She glanced down, unable to meet his eyes. "He plans to make her his mistress."

Rage exploded within him. His skin flushed from head to toe. "We can't let that happen." His breath came in quick puffs.

Katherine squeezed his hands. "There is one way. We can't trust him, he lies with every breath, but he said if I will take her place, he will spare Alexandria when he has her. I will go with you to Carrara, but he will call me back here—upon occasion."

Ian reared back, the shock rocking him to his core. "Why not just violate you now?"

Katherine turned red and looked away. "I think he prefers . . . a more mature, *willing* partner."

"God help us."

She nodded and faced him. "Do we have a choice?"

Ian searched inside himself, wondering if they did. What if Franco never had Alexandria within his clutches and they sacrificed this for nothing? But the duke knew where Alexandria was. He had been watching her for a long time . . . waiting . . . waiting for her to come to him. It made Ian sick.

Of course she would come for them. In some ways she was so like her mother! He took a few short breaths wondering, for the first time in a long time, if God might have a way out that he couldn't see at this moment. But then he saw his darling daughter's face, so sweet, so innocent, so loving . . . the daughter he had abandoned for his wife's passions.

He looked at Katherine's ravishing face, still startlingly lovely, more wretchedly lovely than when they'd married, and he wanted to sob. If there was even the slightest chance he could save Alexandria from such a fate . . . he would do it.

"Do what you have to do." He turned away from her.

She sighed, came up to him, and pressed her head against his back. "I *am* sorry. We should have never started this business. We should have never left Holy Island."

He said nothing. Thinking that she was right about that.

ALEX HUNCHED WITHIN THE FOLDS of her fur-lined cloak, her hands buried in a fur muff, her hood pulled up over her ears. Puffs of vapor came from her cold nose and the cold whipped against her cheeks. But all the cold air in the world was worth this sight—the dawning light of the sunrise displayed on the horizon. She couldn't help the thrill of joy expanding her chest. And she couldn't stop smiling.

"You've caught the bug, I see." Sophie handed her a cup of steaming hot tea.

"The bug?" Alex took the cup and brought it to her face, inhaling the sweet scent.

"For flying." Sophie shrugged, an equal smile in her eyes. "For adventure."

"I was born with that bug." Alex stared up at the white, cloudless sky streaked with pink and purple.

Sophie nodded. "Most women don't know what I am talking about. I seem odd to them, but not to you, I think."

Alex hooted a laugh. "I know that feeling all too well. You are not odd to me, Sophie Blanchard. You are amazing."

"It comes with a cost though, don't you think?" Sophie's eyes turned dark under the dawning light. "I wonder sometimes if I had married someone else—someone safer and more conventional—what my life would have been like."

"But you would have never had all this." Alex took one hand from the muff and extended it toward the magnificent scene.

Sophie looked out at the sunrise and smiled softly. "Yes, but I miss him so much."

"You have regrets, then?"

"Mostly no, but sometimes." Sophie shrugged. "I just wonder about things, and you're the first person I've felt might understand."

"Of course I understand. And of course you wonder about how your life might be different if you hadn't met your husband. I think everyone does that. When I was on Holy Island, stuck out in the 'wilderness' as my husband calls it, I dreamed of all kinds of adventures. I felt constrained there, like my life would never really begin. But now I've had adventures beyond my imaginings. And hard things . . . things I wish I could go back and change."

Alex looked up into the brightening rays of sunshine and sighed. "We all do the best we can. And Sophie . . . God's Spirit is here, on the earth, to help us. When Jesus went back to heaven He said He would not leave us orphans. He said that God would send someone to help us, comfort us. The Holy Spirit. I have found that if I train myself to listen, I can hear

Him leading me and guiding me. He is an inner voice we have to become used to hearing, and then following. If we can do that, at least to the best of our abilities, then we will live the life we were meant to live."

Alex smiled a rueful smile. "Regrets are hard to bear, Sophie, I know. I have some of my own, and I'm sure there will be more to come, but if you had married a more conventional man and led a more conventional life, there would have been other, different obstacles to overcome."

Sophie stood next to her and gestured toward the sunrise. "Yes, well, I can't imagine never seeing a sunrise from this point of view."

Alex nodded. "I am thankful to have seen it once. It is as if we are floating toward heaven."

"I will listen to God's Spirit. Thank you, Alexandria. You are right. I can't imagine trading this view for anything."

THEY HAD CAUGHT A FAIR westerly wind and were heading in the general direction of Italy, taking watches so each of them could get a few hours of sleep. Alex learned to use the compass and alerted Sophie if the wind changed direction too much or if they were approaching any obstacle that would cause them to have to throw out sandbags and ascend. Thankfully, that hadn't happened. Mostly they just floated, looking down at the rows of crops, the vineyards, and clumps of forests as they sailed over western France. The wind carried them at what seemed a slow speed, but they covered far more ground than if they had been traveling by carriage.

On the third evening the sky turned gray and stormy, the feeling of rain heavy in the air. "We will need to ascend quickly and get above these storm clouds." Sophie heaved up a heavy sandbag, peering over the edge to make sure it would land in a field, and then pushed it over the side.

Gabriel quickly grabbed another bag and threw it over. Alex rushed to help Sophie with a third one. "How many should we throw over?" Alex yelled against the rising wind.

A jag of lightning in the distance made Alex jump with a shriek. "That was close!"

Sophie looked at the sky, tense lines standing out around her mouth, but her eyes were level and intent. "Keep throwing them over until I say to stop!"

"Shouldn't we descend, land somewhere, and take cover?" Gabriel asked, though he kept throwing bags overboard.

"No, I've done this before. If we can rise above the storm clouds, we will be out of danger."

The clouds continued to grow dark and so thick Alex couldn't see very far ahead of her. Rain began to pelt the balloon. Alex looked up, her heart loud in her ears. The wind gusted against the balloon, flattening one side and then turning them, making them whirl like inside a top. Another jolt of lightning flashed, seeming right next to them, and then a loud rumble of thunder. Alex could feel it inside her body as well as out. Within moments they were all soaked and freezing, rising up and up into the thin air.

Alex began to feel faint.

"We're nearly high enough!" Sophie shouted from one side. "Just a few more bags."

The clouds began to thin and lighten. Gabriel came over and put his arm around Alex's waist, bringing her close to his side. "Look, it's getting lighter."

Within another few moments, they broke free from the storm clouds and rose higher still to a clear expanse of sky. Above them were the stars, bigger and brighter than she'd ever seen them. The moon appeared a giant, glowing orb, shining down upon them.

Alex peered over the edge of the basket, looking for the now-familiar sight of the distant earth but saw only flashes of lightning jagging down through the swirling storm clouds. She felt caught, suspended in a calm space that was both eerie and beautiful, as if they had crossed over from one life to the next.

Her breath was short though, and she couldn't stop shivering from the snapping cold. She pressed closer to Gabriel. "Have we made it?"

He looked at her lips . . . oh no. "Gabriel, can you hear me?"

He turned her into his arms. "Don't worry. It's the altitude, I think. It seems to either make my hearing better or worse. It should come back once we are on land again."

Alex bit down on her chattering teeth, nodding but worried. What if it didn't? The thought of him going back to the nonhearing world filled her with despair, but she mustn't show that. She must appear confident and full of faith.

"Come along. We have to get you into warm and dry clothes. You and Sophie go under the awning first. I'll keep watch."

Sophie came up to them, her face white with cold and her lips tinged blue but still with those steady dark eyes. "The compass says we are traveling north, which is not ideal but at least we aren't going backward to the east. This storm will cost us some time, I'm afraid."

"At least it didn't cost us our lives." Gabriel watched her lips as they spoke.

Yes, Alex thought, diving into the warmer air under the awning and scrambling for some warm, dry clothes. But had the balloon cost Gabriel his hearing? Would finding her parents cost them so much?

Chapter Nineteen

*F*ranco's well-sprung carriage did little to cushion Ian and Katherine's bleak mood on the road to Carrara and the marble caves. Deep ruts, uneven ground, and a recent storm made traps of sucking mud and slippery roads. The wheels of the carriage veered back and forth like a newborn colt trying to stand for the first time. Katherine gripped the leather strap with a tightly curled hand and stared out at the hilly countryside.

Italy. The hilly valleys of Tuscany with the craggy mountains pressing in on one side and the sparkling waters of the sea on the other. It was one of her favorite places on earth. And she had a lot to compare it with. She and Ian had been to the far corners of the known world—pyramids in Egypt, a silver mine in Brazil where she had learned how to make any number of explosive devices, a family secret in Philadelphia, Australia's new colony to find a missing brother, and more recently—Ireland, Iceland, and back to Italy, a place she hadn't visited since the quest to find a missing painting by Michelangelo. Now another Florentine—Augusto de Carrara—and his mysterious manuscript.

"What do you think is in this manuscript, Ian?" She turned away from the window and looked at her husband on the seat across from her.

"We've discussed it many times. Some sort of weapon. Something powerful enough to control the world." His voice was quiet, the lines on either side of his mouth deep, sad. She felt a shaft of pain knowing she'd brought them to this place.

"He'll trade Alexandria for it. We have to find it."

"I confess I am losing hope. We have spent over a year of our lives looking for it to no avail."

"But we're close," Katherine insisted. "We found Augusto's house in Florence, or the house that was built upon the ashes of his home. We spoke to the town's residents and combed the monastery and what remained of Oswald's library. We know the manuscript was a part of Hans Sloane's collection and that it was, at one time at least, in the British Museum. It came up missing only in 1813, wasn't it?"

"That is another curious puzzle." Ian sat up straighter. "Did Sloane really have the original? It would be so old, over two hundred years. How could something that old still be intact?"

"It exists." Katherine crossed her arms over her chest, narrowing her eyes.

"How can you be so sure?"

"I feel it," she whispered and then raised her chin. "The feeling is stronger than ever this time." She took a short, almost painful breath. "It's as if it is calling to me." She released her breath, closed her eyes, and looked away. She didn't want to see his reaction. She just needed him to trust her.

"For our daughter's sake, I hope you are right." His voice was even, resigned. "Let's think back over everything that has happened."

Katherine sat up and nodded. It was always a good sign when he turned to the analytical side of his nature on any mission.

"Sir Edward Brooke wrote to us and asked us to meet him in London, which we did."

Katherine nodded. She hadn't wanted to go to London, but it was necessary at times.

"Think back over every detail of that meeting with Brooke. Is there any clue we have overlooked?"

Katherine contemplated the carriage roof, thinking of what was said at the meeting. Not much. Sir Edward hadn't even told them about Augusto. He probably hadn't known the author of the manuscript. All he had was a partial manuscript of drawn plans, mathematical sketches that were beyond their time, and certainly beyond Ian's and her knowledge to puzzle out. Brooke had glossed over what the plans were for, just saying that the original had been stolen some years ago from Hans Sloane's collection from the British Museum and they were on the hunt for it. It had last been rumored to have been seen in Dublin, Ireland, in the hands of the Royal Irish Academy, odd lot of fellows there. That had started their chase across Ireland.

"I can't think of anything about that conversation that we haven't already dissected. Can you?"

"No. I can't." Ian ran a hand through his silver-threaded hair in a move so familiar, it brought a pang to Katherine's heart.

She hardened her heart to the feeling. "In Ireland we found the clues to Iceland, where we poured through libraries looking through the sagas."

"Then you found the book, the story about Augusto."

"Yes, his story took hold of me then. That's when I started to feel we were truly on the right path. I knew we had found the author of the manuscript."

"And you left clues for Alexandria. That drawing . . ."

"I'm sorry!" Katherine said. "I had to . . . I knew she would come for us and follow our trail. I had to leave clues to guide her to us. To keep her safe."

Ian leaned forward, elbows braced on his thighs, eyes beseeching. "You may have traded our safety for hers. What if she pays the ultimate price for this mission?"

"No, I won't believe it." She gazed out the window again and said in a voice so low it was barely audible, "All she ever wanted was what we have. I just made sure she got it."

The hills became steeper, the climb rocky, and the road narrow, sometimes hanging on the edge of a precipice. The carriage swayed and dipped as they rode through the village of Carrara and up the slopes of the Apuan Alps. The mountains appeared draped in snow, but it was not snow they approached; it was the marble, the famed white marble of Carrara.

For centuries it had been dug from the earth and used by such great artists as Michelangelo for his *David* and countless other famous sculptors. Buildings, monuments, whole massive structures had been built of Carrara marble. And Augusto had used it too. Sculpted with it and lived in it, deep inside the caves when he'd gone into hiding. If that manuscript was anywhere, it should be here, buried where he had buried himself for so many years. They were close. She could feel it.

"Now that we have Franco's written permission to scout the quarries, I suggest we start in the *Cave di Fantiscritti*."

Ian shot Katherine a wry look. "If the Carbonari aren't guarding it. They would only scoff at a document from a d'Luca. You know them, with their revolutionary ideals." He shook his head. "We still have to stay clear of them."

Katherine shrugged. "Yes, well, it is said to be the oldest part of the mine. If Augusto lived in these caves, which I believe he did, then we should begin in the oldest known part."

"Agreed. Just be careful."

"Of course. You know I always am." Katherine turned and looked out the window at the white-streaked majesty of the mountains that would be their home for the foreseeable future and said a silent prayer, the prayer she always prayed for Alexandria. *Don't let her be like me. Don't let her need anything or anyone—ever.*

Katherine still wanted to save her daughter from every hardship this life would give her. She'd done her best to make her independent and she'd built up a fortune that would always provide for her. Someday she would show her love too, when Alexandria was ready. The little paltry love of another human—thin, watered down by need. But first she'd had to make her strong.

Pray her daughter had learned her lesson well.

She was about to enter the lion's den.

Geneva, Switzerland

ALEXANDRIA TUGGED ON HIS ARM, pointing with bright eyes, mouthing the words, "Isn't it amazing?" She leaned entirely too far out of the basket for Gabriel's comfort so he focused his attention elsewhere.

He looked instead out over the city that was fast coming in the distance and had to agree. The Swiss Alps and the city below was an amazing sight.

Geneva sprawled out before them with stately, multistoried buildings, rows of neat gardens, shrubbery, and trees hugging Lake Geneva, which lay sparkling on the western side of the city. That was a pretty picture enough, to be sure, but then the swell of majestic mountains framed the city, coming closer, the highest mountains he had ever seen.

"Sophie, are you certain we can maintain the height we will need to cross the Apennine Mountain range?" They would have to sail over seven thousand feet for a great distance. It would be cold and the air would become increasingly thin.

Sophie, already adapting to his returning affliction, lifted her chin and spoke plainly. "I have never attempted it, Your Grace. Pray God we are successful."

Yes, pray God, indeed. The thought of crashing into the mountains was enough to make him shudder. Gabriel turned away and swallowed. The clogged feeling in his ears was always there and refused to pop and give him relief.

Alexandria looked up at him with concern in her eyes. How was she feeling about this coming and going of his hearing? He imagined if she were having a physical ailment and how difficult it would be to see that, to watch a loved one struggle and suffer. He mustn't let her worry though, so he smiled and nodded at the coming city, turning her thoughts to other things.

"It is magnificent, you are right. I have a feeling that crossing the Alps will only get more breathtaking—both literally and figuratively."

"Sophie says we will have to land and make more hydrogen in Geneva before we can go over the mountains."

Gabriel nodded. "Yes, and sleep one night in a real bed." It would be good to spend the night in a normal bed and stretch their legs on solid ground.

Sophie let more hydrogen out of the balloon, causing them to float just above the treetops. As they neared the edge of the city, people of all ages began to pour out of the shops and houses, pointing up at them, waving and shouting. They were making quite the spectacle, and Gabriel hoped no one panicked and shot at them. People could behave irrationally when afraid and confused.

Sophie turned a valve and let more air out of the balloon. They were headed for a grassy park area, rows of trees lining either side of them.

"Hold tight and brace yourselves!" She shouted so loud that Gabriel heard a little of it. She dug in her heels and grasped hold of the forward lines. Gabriel and Alexandria grasped the lines on either side to help distribute the weight. The balloon bumped, as if hitting a current of wind, twirled in a half circle and then back again, shivering with the release of the gas.

They jolted forward as one corner of the basket hit the ground. Another bumping jolt where they were airborne again, heading right toward a tree, and then they tottered to the other side, the basket hovering a few feet above the ground.

"Quick, throw out the anchor lines!" He read Sophie's lips, his ears ringing.

He and Alexandria grasped the ropes in hand and threw them overboard. They landed on the ground with a jarring thud, securing the basket to the ground. Sophie let out a little more air and the basket settled firmly on the ground. Within moments they had the balloon secured to the ground in the middle of a grassy park.

Gabriel turned, breathing hard, to see crowds of people coming toward them, some uniformed soldiers and armed, most of them wide-eyed and talking, as if Gabriel and the ladies were ghosts or angels or alien creatures come to visit.

They would have to convince them otherwise and soon. With his hearing so faint, communicating would be a challenge. Gabriel cleared his throat, hoping to hear the sound of it now that he was on solid ground.

He did not.

The crowd closed in. Gabriel climbed from the basket, walked a little forward, and held up his arms. In French he shouted, "We come in peace! From Paris! Genevans, may I present the famous aeronaut Sophie Blanchard!"

He whipped an arm back toward Sophie like a circus master. Sophie climbed neatly over the edge of the basket and swept into an elegant curtsy. The crowd began to smile and clap.

Voices clamored for attention. Gabriel looked to Alexandria, who told him with her lips that some wanted to ride the balloon and others were asking questions about how it could fly. The cacophony of sound burst into color—red and dark swirls of orange, yellows, and browns appeared and then disappeared over the crowd, making Gabriel's head swim. He shook it, panic filling his chest. He had to stay in control of the situation. Inspiration struck with a flash of light blue like a lightning bolt, making him blink hard.

He held up his arms and motioned for the crowd to quiet. "I understand you have questions and some are even brave enough to ask if they might ride in such an air machine. With the cooperation and permission of your city's leaders, we will hold a demonstration . . . and a lottery. One person will win a ride in the balloon. You may purchase a ticket for the lottery for only one franc!"

The people cheered.

"Will someone direct me to the administrator of your city?"

A stocky man, his breath heaving in and out of a barrel chest as if he'd been running, pushed through the crowd.

He stood before Gabriel, swept off a tall hat from his balding white head, and bowed. "I am Monsieur Piccard, the *Président du Conseil*. Most honored to be at your service."

Gabriel gave him a short bow. Alexandria and Sophie curtsied on either side of him. "I am the Duke of St. Easton. This is my wife, Alexandria Ravenwood, the Duchess of St. Easton, and this is Mrs. Sophie Blanchard. We are in need of several things if we might bear upon your good graces."

"Of course, anything! Anything at all. What can we do for you, Your Grace?"

"Lodgings for the night, guards for the balloon, and Mrs. Blanchard needs help making more hydrogen. A scientist or apothecary could help with that perhaps? Someone who might be knowledgeable with such things?"

"But of course. We are at your disposal." He bowed again, a sheen of sweat on his florid cheeks.

"We will pay well, of course, and should you give permission for the lottery, we will donate the proceeds to your city."

"You are too generous, Your Grace."

"Excellent. Then you will appoint someone to sell the tickets and see to the lottery?"

He bobbed his head, looking from Gabriel to the huge balloon. "It will be my honor. You honor our city with your presence."

Gabriel leaned in and lowered his voice. "We are in somewhat of a hurry. We will need to leave tomorrow at the earliest possibility to cross the Alps."

Sophie nodded agreement. "We could give the winner his ride and then leave by midmorning."

The president bowed. "I will see that it is done."

"Very good." Gabriel turned to Alexandria and Sophie with a grin. "Some decent food and a real bed for the night.

How does that sound, ladies?" And a night finally alone with his new wife.

"And hydrogen," Sophie said, her small, serious face like a child's with ancient eyes.

"And hydrogen," Gabriel agreed, taking a lady on each of his arms and following Monsieur Piccard through the parting crowd toward Geneva, a city nestled in the glory of the Alps.

Chapter Twenty

Carrara, Italy

*K*atherine! Katherine, come quick!" Ian held the lantern aloft, the light splaying across the gray-veined white marble, and waved her over.

They were in a winding tunnel deep in the marble caves, where for the last several days they had climbed, clawed, and crawled through the marble quarries. They had circled around since the night before, having slept in the caves and feeling more like burrowing animals than human. Now they were coming toward the far end of the quarry, where they'd never been before. It was still dark, pitch dark, but the air was changing, lighter, a fresher air that had movement to it, and even more encouraging, the tunnel was widening.

Ian crouched under a low ceiling and then burst into a large chamber, a thin shaft of light coming from far above their heads.

Katherine came up behind him and lifted her lantern. They saw it at the same time, a pile of objects that didn't look anything like the stone-carvers' tools they'd seen scattered around the mines.

"Could it be?" Katherine rushed around Ian toward the scattered objects. "We have not seen anything like this!" Her words echoed across the cave walls.

Ian hurried to her side and lifted his lantern high.

Light flashed over the objects—books, canvas paintings, articles of tattered clothing, a comb with some missing teeth. Katherine delicately picked through the pile. Could it be Augusto's things? Had they found his cave? She opened one of the books and saw faded script in Italian.

"Can you read this?" She handed it back to Ian, a natural at languages. He had, on many occasions, helped solve cases with his quick grasp of culture, language, and a sharp mathematical mind. They were polar opposites—him with his logic and her with her intuition. Katherine knew she would have never been so successful without him.

"It's an old book of philosophy." Ian carefully turned the pages. "Socrates is well quoted."

Katherine turned aside with a frown. There had to be something more. Something that pointed to Augusto. Her eyes lit on a ledge of the cave wall where there was a dark form sitting on top against the marble. She walked over and gently picked it off the stone shelf.

The instant she touched it, a flash of light exploded from behind her eyes. She brought it instinctively to her chest, as a mother might cradle a babe, and closed her eyes. Her senses rushed to the fore, grasping. The smell of the parchment overwhelmed her. A chill raced across the back of her neck. With trained patience she metered her breath and raised the leatherbound book to a place inches in front of her face. Ian came up behind her and lifted his light. She opened her eyes and read the inlaid words. *"Il prodotto del mio fuoco."* Katherine looked at Ian with raised brows.

"The product of my fire." His eyes grew round. "It could be."

With shaking fingers, Katherine turned the leather cover. The first page had a faint signature at the bottom of the page. Augusto de Carrara.

Her heart lurched. "It's him! This has to be it. We've found it!" Tears sprang to her eyes. "We can save her now." A little cry came from her throat.

Ian's eyes glassed over, holding both hope and terror. "Turn the page."

Katherine reached for the yellowed page. It cracked beneath the strain, the threads of the binding creaking. She sucked in her breath. No! It was too faded to read, the lines of ink barely visible. A word could be made out here and there, a scratching of a mathematic formula, but it wasn't enough.

She turned page after brittle page—all the same. Illegible scratching! None of the pages had anything of worth to anyone. An ancient, ruined, worthless manuscript.

"Oh, Ian." She set the book back on the ledge and pressed her forehead to his chest. "What are we to do now?"

Switzerland

GABRIEL'S HEART RACED. YELLOW, LIKE an explosion of sunlight, made him shy away from the table of three men beside them at the inn who were obviously well into their cups and laughing uproariously, slapping the table with meaty palms.

He turned, raising his shoulder against the brightness of another sudden streak of light. It was louder than any sound. He turned his head only to see a shot of blue so bright, he brought his arm up, involuntarily, as a man passed by, his mouth pursed in a whistle.

Gabriel ground his teeth and jerked away, only to see bright spots of orange fill his vision as the serving girl set plates and cups on the table in front of them. *Bang, bam, clatter, clatter*—he could hear it in a way that made every sound a bright color in the back of his eyes. His head pounded. Sweat began to course over his skin in a hot prickle. His breath was too fast . . . too much. God help him!

He reared back from the crowded room where they were to have their supper and said to a startled Alexandria and Sophie, "I need air."

Alexandria started to go after him. "Are you all right?"

But he brushed her away. "Just give me a moment in peace. Start without me."

He couldn't explain more, just turned from their fearful faces and stumbled from the color-clad room. He rushed headlong, not minding who he passed or what they said to him, out into the cool night air, the coming twilight, the blessed silence.

He kept going until he was well down the street, toward an open field. The air was calm and cooled his face. He stopped and looked up.

God, there's too many colors. Am I losing my mind?

Streaks of color like he'd never seen on earth raced across the sky in a dizzying array of terrifying glory. Blues on fire, purples so deep he could feel them, greens that oozed with a hue that made him taste the tang of plants, yellows that outshone the sun. White. Bright white.

He shielded his eyes with his forearm, his head pounding. *Oh God, help me. Am I dying? I'm going to die, aren't I? This is heaven, a glimpse of it, isn't it?*

He dropped to his knees in a grassy patch beside the narrow road. *But I don't want to leave Alexandria! Not yet! Please . . . God . . . just a little more time. A child? A life together. God, I want to grow old with her. You only just gave her to me. Don't take her away yet! Please! I'll not love her more than I love You. I promise.*

He clenched his eyes and cradled his head in his arms, just trying to breathe. *Jesus. God. Help. It's not true. I do love her more than I love You. I'm sorry. I can't help it.*

Your will be done. He curled tighter toward his stomach. *But I don't want it to be done if You are going to take me. I don't want to die.*

A sudden lightness filled his head. He felt as if he were floating, like on the balloon but still anchored to the earth.

With a quivering stomach his eyelids fluttered open. He took a long breath and looked up. Glittering stars. An occasional flash here and there, but mostly he just saw the giant expanse of glittering stars and dark sky with the shadows of the mountains in the distance. There was a soft blue and an occasional streak of green or yellow but opaque now, ghostly colors that brought a lump of peace to his throat.

He had a sudden knowing that God was dimming the lights of heaven so he could bear to see it and Gabriel chuckled, a sound as deep as the night . . . a sound he *heard*.

His chuckle turned into a laugh. He could hear again! He didn't know how well yet and he didn't care. He was tired. Tired of carrying it all, the weight of what he could and couldn't hear. The weight of the rise and fall of emotion that followed in the wake of his affliction's path. He couldn't care anymore. It was too much for his human flesh and he recognized it in a flash. He had to let go . . . again. He had to live with whatever God gave him in this moment. Nothing less and nothing more.

He was as Isaac. Laid out on a stone altar about to be sacrificed, waiting to see if today an angel of the Lord would stay death's blade or if today would be the day he crossed over to the other side. It was hard, living on the constant razor's edge of not knowing from one moment to the next if his affliction would return, become permanent. Harder than anything he had ever tried to do—everything had always come so easily to him. But this affliction, it made him pant like a gladiator in the ring with roaring lions. The difference was he had to stop fighting and trust God, fully, completely, that God would do what He wanted with their lives.

It was near impossible except for the breath of hope and grace that swirled around him. He rose, staggered onto his feet, and turned back to the inn.

What to tell Alexandria? He would have to explain his abrupt departure. Was it time to tell her about the colors?

ALEXANDRIA BREATHED A BIG SIGH when Gabriel walked back through the door of the inn. She had just been about to excuse herself to Sophie and go in search of him, but now he was coming toward them and the look in his eyes was—intense. Intense and intimate. A deep connection pulsed through the air between them as he came closer.

Heat rose to her cheeks. She looked up into his eyes, concern and love for him filling her chest. "Where did you go? I was beginning to worry. Are you all right?"

He sat next to her and took her hand, brought it to his lips, and kissed her knuckles. He bowed his head over her hand and closed his eyes, eyelashes so thick they made inky black smudges against his high cheekbones. "I have something to show you. Are you finished eating?"

She nodded, glancing at Sophie. They shouldn't leave her alone.

"We aren't staying the night here. I've been given directions to a villa, Cologny at the Villa Deodati at 9 Chemin de Ruth, where the poet Byron once stayed. There is a carriage awaiting us."

"Oh, that was kind of them." She hadn't been looking forward to staying in a crowded inn, possibly with Sophie and other women lodgers as bedmates. Anticipation coursed through her when she thought of being in a villa—with Gabriel—alone at last.

Alex looked at Sophie. "Are you ready?"

"Yes." Sophie stood to follow.

"Come along, then." Gabriel held out his arm. "I've made all the arrangements."

It was dark when they stepped from the inn, but when Alex looked up into the sky, seeing a thousand twinkling stars with the heights of the dark mountains around them, she took a sudden inhale. "It's so beautiful here."

"Magical." Sophie looped her arm through Alex's. "I wish we were sailing over them right now." Her voice was soft and filled with longing.

Gabriel laughed. "Do you not ever prefer to be earthbound, Sophie?"

The fact that he had heard her slammed into Alex, causing her to turn toward him with raised brows. Sophie had been facing away from them when she spoke, and her voice had been so quiet. How was Alex to keep up with her husband's latest change? He nodded at her silent question while Sophie answered it.

"I find it is less lonely when I am flying, Your Grace." She gave them a small, humble smile.

"Have you thought of remarrying?" Alex asked as they climbed into the carriage.

"Oh no. Can you imagine? What man would suffer an aeronaut for a wife?"

"Another aeronaut perhaps?" Alex settled in across from Sophie next to Gabriel, who took Alex's hand and lightly squeezed it.

Sophie gave a soft laugh. "There aren't many of those to choose from. None a bachelor that I know of."

"Perhaps His Grace knows of someone with an adventurous soul. Gabriel?" She turned to him with a mischievous smile.

"I shall give it some thought." He squeezed her hand again. "You'll have made me into a matchmaker too, will you?"

"Too? Whatever have I already made you into?"

"Ha! Any number of things I've never been. Adventurer, investigator, antiquities expert—at least on all things regarding Hans Sloane. Let's see, husband—"

"Father?"

His head jerked toward hers. "Father?"

Alex burst out laughing. "Not yet. At least not that I know of . . . yet."

"You will tell me the very minute you suspect anything of that sort."

He was so serious she tried not to laugh again. Smoothing back her smile, she nodded, pasting a serious look on her face. "Of course, Your Grace."

"I mean what I say, Alexandria." The growling panther in him came forth and raised his brows, green eyes glowing.

"Oh, dear. I didn't know you were going to turn into a tyrant. And right here in front of Sophie!" She smiled at him, that slow, melting smile that held a hint of heat and fire beneath it. That promised things to come. Things they'd made up together. Things that belonged to only them.

His face relaxed into an equally slow smile.

Sophie coughed into her gloved hand and looked out the window. Alex felt a little bad about that, but for goodness sake—she was on her honeymoon after all.

Chapter Twenty-One

Carrara, Italy

"What's that you have?"

Katherine spun around, the note gripped in her hand. "The duke wants us . . . he wants *me* . . . to come back to Malaspina Castle and report our findings."

"And get into his bed!" Ian cursed and swung his fist into the bedpost in their rented house in Carrara. The bed shook with the impact.

Katherine took a long, shuddering breath and walked over to the fireplace where she threw the note in, watched it curl and turn into dark flakes of ash. She had known this moment would come and had been somewhat surprised Franco had waited this long. She had refused to think of it, pushed it to the far corners of her mind, and concentrated on finding Augusto's cave. But now that they had, and found the manuscript worthless, useless, illegible, and crumbling under a single touch? "I'll tell him we haven't found anything yet."

"Pray God he believes you."

"He will." She narrowed her eyes at the flames.

"Oh, of course. I forgot how vast your powers of persuasion can be."

She swung around, her dress flying out. "Ian, stop this. What would you have me do?"

He rubbed his hand over his face. "I'm sorry. It's not your fault. It's just that I can't bear the thought of it."

Katherine rushed over to him. "Nor can I. So we will not think of it. It's just my body."

"What if there's a child?"

A moment of shocked silence descended and then Katherine gasped out. "I'm too old."

Ian took her chin in his hand and lifted her face up into the light streaming in from the window. "You are not too old. We have been very . . . careful. He will not be. He will not care."

Katherine ripped away from him. "Don't make me think of it. Not like that. I can't go through with it if I do."

"Maybe you shouldn't. We could leave, take the artifacts and manuscript from Augusto's cave back to Sir Edward and the prince regent. It's not our fault the manuscript is illegible. We've done our job."

"And what of Alexandria? Do you suggest we just leave her to him?"

"Of course not! We'll find her ourselves. Before we go back to England. We'll take her home where it is safe."

"You don't think he'll come after us? If we double-cross him in such a manner, he will have us all killed."

Ian paused, stared deep in her eyes with a sad desperation that made his face seem years older.

"You know it's true," Katherine whispered. "We have to play the game out. We have to find something to give him, perhaps something we conjure up ourselves, something that will make him let go of Alexandria." She wrung her hands.

"Ian, dearest, he has eyes and ears everywhere. He will track us all the way to Holy Island. Unless we find something of worth to give him . . . we will never be safe again."

"We'll give him the manuscript we found. Tell him the truth."

Katherine's laugh was as brittle as crackling ice. "The truth? Does anyone really know the truth about Augusto and this invention? The truth died with him but Franco won't settle for that. He'll have all our blood on his hands digging for it, searching for it. I know him, his type." She swallowed and looked away. "Ian, I've seen it."

"Fine. Go to him." Ian came over and spun her toward him, his eyes glittering with fear and hate. "You've done this. You've brought us to this." Before she could answer he turned away from her and grabbed his hat, a dark gray felt hat that made him appear every inch the adventurer, the one he wore when they were treasure hunting. The one that made him look rakishly, devilishly attractive to her. He placed it on his head and without a backward glance, through the sheen of tears in her eyes, she saw his blurred form stride through the door, slamming it behind him.

She stood there, her throat aching with unshed tears. When was the last time she had really cried? She couldn't remember. She had always been strong. She had to be strong. She stood taller, lifted her chin, and demanded the tears away.

Even now it felt safer to be that woman.

Emotions, weakness, truth? Those were the inheritance of the rich—people rich in security, rich in love, rich in faith. She'd built security with the work of her hands, the sweat of her brow, and love in a marriage to a man besotted with her. But faith? God had not protected her so how could she have faith in Him now or ever?

She gritted her teeth and reached for her trunk to pack her clothes for Malaspina Castle. She slid satin dresses in among lace-edged undergarments. She didn't plan to give Franco any reason to say she had failed to keep her side of the bargain.

IAN KNELT AND BOWED HIS head in the Carrara Cathedral until his knees ached. He kept his eyes tightly clenched. *Lord, show us the way out or the way through. Don't let Katherine have to commit this sin, this horrible thing, I beg You. We commit ourselves to You. Tell us what to do. Show us the way. Light our steps. God! Save us and keep Alexandria safe. Bring her safely to us.*

And Lord? There is something in me that is telling me not to give up on Augusto's cave. I don't know what that is. I'm not usually the one with "feelings" about things but this just won't go away. If there is something—something we've missed—help me find it. While she's gone . . . I don't know how to endure it! I'll keep looking. Just help us, please. Give her a way out.

Geneva, Switzerland

CANDLELIGHT GLOWED ON HER SKIN, making it shimmer with the flickering light. Gabriel leaned over her and closed his eyes. Wafts of lavender and *her*, a distinct perfume that was Alexandria, drifted from her hair and skin toward him in the enormous bed they had been given in the master's bedchamber of the Swiss chalet.

"Why do you love me?" Her sky blue eyes opened with the question. She looked serious, as if she doubted it. Too serious for a pat answer.

He lowered onto his elbow, lips inches away from hers, and cocked a brow. "Why do you love *me?*"

She pushed against his shoulder with a laugh. "Not fair! I asked first."

"Well." He dipped his head toward her neck, kissed her beneath one ear, and then delved lower, into the nooks and hollows of her collarbone. She stretched out her neck to give him better access and sighed.

"Let us count the ways, shall we?" He murmured against her throat.

She nodded once.

"One—I have been waiting for you for what seems like centuries." He hovered over her lips but didn't kiss her, just stared deeply into her eyes. "I knew something was happening after your first letter. Those poor"—he kissed her with a little peck—"diseased sheep." Another peck. "And the well that had run dry." Another peck against her lips that were now smiling. "The leaking roof." A longer kiss against her laughter.

She turned her head aside. "I was very . . . audacious, wasn't I? Looking back, I can't believe I wrote those things."

"Oh yes. I found your letters very charming . . . utterly irresistible." He dipped his head again, his lips skimming the edge of her jaw. "I recognized somehow that I'd found someone rare and wonderful when I read that first outlandish letter. Imagine my shock when later I discovered that you had tricked me."

"I didn't want to!" She started to rise, met his chest over hers, and fell back onto the bed with a frown. "I had no choice."

"Hmmm." His voice was a low purr. "Perhaps I should refresh your memory." He leaned up in a sudden move. "You told me you needed money for sheep and wells and pens and a leaking roof that covered that excuse for a castle." He murmured deep within her ear, "my little liar," and then ran a trail of kisses back to her lips.

"I did need those things!" Her voice came in a laughing gasp.

"Oh, yes. You needed your allowance for those things, did you?" He took her wrists in a sudden move and pushed them gently by her ears.

"Well yes, if I hadn't had to go after my parents, I would have spent the money on those very things." Her eyes flashed with indignation.

He chuckled, couldn't help it, and ran his fingertips down her side, making her shiver. "Sweet, conniving, adventurous . . . *wife*." He couldn't stand it any longer. He turned them on their side before she could really feel his weight, and then kissed her in earnest.

"I can't believe you found me. I was so far from anywhere. I didn't think I would ever find a husband."

"We can thank the regent for that."

"And God's providence. I think people were praying for me to find a husband."

"To get you off their hands?"

"Well, yes." She gave him a rueful smile that made his heart lurch. "And to give me something to do."

Gabriel brought her closer and chuckled. "I will most certainly give you something to do."

They had the crossing of the Alps tomorrow. They had the finding of her parents. They had a lifetime of challenges and his affliction that would give them highs and lows of experiences together, but tonight they had each other.

Chapter Twenty-Two

Katherine turned from the huge fireplace, a stone monstrosity that was at least three feet taller than she was. It had a paltry little fire flickering against the cold stones in odd juxtaposition to its scale. She'd been brought to the private drawing room that connected to the bedchamber of Franco II, brought and told to sit until he arrived. The room had a musky, cloying scent that made her reach for her handkerchief to cover her nose.

Decorated in deep brown and rose velvet, every surface was covered in something soft, something sensual—an Indian scarf; a Moroccan rug; French chairs with pinioned, cushioned seats and the lush, curved legs of the Louis XIV design. There were mirrors—the frames all shimmering in gilt, silver, bronze—the shape of the frames curved and luxurious. If painted wood and metal could be luxurious, these were, and they were everywhere. Paintings flickered to life in the candlelight from the many branches of gilt candelabra. And it was the candles on the tables, she finally realized, that smelled so horribly. She walked over to blow them out.

"You prefer the darkness?"

His voice was violent velvet.

Katherine leaned over and blew out the three candles of varying heights on a small, elegant table. "You've had them scented. I don't like the smell of it." She straightened and turned to face him.

The remaining light in the room threw his face into stark relief—one side lit while the other side was shadowed. His beard was too sharp; his cheeks, hollowed; his eyes, black and unreadable except for the malice emanating from him, so strong she could almost see it, could certainly feel it, like an evil force advancing, a cloud of darkness coming to consume her. She swallowed hard and took a step toward it.

She tilted her chin and raised it, eyes shuttered to her soul. "The room reeks of musk, Your Grace." She said it like a deep caress.

"I vow you will learn to like it."

She raised one brow. "Will I? Perhaps. I have learned to appreciate many things I have found revolting." She shrugged. "For one reason or another." She moved in a graceful sweep around the settee, her hand skimming the cushioned top. "You must be curious of our findings." She slanted him another look, retreating a bit further into the flickering shadows of the room.

"Oh, yes. I am curious about many things." He gestured toward one of the thickly upholstered divans. "I'm most curious, at this moment, about your response to me rubbing your feet."

Katherine laughed. "I hadn't thought you to be so staid in your peccadillos."

"I assure you, Lady Featherstone. It is one of my more lethal talents."

Katherine paused, looking across the color-drenched, scented room at him. *Fear*—a quick pulse in the base of her throat rose to flush her cheeks. She drew in tiny breaths and followed his coaxing hand to the deep cushions of the divan.

He knelt in front of her, placed a thick pillow under her feet, and flipped the hem of her skirt up onto her knees. He took one slippered foot and eased it into his hands. With the lightest of movements he pulled the ribbon free of its knot upon her ankle, stroking and warming the silk of her stocking as he slid the slipper free. She jerked her foot away, but he snatched it back into his hands with a hard grip.

He took her foot into his hands and began rubbing in tiny circles around the heel and then arch.

She set her teeth and stared into the eyes of the woman in the painting on the wall across from her. Her mind groped with questions about her—reaching, desperate for anything to distract her fear. Who was she? Had she been happy in life? In this castle?

He deepened the pressure, pushing into the places in the muscles that she hadn't known were tight and stiff. An unraveling began deep within her. She turned her face away, trying to stop it.

He chuckled. A deep and dark chuckle, filled with velvet softness. "You weren't meant for the likes of him." He reached for her other foot as he pressed his cold lips against the inside of her stocking-clad knee. "You know it. You see these things, don't you? You *feel* them. Look deep within. Test what I'm saying. He was only a stepping-stone to your true destiny. Katherine . . . I understand you. You belong with me."

"Katherine." His hands drew up her skirt toward her thigh.

She jerked away.

"Come now. You know you want this." He drew her stocking down and then off, caressing her bare leg with his hands.

"Tell me, what have you found thus far? Augusto's cave? My spies have reported that you stayed the night deep in the tunnels. Did you finally find it? Do you have the manuscript, my love?"

Katherine shook her head and in a sudden move, she leapt away from him, her eyes narrowed and haunted. His eyes, his touch, his voice were deceiving traps. She had to remember that. "The mines are vast. We need more time. We haven't found anything yet. We have to have more time."

His face turned feral, like an attacking wolf. His lips curled back into a snarl. "You're lying. I can feel it. I feel things too. We're connected, Katherine, whether you like it or not."

Horror rose to her throat. Could he really *know* her like that? Could anyone? She hardened her eyes. "I speak the truth."

He rushed her, crushed her back into the soft cushions of the divan. He pressed into her neck, hard, his breath quick and fast against her pulse. "You will tell me." He breathed into her ear making fear a living thing. Memories of the time before rushed over her, a crawling sensation down her spine and a deep quivering emptiness in her stomach. For the first time in all her treasure-seeking travails—she felt she might be sick. She was going to fail. This was beyond her capabilities, beyond her ability to deflect and control.

"You will . . . tell me . . . everything."

Katherine turned her face away, tears streaming down her cheeks. The sobs she'd been holding back for so long pulsed against the barriers of her heart. She struggled against it, against him as his arms pinned her. She broke and prayed.

God, oh God . . . save me from this evil. I thought I could do it without You.

I cannot.

He reached for her skirt and brought the satin hem to her waist. With a small smile he reached for either side of the neckline of her dress, ready to tear it apart.

"No." She kicked out and pushed against him with her arm, her elbow, turning toward the edge of the divan, feeling the wood frame beneath the cushions like a cage.

"No! What do you mean by *no*? Do you mean no to your daughter? Her first thing she will know will be me . . . ravishing her." He leaned close in a hoarse whisper. "Do not doubt it. And do not ever think to tell me no."

Despair made a darkness so deep it chilled her to her core, a drowning feeling, sinking and smothering under the depths of his words. He would be the end of the Featherstones; she would have brought them all—Ian, Alexandria, and her—to their demise. *She* cost them this. Brought them to this place of ruin. It was all for naught. It was . . . hopeless.

Franco saw her defeat. She could tell by the look of triumph in his eyes. He thought he had won.

And that made her mad.

Katherine changed, a small but integral change. Something that at first only she could feel. She pressed back into the cushions, looked up at him, and shot him with a sinister smile of her own. She chuckled, dark and low, from that place where she really lived. That place that knew things . . . saw things . . . understood beneath the surface. "I thought you wanted a willing partner. I didn't know you were nothing but a brute."

"You dare insult me?" But there was an odd light to his eyes now. A new light that said he understood the rules had changed. That despite her obvious physical weakness, she was now challenging him.

"I thought you liked games . . . and challenges." She sat up further, her hand against his chest.

He chuckled. Changed. Came down upon her body in a liquid way, a melting way she hoped she could coax and control.

God help her if she couldn't.

A sudden banging on the door broke their breathy silence, just as he'd been reaching for her leg. Franco rose up and off her. Katherine scrambled back, straightening her dress and brushing the loosened hair from her face. Her gaze flew from him to the door. It banged again. Louder still.

He jerked away, veered toward the door, and then swung it wide.

Katherine gathered herself, pushing her clothes into neat folds of convention, sat up straight, and wiped any trace of tears off her cheeks. She lifted her chin. On the other side of the door a man of the church, a man dressed as a bishop, handed a letter to Franco and, with a sidelong glance at Katherine, a moment of revulsion lighting his eyes, he bowed and left.

Franco turned, shut the door, and unfolded the missive, ignoring her. He stood silent for a long moment, reading it. Another long, silent moment while she sat there watching and waiting, and then he folded it back up and smiled at her.

It was the coldest smile she'd ever seen.

"I am to see the pope . . . immediately."

Katherine nodded, saying nothing.

"You've won yourself a reprieve." His voice lowered to that velvet hiss. "A very brief reprieve, my love."

"I should go back. Keep looking for the manuscript."

His eyes narrowed.

"I tell you the truth, Your Grace. We haven't found it yet. I swear it. We need more time."

"Very well. I will send for you upon my return. I hope by

then, for all your sakes, that you will have a different answer." He took sudden steps toward her, grasped her chin in a tight grip, and raised her face so they looked each other in the eyes. "I will have you, one way or another." He leaned closer, his breath hot in her face. "But that will be only a bittersweet moment for us."

He smiled. "I will have your husband and St. Easton too. They will tell the truth. Love blinds men like them. They will find it for you if it exists."

St. Easton? What could he mean?

He gripped her chin harder and pressed his mouth against hers.

Katherine burst out a choked sound as he tore free. She watched him turn and stride from the room in a dull daze . . . as if time had slowed down and she could hear the ticking of a clock that was part her heart's beat and part her stomach's dread.

A reprieve, but a short one.

She had to find Alexandria.

THE CARRIAGE SWAYED OVER THE road in its haste toward the famed Geneva doctor that the Président du Conseil had mentioned could help Gabriel with his "headaches." He had asked Gabriel if something was troubling him the day before when they discussed lodgings and the lottery, probably the result of Gabriel startling so easily and pressing his fingers against his temples.

He couldn't help it. It was distracting . . . and frightening. The colors came with a frequency that made him feel as if he was speeding toward an inevitable event—a fatal event.

Even now, as the coach bumped over the road, he saw splashes of yellow coming from the wheels as if they were plowing through water puddles, creating streams of water and droplets on either side. He closed his eyes and took a long breath.

Perhaps this would work.

Perhaps this was God's plan.

The president had expounded upon Dr. Von Travers's talent as one would a prophet of old. It was worth the chance, the time taken away. Gabriel had instructed Sophie and Alexandria to go ahead with the lottery and the balloon ride without him. He couldn't let this opportunity pass by and never know if this man could help him.

The thought of something happening, something going wrong with the winner's ride wouldn't quite go away, but he pushed it aside. Sophie had been piloting her balloon for years. She didn't need him. But still . . . Alexandria. He hated to leave her alone, even for a little while. Dangers lurked everywhere, even this far from France.

The coach turned down a side street and stopped in front of a quaint-looking cottage nestled among other similarly shaped cottages. The door to the carriage was flung open and he stepped out, adjusted his coat, and placed his felt hat on his head. As the door shut behind him he saw green, bright and almost alive, burst from both sides of his peripheral vision. With a deep breath, he took the steps to the door.

His knock on the door made orange sparks fly from his knuckles. It wasn't appearing just with music anymore, something that hadn't been so bad, especially when he couldn't hear the music. Now it was, at times, almost any sound making the colors. And it was too much. He needed help.

The door opened to reveal a little white-haired man with tiny spectacles perched on a large nose. He wore a wide, white apron bulging with metal devices and cords that spilled over to dangle to his knees. He squinted up at Gabriel, his eyes seeming to take a long time to focus.

"Yes? What is it you want?"

"I've come to see Dr. Von Travers. Is he in residence?"

"In residence? Well, he lives here, if that's what you mean. What's your business?"

Gabriel glanced around and noted a few passersby. He wasn't about to explain his affliction on the front stoop. "Ah, it's somewhat of a . . . delicate matter. Might I see the doctor?"

"You're not blind, are you?"

"No."

"Well, then you're seeing him!" The man turned abruptly away and wandered into the dark interior.

Gabriel broke off a laugh and made his way into the room after him, closing the door behind them. They came to a sitting room, well, that was his best guess. The room was cluttered with various paraphernalia. Books, loose papers with writing scattered across in the most illegible manner, instruments—some looking more medical and others from differing branches of science. And stacks and stacks of papers.

"I've not cleaned out the examining room yet." The man patted his apron, which gave a clinking sound, and looked around the room as if seeing it for the first time. "My housekeeper left me, you see." He shrugged. "Third one this year." He waved his hand toward the sofa. "Just clear a corner, would you? Squeeze in and don't interrupt too much, you see?"

"Yes." Gabriel cleared his throat. "I think I do." He perched on the arm of the loaded-down furniture.

"What seems to be the problem with you?"

Gabriel was at a sudden loss for words. Where to begin?

The man squinted at him. "Start with what ails you and we'll work backward."

Gabriel nodded. Seemed a good enough plan. "I see sound in colors."

The man's eyes lit up like a storm-laden night. "Go on."

"Well. Nearly a year ago I had a terrible, exploding feeling in my brain, or in my ears, I'm not certain which, but I woke up the next morning stone-cold deaf."

"Interesting. Interesting indeed. What else?"

"In the months that followed my hearing came and went. I was traveling a great deal and it seemed to change depending on where I was. I went north to Northumberland and my hearing improved. Then on the way to Ireland aboard a ferry, I lost it again. I get horribly seasick, you see, and my ability to hear would either become better or worse when aboard a ship."

"Why were you traipsing about the countryside with an ailment like that anyway?"

Gabriel flushed. "That's another story altogether. Shall I continue the one I'm telling?"

"Ah. A woman. Yes, yes, go on."

"In Ireland I started seeing colors. Well, no. Actually, I saw them for the first time when I was sword fighting with my instructor in London. Then when I went to the opera. And at a pub in Ireland, I saw the music as colors. At first it was mostly with music but now"—he looked at the doctor with genuine despair—"it's everywhere. My hearing returned recently, on a ship from Dover to Calais, and I thought, I hoped, it would remain. And then—" He paused. Would this man believe him? How could anyone believe such an outlandish story. "This is going to sound a bit foolish."

"As if it doesn't already!" The doctor dug into his apron and pulled out a wrinkled handkerchief, which he loudly blew his large nose into. "Yes, yes, go on."

"Well, I came here from Paris by hydrogen balloon."

"The balloon? I saw it. That must be some kind of travel-ing device. What's it like?"

"It's actually very peaceful. The view is unimaginable. The sunrise and sunsets . . . well." He shook his head. "Something happened when we were high up in the air. My ears felt clogged as if they wanted to pop. Alexandria, that's my wife, said her ears popped and Sophie, that's the aeronaut who is flying the balloon, said that's normal. But mine wouldn't pop and clogged instead so I couldn't hear again. Once we landed in Geneva, my hearing returned, to some degree, but the colors. They are everywhere." He stared down at his clasped hands and added his greatest fear aloud in a low voice. "I fear my mind is going to . . . snap."

"Let's take a look, shall we?" The doctor dug through his apron and then brandished a long, tubular metal piece with an odd mirror on the end. With a touch so gentle Gabriel could barely feel it, the doctor inserted it into his ear, turned a small lever, and leaned toward the mirror with one eye. With another hand he held up a light and shined it into the mirror.

Gabriel sat very still, heart pounding a steady rhythm he could feel against the instrument. Another tiny crank, sounding like the click of gears, and then the instrument went deeper, the doctor so close Gabriel could almost feel the whis-kers of his beard against his cheek.

With another fluid movement, Dr. Von Travers backed away. "Hmmm. Interesting. Very interesting," was all he kept saying.

He repeated the process on the other ear. Gabriel tried to relax, remain still and patient. This doctor was slow, methodi-cal. He pulled out a notebook and jotted down little scribbles as he went.

After coming in front of him, he leaned his face close to Gabriel's and hummed a note. "Can you hear that?"

Gabriel nodded.

"Any colors?"

"Blue. A deep, cerulean blue."

He jotted that down. "Close your eyes."

Gabriel complied.

He hummed another note, a half step higher.

"A shade lighter blue." Gabriel kept his eyes closed but knew he was writing that down.

The doctor hummed a lower note, so low that Gabriel could barely make it out. "The sound is muddied but I see a deep orange." Gabriel took another breath, anxiety and an uncomfortable feeling making him want to get up. He didn't.

The doctor hummed a lighter, higher note.

"That one is clear. Like yellow sunlight. White-yellow. Pure. Bright but I can look right at it."

"Amazing." The doctor reared back. "Open your eyes."

Gabriel tried to keep the mix of hope, desperation, and skepticism from his eyes. "What is it? Do you know why this is happening?"

The doctor gazed deep into his eyes, not blinking or flinching. "I haven't seen this before, not exactly, but something close. I believe you have a rare altitude and atmospheric pressure sickness."

Gabriel raised his brows.

"Your body . . . your ears." He tapped Gabriel's ear. "It does not cope with the changes in the air, in the" he held his arms wide—"great expanse."

"What do you mean, the great expanse?"

"The expanse of the heavens, the air and atmosphere between the earth and heaven, or so I like to think of it. The place that involves weather changes, height and depth changes, gravity's pull." He held out a hand as if trying to explain it. "Uhm. Let's see." He looked up as if struggling for the words and then back down at Gabriel. "Your constitution . . . it doesn't change with the atmospheric changes very well. The colors?" He shrugged. "I am sorry. I do not know why you see colors, but perhaps it is connected. Perhaps not."

"Is there a cure?"

"Hmm." He shrugged again. "Stay in one place? Lead a quiet life." He suggested with a smile. "In a calm place where the weather doesn't change very much, at sea level. I am sorry. It is my best advice."

Gabriel closed his eyes, fighting the tightness in his throat. A quiet life? One place? *God? How is that possible? What were You thinking matching me up with the epitome of an adventuress? I'm to stay quiet, calm, and peaceful, in one spot?* He felt like kicking something.

"I do have a tea you can try. It might help . . . a little." The doctor scurried away to fetch it. Gabriel was tempted to get up and leave but he didn't. If it helped some he would try it, and in the meantime, pray he didn't snap. Pray he could cope with the colors until they found Alexandria's parents. Until they found this perfect landing spot.

He had a sudden yearning for Bradley House in Wiltshire countryside, his childhood home and county seat, and laughed at the irony. A more rainy, weather-changing place probably didn't exist. He was doomed to cope or hide.

And the sad truth was—a part of him, the part that felt like his hide had been worn thin by the potter's wheel, longed to hide.

Chapter Twenty-Three

"Jan?" Katherine opened the door to their little rented house in Carrara and stopped, waiting for an answer. When nothing came forward, she took a long breath and closed the door behind her. Walking forward she let her bag sink to the wooden floor with a soft thud, walked to the fire, and reached for the decanter of wine on the side table. She kicked off her shoes as she went, skimming the cupboards for a glass, shrugged off her cloak, letting it puddle in a dark pile on the floor, and then sank into a chair at the table.

With another long breath, she leaned back her head and pulled the pins from her hair that had been adding to her headache during the journey from Malaspina Castle. Long and dark with no strands of gray, smelling of her daughter's rose hair tonic, it fell in waves around her and over the back of the chair.

She poured the wine, set her feet upon another chair with a stretch of her arches and then an upward curl of her stocking-clad toes, and raised the aromatic drink to her nose. For a moment she just inhaled the scent, eyes closed, so tired and aching from the journey that she could hardly think.

"Did you enjoy it?"

His voice came low and deep from the other side of a tall wingback chair. Katherine opened her eyes and sat up, turning toward his dark shadow. "Nothing happened."

"You lie to save my feelings." His voice was clogged with emotion.

Katherine set her glass down hard and turned further toward him in her chair. "I do not lie. Well. Not to you."

Ian got up, came around the chair, and stared at her, his head turned half away as if he couldn't quite look at her yet. "What happened, then?"

"I got lucky, I guess." She laughed, cold and dark, not thinking to tell him of her prayer. Not yet ready to credit God with her timely salvation. "He was about to. He had his hands on me. And then someone knocked on the door. He got a letter from the pope. Right before. He was called away . . . immediately."

She picked up her glass and took a sip, staring down into the dark liquid. "It is but a small reprieve. He wants us to continue searching. I told him we hadn't found the manuscript but still had hopes it would be in the marble caves. I told him we thought we found Augusto's cave. He has given us a little more time."

Ian rubbed his forehead and breathed hard. "An answer to prayer."

"Perhaps."

"Katherine, I've been doing nothing beyond praying, fasting . . . and combing through every rock and crevice of Augusto's cave."

"Have you found anything new?"

He shook his head. "Anything of paper has turned to dust or becomes dust in your hands if you try to pick it up. Some of his paintings survived, but I doubt Franco will care about those."

"No, certainly not."

"I did have an idea. It's . . . risky at best."

"What is it?" Katherine lifted her head, a spark of hope in her heart.

"We could make our own copy. Possibly find someone to help make drawings and calculations, something that looks like that partial manuscript we were shown."

"He would know it for false as soon as he decided to build it." She turned away, gazing into the fire, dead inside.

"Yes, but it would buy us time. If we could wait until Alexandria arrives, watching him in secret, then give him the manuscript, before he has time to do the harm he is planning you or her. We might escape with her."

"He would come after us, but I'm getting desperate enough to try anything." Katherine stood and walked over to her husband. She wrapped her arms around his waist and leaned her head into his solid chest. "I'm tired and I don't know what to do."

"That's a first." Ian leaned his cheek into her hair.

"Yes."

"God will make a way . . . we must follow His leading one step at a time."

Katherine didn't say how terrified that made her feel. She didn't tell him that she had never really trusted God or him, never trusted anyone. Ian probably knew it, but they never spoke of it. The walls around her heart were high and thick. After the defilement by a friend of her father's and the pregnancy, the birth and death of her son—how could she trust?

She clenched her eyes against the pain. No one would ever hurt her again like that. No one could hurt her anyway because she didn't expect anything of anyone; she didn't let them love her. She hoped she had taught Alexandria that lesson as well.

WHEN GABRIEL STEPPED FROM THE carriage, Alexandria waved wildly from the basket of the balloon, calling him over. His return was perfectly timed as they had just landed from giving Mr. Gerhard Lindberg and his wife, Filippa, who he insisted must come along with them on their winning voyage up into the air. The balloon had remained tethered to the ground by a long rope, flying upwards of two thousand feet so the Lindbergs could marvel at being so high in the air without them actually traveling away from the town.

They had babbled excitedly, Mrs. Lindberg clinging to Mr. Lindberg's arm and shrieking with fear and delight as the lake turned into a pond, the town shrank into dotted brown houses, and the trees into mounds of brush. A sunrise had lingered beyond the mountains, casting a rosy glow against their pale rock faces and causing them all to stare in wonder at the beautiful sight.

Gabriel made his way to her through the lingering crowd. "How did it go? Are we ready to depart?" He swung up and over the basket, landing beside Alexandria.

"They thought it was magical. The sunrise was perfect."

"And I was able to find an easterly wind, Your Grace. If it hasn't changed and continues as we rise above those mountains, we will indeed be in luck."

"We could use a bit of that. Let's be off, then." Gabriel directed to the waiting men to loosen the tethers.

They waved and waved to the cheering crowd, the balloon filling and billowing with its new store of hydrogen. Sophie had such help and support in her efforts to make the new supply, that it hadn't taken them long at all. It seemed the fair winds and generosity of these people was indeed blessing them with a good beginning to this last part of the journey.

"How did your visit with the doctor go?" Alexandria asked as soon as they were high enough to turn away from the crowd.

Gabriel quirked one brow and gave her a self-deprecating smile. "He gave me tea."

Alex wrinkled her nose. "Another tea?"

"Yes." He shrugged. "I'll try it, I suppose. We will be going higher than ever to cross the Alps, some seven thousand feet. I confess I am concerned." He pressed his lips into a line.

"We don't have to use the balloon. We could go back to Geneva and hire a carriage." The thought of her quest for her parents being responsible for him losing his hearing again, possibly for good, was beyond imagining.

Gabriel shook his head. "It would take weeks to get to Florence by carriage. It will only take two days to cross the mountains in the balloon." He kissed her forehead, his hand lingering at her back. "God provided us this way. I know He is leading us. And I feel an increasing pressure to hurry. I don't want to frighten you, but we need to get to your parents, beloved."

Alexandria swallowed hard and nodded. He was right. She felt it too. "Just talk to me, okay? Tell me what's happening with your hearing. Let me share this burden with you."

His green eyes took on that particular gleam that made a strange warmth fill her, that admiring, loving, heated glance. "Actually, I do have something I haven't told you. It was part of the reason I went to see the doctor."

Alarm shot through her. "What is it?"

He looked down. "I don't know that you'll believe me. I hardly believe it myself."

Alex glanced at Sophie, who was working the valves of the balloon and probably couldn't hear them if they kept their voices low. But what if she could hear? It sounded like something Gabriel didn't like to talk about. But she had to know, now that he had alarmed her. She leaned in toward his ear and lowered her voice. "Of course I will believe you. Tell me, please."

Gabriel turned toward a flock of birds flying by at nearly eye level and pointed. "Do you see those birds?"

"Yes, of course."

"Can you hear them?"

She paused, listening for any sound they made. There was an occasional squawk and the slightest sound of rustling, flapping wings. "I can hear them flying."

Gabriel took her hand, still looking at them, and squeezed it. "I can *see* the sound you are hearing."

She wrinkled her brow at him.

"That flapping sound looks like streaks of blue following them. And when they call to each other, it is a sharp, bright yellow burst that quickly disappears. It's hard to describe, but since losing my hearing, I have been increasingly able to see sound through colors. Especially music. It started with seeing music."

"This has been going on that long? Why didn't you tell me? Is it dangerous? Does it hurt? What does it mean?" She was confused and upset. Fearful and angry all at the same time, making her pull back and look into his face.

"This is why I didn't tell you. I didn't want you to worry."

"But I'm your wife. What else haven't you told me?"

"Nothing. Don't be so alarmed." He gave her that half-cocked smile and shrugged. "Aside from nearly driving me mad, it isn't so bad."

"Tell me everything."

"Shortly after losing my hearing, it started when I was sword fighting with Roberé Alfieri, the master swordsman who

I train with. It terrified me then. I thought I was going mad or my mind had snapped. But then, it happened again when I heard music . . . the opera. After the initial shock wore off I actually enjoyed seeing the music, especially during those times when I couldn't hear the music.

"You may not know how much music has always meant to me. For some time it meant more to me than God even. I couldn't play it, though I studied and practiced for decades, but I loved music in a way that some men take snuff or love their brandy. I *needed* it. When I lost my hearing, I despaired of a life without it. Then at the opera, I saw the colors and it was like God had given music back to me, but in a different way. I—"

"You learned to experience it in another way. I saw it. On that day in the piano room, our first kiss. You played so beautifully then. It was almost as if you were one with the music."

"Yes." Gabriel's voice grew intense. "That's exactly it. It is so difficult to explain but you understand, you know me."

"But now you see colors all the time? That seems . . . frightening." She squeezed his hand again.

"It is disconcerting." He looked down at their hands, his thumb rubbing the outside of her thumb. "Since being in the balloon it is happening more frequently. When we landed in Geneva, it was almost every sound. I thought I would go mad, but then the hearing came back too. There is a connection but I don't know what it is. And I'm not sure I want to lose the colors, not completely. Just not this constant stream of them. That's why I went to see the doctor."

"What did he say? About the colors. You told him about them, didn't you?"

"I told him everything. He thinks it is an atmospheric-pressure problem. When there is a change in altitude, the weather, my body no longer adjusts to the constant, varying degrees of change. He said something about the expanse, the place of space between heaven and earth and how most people are able to cope with changes in this space. They might have clogged ears or stuffy noses or some symptom, but they eventually adjust. My body no longer makes those adjustments and somehow, though I think the doctor has only scratched the surface with his diagnosis, somehow my hearing fluctuates and these colors, the frequency, that changes as well."

"So the balloon is not good for you!"

"Neither are ships or traveling at all! I'm to find a spot on the earth where there is little elevation and little change in weather and stay put. That was his advice."

"Then we have to find that place. We have wealth. We can find something like that, can't we? Gabriel, I can live anywhere as long as we're together." Alex didn't care that Sophie was openly listening now. They had to find a way to make Gabriel normal again, comfortable.

"A cushioned cell? Is that my fate, then?" His eyes filled with pain.

A long moment fell between them while they judged the future in each other's eyes. "You have already traveled the world, haven't you? What do you have left to see?"

"*You* travel the world."

"Oh," she said on a breath. He would give up his comfort for her. He thought she wanted to be an adventuress, a treasure hunter like her parents. And why wouldn't he? That's all she had talked about since she met him. She hadn't told him how much she had grown used to the idea of staying in one place and being his wife. She hadn't said it.

Tears threatened her eyes. "I don't need to see the world. Not anymore." Alex reached up and cupped his cheek with her hand. "After we find, no *rescue*"—her grin wavered—"my parents. I want to settle down and have a family."

Gabriel's brows rose. "Stay in one spot? You can't mean it."

"I do. And lots of children. Or at least three."

"Tied down with children clinging to your skirts? Who has come and replaced my wife with this creature?" He chuckled. "Don't say it for my sake. I knew the trouble you would be." He gave a fake shudder. "A bored duchess."

She playfully slapped him on the shoulder. "I speak the truth."

"We'll retire to the crumbling Lindisfarne Castle on Holy Island where you grew up. My hearing returned there and I wasn't seeing many colors. We'll buy it from your parents and have a passel of children and raise sheep." He chuckled. "Of course, I'll have to renovate the place to make it habitable."

Alex shook her head. "I can't imagine that Holy Island is a place with little change in the atmosphere and yet . . . it *is* always dreary there and with hardly any elevation. But I must warn you. The people, they are quite dreary too. You'd not miss the London social whirl?"

"Not at all. Would you?"

She frowned. "I do love your sister Jane. And I think a wedding between her and Meade is not far off."

"I'm not an invalid. We could visit upon occasion. You haven't even seen Bradley House yet. We could stay there when the weather is good."

"It sounds rather perfect." She reached up and kissed his lips. "I know you want to give me what I want and what I want is to give you what you need."

"What do you need?"

"You've already given me everything I need except for one thing—finding my parents. And you've promised me that." She looked up at him with wide, anxious eyes. "A duke's promise."

He squeezed her tight against his side. "A duke always keeps his promises." He said it with conviction, his face settling in lines of determination. "The air is getting colder." He leaned over and pressed his warm lips against her temple. "Better get into your warmest wraps. The air is thinning too. It may soon become hard to breathe."

Sophie said her first words then. She checked her apparatus and turned another valve. "We are about to go higher than I've ever flown, Your Graces. Hurry to bundle up. It's time to throw out more sandbags."

Alex considered the coming mountainside dotted with dark trees below and draped in snow along its jagged rocky peaks. The future and where they would live could be discussed later. It was time to fly over the Alps and the Grand Saint Bernard Pass. Napoleon had crossed over this pass with his vast army a few years ago. But they would not need the pass. God willing, they would fly on the wind over one of the greatest mountain chains in the world in an air balloon.

They would make history to get to her parents.

Chapter Twenty-Four

*I*t's s-s-so c-c-c-cold." Alexandria blew on her mittens, trying to warm her fingers through the thick yarn with little effect.

Gabriel pulled her back into his chest and wrapped his arms around her, hugging her to him. She looked up at him with a small smile hoping it disguised her worry. They had thrown several sandbags from the basket and were now sailing over the peaks of the Alps, and she could feel the difference. Her breath wasn't as deep and her nose and face were tingling with cold.

If she was feeling the effects, she could only imagine that Gabriel was feeling it even more, not that he complained. Every time she inquired how he felt, he grew brusque and brushed her off. She quickly understood that he didn't want to be coddled, and she didn't want him to regret telling her about the colors and what the doctor had said, so she clamped her chapped lips together and just shivered in his arms.

Sophie, too, wasn't looking good. Alex wished she had someone to hold her and help keep her warm. And why not? He motioned her over. They could all huddle together.

"Sophie, we seem to be going in the right direction. Come over and get warm."

Sophie held her compass out and studied their direction. "I must keep a constant eye on the instruments, Your Grace. Any change in direction might require an ascent or descent. We don't want to land on the Alps and become stranded there. It would mean our deaths." She said it in a matter-of-fact way, but the words still made Alex's heartbeat speed up.

"Oh, yes, of course, you're right." Alex shivered anew. "But Sophie, you look so pale. How are you feeling?"

"Once, when I was at about six thousand feet, I fainted because of the cold and the thin air, but that was during the winter. The cold is not as bad this time of year."

"You fainted and just floated in an unmanned balloon. Goodness, what happened?"

"When I regained consciousness I had no idea where I was, but I was still in the air and had drifted down toward the ground. Thankfully I landed close to Naples and reached help." She nibbled on a finger with a small smile. "My ears were frostbitten and still ache when they get too cold. That's why I wear this fur hat pulled low over my ears."

"Well, it looks quite good on you, anyway." What a plucky thing Sophie Blanchard was. Alex looked out at the surroundings, seeing mountain ranges stretched out all around them as far as she could see. They were so pretty with their snow-capped points of rock jutting through the snow, rising and falling in graceful slopes of stone. A deep shiver ran through her body as if a wind had buffeted against her, but she could not feel the wind, traveling with it as they were. Only crystal cold air that snapped her breath away.

"Alexandria, let's get you under the awning and under some warm blankets."

"But I don't want to m-m-miss the sights. It's too wonderful."

"Just for a little while to warm you up." When her mouth hardened in a mulish line, Gabriel frowned. "I insist."

"Oh, very well. But only if you tell me how you are really feeling. Perhaps we should take turns warming up."

"I'm fine, really. The colors were worse when we were closer to the ground, but now they have quieted some. I am a bit out of breath as you and Sophie are, but it's manageable. Sophie, go under the awning with Alexandria for a little while. I'll keep a close eye on our direction."

Sophie hesitated and then handed him the compass. "Call me if there is any change."

"Of course."

Alex grasped Sophie's arm and dragged her under the awning where the air was immediately warmer. "Here." She handed Sophie a thick fur robe. "Get close to me and we'll put this on top first, then those other blankets over the fur." Soon they were ensconced in warmth.

"Sophie, what was your husband like?"

A soft smile formed across her lips and reached her eyes. "His motto was *sic tier ad Astra*—'reach for the stars.' He was a good man, a kind man. He loved his country and wanted to make France proud. When he flew in the balloon, all his cares washed away and he was free."

"How long were you married?"

"Only four years. He taught me though. He didn't think a woman shouldn't be able to fly. He wanted to share it with me."

Alex squeezed her arm. "I'm sorry he is gone."

Sophie took a long breath. "As am I."

They snuggled under the wraps and soon dozed off to sleep.

A sudden shout from Gabriel made them both scramble out of the blankets. The cold was like a fierce slap in the face. "What is it?" Alex turned around and saw a thick fog rolling away. Beyond it was the rock face of a mountain coming right at them.

"I didn't see it with all the fog and then the wind dipped suddenly! We lost our height in seconds," Gabriel shouted over at them.

Sophie sprang into action, grasping the string attached to the valve and tying it fast. "Throw the remaining ballasts overboard. We have to rise quickly!"

Alex and Gabriel rushed to the sandbags, Gabriel lifting them unaided while Alex struggled to get even one up and over the side. Soon Sophie was at her side taking one end while Alex hefted the other. The balloon rose but the wind was strong, pushing them toward the cliff face. Alex looked down and swallowed. What would happen if they ran right into it?

Another three bags and the balloon practically leapt in the air. Gabriel threw the last one overboard. "It's not enough! Throw out anything we don't absolutely have to have!"

Alex glanced around the interior of the basket in a panic. Her gaze lit on her trunk. It was the heaviest thing on board after the sandbags, but her clothes! How was she going to replace them?"

Gabriel looked at her and nodded. "Both trunks. Take out the money and traveling documents first. Hurry. Keep the food, water, and blankets. Anything else must go."

Sophie grasped one side of the heavy trunk while Alex grabbed the other. After removing the most important articles, they rushed it over to the side, lifted it, and pushed it over. Alex peered down as it spiraled through the air, bouncing off the mountainside, opening, all her beautiful gowns spilling out like colorful silken handkerchiefs. They seemed so small. She turned and saw that the wind had changed their course. "Gabriel!"

They were headed straight for a mountain peak. Its sharp point looked deadly.

Out of the corner of her eye, she saw that Gabriel was ripping the striped awning off the side and tossing it over. Another trunk, Sophie's, went next and then they dumped two heavy ropes and the baskets that held the food.

Sophie gripped one of the lines and tugged on it as hard as she could. She let out a squeak as the bottom of the basket grazed over the top of the mountain. Alex could feel it under her feet, feel its sharp solidness. *Dear God, let the basket hold together or they would all spill out and down the mountainside toward their deaths.*

Her heart pounded like a trapped rabbit. She clung to the line next to Sophie's.

"Jump!" Gabriel commanded.

Just as the basket hit the point, bounced, and looked ready to hit again they all jumped up. They cleared the razor edge just in time, the basket coming down on the other side, shaking and hovering but meeting only air.

"We did it!" Alex's face broke into a huge smile.

Sophie sank down, shaking from head to toe, but smiling now too.

Gabriel boomed with laughter. "Bravo, my girls!" He came over and pulled Alex into his arms. "That was close. I thought I would lose you." He buried his face in her hair and held tight to her.

"I was afraid I would lose me too!" Alex laughed, still shaking but jubilant.

"Sophie, I think we've had enough ballooning. Let's land at the first town we see. I believe we will take a carriage from there on." Gabriel held Alex tight and kissed the top of her head over and over as the mountains faded behind them.

SHE WAS TOO COLD, HER lips blue and her dark eyelashes feathery shadows against her pale skin. She moaned and turned in his arms, the sound causing a shrieking ringing in his ears and dark splashes of color flickering like death around the inside of the carriage. The road from Alessandria, Italy, was rough, their hired carriage jerking from side to side making it difficult to keep Alexandria from sliding off the leather seat.

Gabriel wrapped the blanket tighter around her and leaned down to press his lips against her forehead. A fever. *Feverish* was the better word. Her whole body shivered in a sweat-soaked bundle, her hair spilling over his legs in dark waves, wet near her scalp. A new kind of fear gripped him, making the muscles of his stomach turn over. She hadn't been right when they landed in Alessandria—its air hot and humid after the frigid temperatures of the Alps. He thought the heat would do her good but she worsened.

He'd led her to an inn, made her drink plenty of water all the while trying to ignore the bursts of color from the noisy room, but she kept saying she just couldn't get warm so he couldn't leave and find relief in a quiet place. He gritted his teeth against the colors, his hearing coming in and out, and barked out orders.

Provisions, the finest carriage with a dependable driver, clothing if it could be had, and whatever aid Sophie might need.

"Sophie, I want you to have this," he'd said to her at the dinner table the night before. He passed a heavy purse full of coins over to her.

Her eyes widened at the weight of it and she started to protest.

"You risked your life for us. I know you miss him, but this is a dangerous business you are in, Madame Blanchard. I want you to have the opportunity to retire if you would like to."

She bit down on her bottom lip and shook her head. "I don't know."

"Well, now you have time to think about it. Now, you can continue to Florence with us or return to France. I have arranged for the local blacksmith to help you with anything you need. He has already been well paid, so whether you decide to attempt the journey back by that balloon of yours or by wagon and haul it back, that is your choice."

"You are too kind, Your Grace." She looked at Alexandria, who had a sheen of sweat on her face and the pallor of death about her. "I am loathe to leave her. Do you think she will be all right?"

"I am fine." Alexandria waved a hand in the air. "I just need to rest a bit and warm up and this town is perfect for that, isn't it? Why it must be eighty degrees here."

Sophie agreed to go back to France by way of wagon, stating that she didn't want to attempt another Alps crossing, especially by herself. The women had a tearful good-bye the next morning, but when Gabriel suggested Alexandria go back to bed after seeing Sophie off, she had gotten that mulish line to her lips and shook her head.

"I can sleep in the carriage just as well. You know we have no time to lose."

It was true and so he had let her talk him into leaving that day. Now, two days later, he was worried he might have made a mistake.

He leaned his head in his hand and stared out the window at the stunning scene. They had been following the coast, the glittering Ligurian Sea stretching beside them with a blue so clear and deep it made a calmness come over him just looking at it. On their other side the colorful houses seemed to spring from the rocky cliffs in jagged rows beside winding, narrow streets. It was one of the most beautiful places on earth and his wife was missing it. He took a deep breath and prayed, then tried to give her more water.

The next day they rattled into a tiny village with one inn. Gabriel carried Alexandria inside, much to her protest, but she was too weak to really fight him. After settling her into the innkeeper's own bedchamber at his insistence, Gabriel nearly collapsed himself. "Is there a doctor in this place?" he managed, sitting on the edge of the bed and swaying, dizzy, trying to remain upright.

"No, *signore*. The closest physician is in Massa."

Gabriel nodded. "That is where we will go then. Bring lots of water, please. Might you have some broth?"

"I make you some tea. Very good tea."

The comment reminded him for the first time of the tea the doctor in Geneva had given him. Alexandria seemed to be suffering from the effects of this altitude sickness too. Might it help her? "Just bring hot water and broth, please. I have my own tea." Gabriel reached in his pocket and took out the delicate packets.

After the man left, Gabriel lifted it to his nose, smelling the pungent odor. It was worth a try.

His own head spun when he turned to look at Alexandria. She had crawled up to the pillow and lay there fully dressed on top of the coverlet. "Come now." He ignored the ringing in his ears as his voice echoed inside his head. "Let's get your shoes off at least."

She said nothing as he bent to the task. How had they come to this? Their only belongings were the clothes on their backs and the money he had left. He might draw funds from the bank at Rome, but he had no intention of traveling that distance. Best to send someone with his seal and see what that could offer them. They would have to have some clothes made up in Massa. There had been little to offer them in Alessandria.

The man returned with a pot of hot water and two bowls of broth. Gabriel gritted his teeth and hauled Alexandria into a sitting position, demanding she wake up and drink some broth. She was weak but able to spoon it into her mouth while he made the tea.

"Gabriel, I think I am going to die." The spoon clattered against the side of the bowl as it dropped to the tray.

"You are not going to die. We just need to get you adjusted to land again."

"Is this how you feel? If it is, I think I would want to die. I don't know how you bear up under it."

He didn't tell her he had felt far, far worse. She was having trouble regaining a proper temperature, had caught a fever because of it . . . at least that was his best guess. Thank God she didn't have the dizziness, the nausea, the vertigo, the ringing and piercing in her ears. Thank God she didn't really know.

He came over, colors making the room swirl with light, too much, too often. He sat beside her and gathered her in his arms. Then he held out her cup of tea. "Let's try this tea the doctor gave me, shall we? It might be just the thing."

Alexandria took it in trembling hands and drank it down quickly. She leaned against his shoulder and closed her eyes. He took her cup, set it on the side table, and sipped his own tea, tasting strange but not entirely unpleasant.

They couldn't give up. They were so close!

God, where are You? We need You now.

He lay down next to Alexandria and pulled her close. A few moments later he was fast asleep.

Chapter Twenty-Five

*G*abriel." Alex sat up and shook his shoulder, pushing the hair back from her shoulder and leaning over him. "Gabriel, wake up."

He rolled over onto his back, threw one arm up over his head, and let out a soft groan. Her gaze traveled over the dark stubble on his chin, his handsome face so rugged yet boyish in sleep. She leaned over and kissed his lips. "Gabriel, I'm feeling remarkably better. We must take to the road, my dearest."

His lips broke into a small smile, eyes still closed, lashes thick and inky black. She leaned closer to his ear and placed a kiss just beneath it. "Can you hear me? The tea. I think it has restored me to health."

In a sudden, swift move, he grasped hold of her and turned them so he was above her, his arms braced on either side of her, muscles standing out, head dipped toward her throat. "That is good news indeed." He looked up and squinted for a moment, turning his head to one side and then the other. "I do believe that tea has done me good as well. Shall we have another cup before departing?"

"It couldn't hurt, could it? What did the doctor say it was?"

"Something about a cocoa plant. From South America." He bent his arms and hovered over her, kissing her with a more serious intent. "Whatever it is, I'm feeling remarkably rested."

Alex closed her eyes and thankfully agreed.

A little while later they had partaken of a breakfast of day-old bread and strawberry jam, figs, and another cup of their tea down in the common room of the inn. Alex felt a rush of energy she hadn't felt since leaving Paris. "Gabriel, if we hurry, the innkeeper said we can be in Massa by evening. It's a much bigger city and we'll have a better chance to find everything we need there. He also told me it is close to Carrara and the marble caves. I know my parents were last seen in Florence, but they may have gone to Carrara as well. We can ask questions in Massa and Carrara before going on to Florence."

Gabriel nodded. "Excellent thinking."

"If we take horses instead of that old coach, we could get there even sooner."

"Are you sure you're feeling well enough to ride? I know it's not your favorite mode of traveling."

"I'm feeling wonderful. And I am riding better too. It just takes some practice. And after throwing our belongings overboard, we don't have any heavy trunks to carry with us."

"Very well. Let's see to the horses."

Within the hour they were on the road to Massa.

THE ROAD SOUTH TURNED INLAND, easterly, with a light breeze at their backs. The air was cooler, sunny, and perfect, a beautiful day to be out on horseback, riding under the shadows of the Apuan Alps with the sea and long, sandy beaches still visible to the west.

Alex took long breaths of the Mediterranean air and felt a sense of well-being she'd never known. There was a peacefulness here that made her muscles ease and her heartbeat slow. Just looking at the surroundings made her happy, euphoric even. Her gaze soaked in the changing gently rolling hills of vineyards, farms with rows of olive trees that stretched out in serene beauty on either side of the road, and then later, the beginnings of a city—a colorful stone city under the soft rays of the Tuscan sun. She found she could hardly summon anxiety on behalf of her parents.

They were on the right path. They were doing the right thing.

God was with them here.

Alex felt it as strong as her heartbeat, and when she looked over at Gabriel, into his green eyes that had softened with the miles slipping behind them, she knew he felt it too.

Closer to the city they passed old Roman parishes where Gabriel told her thousands had stopped to worship on their pilgrimage to places like Santiago de Compostela in Spain; Reims, France; and Canterbury in England. Alex held her breath in wonder as they rode beside remnants of medieval castles, courtyards of sandstone, and marble sculptures by renowned Renaissance sculptors.

Farther into the town there were shops with clay roofs selling all manner of art from pottery to paintings. The feel of Renaissance still hummed through the air, making her wonder if they would, at any moment, come upon Michelangelo or a group of theologians, poets reposed under a stand of cypress trees. It wouldn't have surprised her, so thoroughly did the air itself spark of mystery and inspiration. As their horses' hoofs clattered over the cobbled road, a love for the place welled through Alexandria's heart that made tears prick her eyes.

The main road became crowded with people the closer they neared the square. Gabriel had a guarded look about him now. He sat tall upon his black steed, his gaze sweeping back and forth over the groups of people.

A sudden thought gave her pause—what if the Spaniards that had been following them since Ireland were here? King Ferdinand *had* asked the prince regent to turn them over to him, a fact that the regent had deflected. But the Spanish king had been very angry Gabriel had escaped and destroyed his ship and all those Spanish soldiers in Iceland. And that was beside the fact that Ferdinand was determined to get his hands on the manuscript. Alex felt for the handle of her pistol, her fingers grasping in her pocket for the shot pouch. There. She was as ready as she could be.

They came to the square, or Piazza Aranci, an even more crowded place but striking with its enormous buildings lining the four sides of the square. They rode through double rows of orange trees laden with summer fruit, the smell of it tangy and ripe in the air. A royal coach stood outside an enormous red building with white marble columns and trim—a long, rectangular palace that took up the length of one side of the square.

"That's the Palazzo Ducale." Gabriel motioned to the marble columns surrounding every window. There must have been hundreds of them in even rows three stories high. What did one do with so many rooms?

A commotion sounded behind them. A royal carriage came up surrounded by white and scarlet-clad outriders. The crowd swelled toward the scene, one group of men seeming rough and intent, pushing around Alex's horse to get near it.

"What's happening?" Alex managed to jerk on her horse's reins and keep them from getting trampled.

"Not sure." Gabriel stilled her with his hand. "Stay back."

She tried to obey. She really did, but the horse was growing skittish and hard to control.

The crowd pushed them closer to the scene rather than farther away. A footman opened the door and let out the carriage steps. A man, dressed in a uniform of white and gold, an insignia of the Austrian Order of the Golden Fleece around his neck, stepped from the conveyance with a regal mien, chin up, and eyes narrowed, turning his face back and forth and studying the crowd with a faint snarl about his lips. His gaze caught hers and he paused.

A shiver ran down Alex's spine but she lifted her chin and met his stare. She refused to look away. He smiled at her then, a small, cold smile that chilled her further. It was as if the sun had been covered by a dark cloud, its light now turned chilly and malevolent. She looked away after all, thinking to turn her horse and get out of the crowd.

Impossible. She was blocked in. A hard-looking man, whose gaze was locked on the man from the carriage, slipped around the head of her horse and edged through the crowd toward him. As he turned to push through, Alex saw the flicker of a long knife in the man's hand. Her gaze flew to Gabriel's, who was regarding her with concern. She pointed and mouthed the words he could understand because of his long practice at lip reading. *That man has a knife!*

Gabriel looked to where she pointed, pausing. The man was pushing his way to the regal man who must live in the palace. He had his back to Alex and was saying something to one of his footmen.

Gabriel turned toward Alex, nodded that he saw the knife, and ordered her to stay back. He dismounted and started after the man, right in the middle of the commotion of the crowd.

"Gabriel, no! Come back!" Alex strained forward to see as he disappeared into the crowd. What had she done? She didn't want him to go after the man. Only to be aware that he might be there for them.

It didn't look that way though. She stood in her stirrups to better see what was happening. The man was almost to the Italian. He was lifting the knife. Was he going to stab him? Right here in front of everyone? It would be madness, a death sentence. And where was Gabriel?

His tall black head moved quickly through the crowd. He was almost there.

Remembering her pistol, she took it from her pocket. She poured the powder with shaking hands and pushed down the lead ball with the ramrod, not knowing how she would use it in such a crowd but knowing she could not let Gabriel risk his life. She cocked it and lifted it.

The man was right behind the Italian and lifting his arm high. Gabriel was only steps behind him. Some in the crowd saw Alex's firearm and others must have seen the knife, for the crowd suddenly began to shout and scatter. Alexandria ignored the commotion. She kept her gaze and the point of her pistol trained on the man with the knife.

Time slowed. A breeze blew through the courtyard, parting the clouds. Tuscan sunlight spilled across the people, the glint of the knife rising, rising into the air. The light reflecting on the knife shot into her eyes, momentarily blinding her. *Gabriel, get out of there!*

A distressed sound escaped her throat as Gabriel reached the man, his arm plunging toward the Italian's back. Gabriel reached around, his height and reach so much greater than the man with the knife, and shoved the Italian out of harm's way with a mighty heave. He stumbled, almost fell, and then righted himself, but he was out of the way of any danger.

Spinning around, Gabriel elbowed the man with the knife in the stomach while his other hand grasped the man's forearm holding the knife. The knife fell from his hands. The crowd backed away with shouts and screams.

"*Il dio li conserva,*" a woman next to her yelled. "*Uccidono il duca!*"

Something about "God help" and "the duke" was all Alex could make out of that. So this man was an Italian duke?

Where was Gabriel? Was he all right? Her arm lowered, the pistol pointing at the street without her realizing it. She lifted in the stirrups again for the best view, seeing that the Italian duke's men had taken the man with the knife down to the ground and were beating him. The duke was clasping Gabriel's hand and smiling . . . a smile that made Alex's stomach roll with dread.

Alex swallowed hard, the earlier chill returning with a sickening feeling. This duke was not to be trusted. She could feel it.

She kicked her horse's ribs, the pistol ready in her hand, and commanded her steed toward the scene. The crowd parted, fear in their eyes, looking at her as though she had gone mad, their faces shocked at such actions from a woman. She guided her horse up to Gabriel and the duke.

They both stopped talking and watched her approach. Gabriel's eyes were wary, gazing deeply into hers. She looked away . . . at the Italian duke. His eyes were pleased, as if he had hoped for such a reaction. The sudden knowledge that she was failing this test made her even angrier. She glared at the duke.

I hate him.

A loathing she had never felt before filled her, puffing out her chest as if to make a shield around her heart. Her eyes narrowed on the man. His eyes stared back at her full of death. She didn't know why, couldn't fathom why, but she knew as deeply as she knew every crevice of her childhood home on Holy Island that this man was dangerous. Not the typical kind of danger they had run into thus far . . . no, no. This man was particularly dangerous to the Featherstones, her family. And she wanted nothing more than to raise her pistol and shoot him right between the eyes.

"Alexandria, what are you doing?" Gabriel's terse voice shook her from her trance. She swallowed and jerked her head toward him, realizing she had, indeed, raised her weapon toward the duke's head.

"She was trying to save me. Weren't you, my dear?" He tucked his narrow chin but kept his eyes on her, a curve of his lips indicating a smile. His soft, even voice made her flesh crawl.

She said nothing. She couldn't. Her heart still pounded with loathing, with self-preservation. She saw it so clearly and she didn't know why. This man was no threat to Gabriel, the Duke of St. Easton. He would see Gabriel as an equal and thought of nothing but alliances and bribes when it came to another of such status.

But the Featherstones? She felt like the world had stopped for a moment—this evil showing her, for the first time, their good. They were the guardians of treasure, truth seekers, *God's chosen*. And this man saw it too. In some way he sensed it and wanted to take what they had into his hands. He wanted to twist it and use it and destroy it.

He's been waiting for me.

He knows who I am.

Her breath was coming too fast. She felt the pistol slip from her numb fingers. Heard it clatter to the cobbles in an odd, echoing way. Her head felt too heavy, bobbed upon her shoulders. Was he saying they should stay with him? At Malaspina Castle?

No, no! Gabriel, don't agree. They couldn't stay with him! Her breath rasped, scant and short.

She slipped from her horse into blackness.

Chapter Twenty-Six

A lexandria, wake up." Gabriel's voice was soft and deep but with a hint of fear in it. Where were they? And ugh. What was that smell? Something with a strong scent was thrust under her nose. She turned away from it with a groan.

"She is coming around." This voice was different, dark with a rasping edge. Alex cringed away from it and opened her eyes.

"Gabriel?" She turned her head toward him and winced. Her hand came up and touched the place of pain on one side of her head. There was a lump the size of a goose egg and dried blood in her hair.

"You fell from the horse. I tried to get to you in time but you hit the ground. Our host has sent for a physician." Gabriel explained in a rush. "How do you feel?"

Alex looked from Gabriel to the dark form of the Italian duke standing behind him. "Where am I?"

"You are at my home. Malaspina Castle. I insisted you accept my hospitality after your husband saved my life. You must stay here as my guests for as long as you wish."

Her gaze flew to Gabriel who nodded at her. "Do you remember our journey, my dear? We've been traveling through Italy on our honeymoon trip?"

Alex tried to sit up. "Yes, yes of course." Her head ached but she couldn't abide lying here in such a position of weakness. "I don't know what came over me, a spell of dizziness I think, but I'm fine now."

The duke took a step forward. "Please, don't get up, *signora*. Perhaps you are expecting a child. My wife suffered from dizzy spells while with child. We must let my physician examine you."

Alex gasped. The fact that he might be right struck her like a blow. But she had no intention of being examined by anyone connected with him. "Thank you, Your Grace, but I am perfectly well—"

Gabriel frowned, new worry in his eyes. "The duke is right, my dear. Lie back now and rest a little." He squeezed her hand. "Perhaps something to drink?"

The duke rang for a servant and requested tea. Alex tried to ignore his presence. She turned away to lie back on the pillows and closed her eyes. She did not want to know whose bedchamber they were in and she did not want to look that man in the eyes, but she knew Gabriel had a plan and for now she would just have to play along.

Minutes later a tall, thin man with dark coloring hurried into the room and bowed to the duke. "Your Grace. I came as quickly as I could. How may I be of service?"

"The Duchess of St. Easton has fainted and fallen from her horse. She recently revived but has a nasty bump on her head."

"Oh, such a pity. That such could befall such a beautiful signora."

Gabriel stood to make room, frowning at him. The doctor came over to the side of the bed and perched on the edge next to her.

"This is Doctor Forsythe." The duke stared at Alex, eyes as hard as diamonds, glittering black diamonds. "We will leave you to examine her. St. Easton, if you will come with me, then we can continue our discussion of the Featherstones. As I said, we have heard of an English couple sleuthing about the caves in Carrara . . . but they've seemed to have disappeared."

"You know of my parents?" Alex sat up and pushed the doctor's hands away from her head.

His dark gaze swung back to her and a twist of a smile formed on his blood-red lips. "Just a rumor. If they were here, I fear some misfortune has befallen them. They haven't been heard from in so long."

Alex made a sound of distress, looking at Gabriel.

"Forgive me." The duke gushed now. "I only wanted to prepare you should you discover bad news. Please, allow me to throw a small party on your behalf. Tonight. In your honor. I do owe you my life."

Alex cast a glance at Gabriel. As badly as she wanted to flee this place, a party might help them hear news of her parents. There would be more people to question. Gabriel gave her an infinitesimal nod. He was thinking the same thing.

"I suppose that would be nice," she murmured, plucking at the coverlet while the doctor went back to cleaning her head wound.

"Wonderful. I will have gowns sent to you to choose from, as I understand you were put upon by thieves and have need of a new wardrobe."

After grinding her teeth, she looked at the man and made herself say, "That is so kind. Thank you, Your Grace."

The doctor finished his examination and sat back. "Your eyes look clear, Your Grace. Are you having any difficulty remembering anything?"

Alex shook her head. "Just an aching head. I do so wish to sleep."

"You mustn't sleep." The doctor shook his head, dark eyebrows drawn together in a school master's lecturing mien. "Injuries to the head can have lasting effects not seen right away, and sleeping is the very worst thing right now. You should be watched for the next several hours."

"But I feel fine. I can remember exactly what happened."

"Yes, you were very lucky, but nonetheless, no sleeping until after the party. You may rest quietly though."

"How am I to rest quietly and not fall asleep?" Alex grumbled.

"I will stay with her and keep watch, Doctor. Thank you." Gabriel took a step closer and edged the doctor out of the way, sitting next to Alex and grasping her hand. "I will not let anything happen to her, my dearest wife." He brought her hand up to his lips and kissed her knuckles.

"I will leave you to rest then. Until tonight." The duke gave a bow of his head and turned to go.

When the door shut behind them, Alex let out a long breath. "I don't like him, Gabriel. Do you think he is telling the truth about my parents?"

Gabriel whispered into her ear, "Speak quietly, beloved. I suspect he has eyes and ears everywhere."

Alex cast an anxious glance around the decadent room. Heavy curtains were drawn over the windows and only two small candelabra were lit. The darkness in the room swallowed the low, flickering light. "Where are we and who, exactly, is he? Can we open those curtains?"

"Yes, of course." Gabriel rose to the task while explaining. "We are at Malaspina Castle and he is Franco de Luca, the Duke of Massa and Carrara among other titles."

"Do you think he knows about the manuscript and my parents?"

"He might. As you know, there are only two places we suspect your parents have been looking for the manuscript—in Florence, Augusto's hometown, and in Carrara, just a few miles from here, where the marble caves are. That is where Augusto lived for those years he went into hiding. Since Florence is another two or three days' travel from here and Carrara is so close, I agree that we should spend a little time looking for clues here." He came back over and sat beside her.

"And the social gathering tonight will be a good place to start asking questions."

"Be careful, Alexandria. This man is no one to trifle with."

Alex closed her eyes and shivered. "Believe me, I know."

THE MUSIC OF THE ORCHESTRA made swirling hues in every color of the rainbow. They danced about the ballroom, filling it with pulsing colors. Gabriel clenched his teeth and tried to ignore them. Able to hear the music, they were more of a distraction now than a thing of beauty. He looked at the instruments—flute, pianoforte, harp, and violin—and knew, without a shadow of doubt, that he could pick up any of the instruments and play them perfectly, following the patterns of the colors.

It had been what he had always dreamed of, always wanted but could never have. And now, oddly perhaps, he didn't care. Life had changed so much that he had new dreams, dreams with Alexandria, dreams of health and family and love, finding God's perfect path for his life. Perhaps one day he would play the music he'd wanted to play so badly, but today, tonight, he had a mission to accomplish.

A promise to keep.

With his wife on his arm, looking ravishing in a rose-colored gown with gold trim, her hair piled high in curls, jewels loaned by Franco dangling from her ears and around her throat, Gabriel led her into the crowded ballroom determined to fulfill that promise.

Small party indeed. The vast room was crushed with elegantly clad people. Northern Italy's finest must have rushed to the city. His gaze caught Franco across the room, standing beside a beautiful but stern-looking woman who must be his wife. The Italian duke waved them over, staring with a hint of lust-tinged eyes at Alexandria.

Gabriel didn't like that, the way Franco undressed his wife, the way he watched her and stared at her with hungry-looking eyes. It was all Gabriel could do not to throw down his glove and challenge the man to a duel. Or better yet, place a fist in his face, but he restrained himself and led her over where they both bowed.

"La, Your Grace. Such a party. However did you manage it on such short notice?"

Gabriel smoothed back a grin. Alexandria's acting talents never failed to amuse him.

"It was no trouble at all. And may I say you are seeming much restored from your fall."

She waved her fan and smiled at him, batting her eyes and making Gabriel want to either kiss her or strangle her, he wasn't sure which. "Yes, as I said earlier, I am fine. Thank you." She looked aside as if annoyed, which made the duke chuckle. Gabriel ground his teeth and tried to ignore the dark color coming from the man's laugh.

The duke introduced them to his wife, who mostly ignored them, and then the ladies and gentlemen in the vicinity, but he didn't take long to ask Alexandria to dance. Gabriel nodded at her questioning look, not liking it—hating for her to leave his side—but they had agreed to separate and circulate, all the better to probe for information about the Featherstones.

After a turn about the room and no one having ever heard of the name Featherstone, or at least not admitting to it, he decided to take a stroll through the castle. Alexandria was in a public place, the most sought-after woman there, dancing with every man in the room it seemed and causing a streak of pure jealousy to course through him when he saw her laughing and smiling.

It was just as well that he left her to her act for a time. If anyone could get someone talking, it would be her. And she was smart enough to stay in the crowded ballroom. He could leave for a little while and not be missed. He moved swiftly and silently down the long corridor, peeking into the dark, empty rooms, salons mostly. The castle was enormous, but ah, here was something. The duke's study perhaps?

He walked in and closed the door behind him. There was a small fire in the grate giving off enough light to illuminate the desk, where various papers were neatly stacked. He hurried around and picked up this one and that. Odd. There were so many maps. Maps of Europe and Italy with directional lines written on them. They looked like military maps. Marching campaigns.

He set them aside and picked up a letter. It was to the pope, Pius VII, and written in French. His heart began to hammer in his chest as he scanned it, words like *manuscript, secret meeting, Kings of Russia, Prussia, and Austria, a Holy Alliance and weapon* jumping out at him. His grip tightened on the last paragraph.

As soon as I have the girl, the Featherstones will have to give me the manuscript. My spies are reporting that they are searching night and day, frantic to find it. We will soon be in possession of the most powerful weapon in the world and shall rule it together in an age of peace.

The letter began to shake in Gabriel's hand. He slowly lowered the letter and picked the maps back up. It was a military campaign. They were plotting to take over the world and together, with a weapon of such power, if the manuscript truly held such plans . . . they just might be successful.

And the girl?

Of course that was Alexandria. Franco knew who she was! He had to get her out of there!

He hurried from the room and back down the corridor toward the ballroom. Once inside, the colors overwhelmed him, the music too loud. His breath came and went in puffs, his gaze frantic, searching the room. Where was she? And where was Franco? Panic crawled down his spine.

He stopped a servant. "Have you seen the duke and my wife? Where are they?"

The servant shook his head, but his eyes were fearful and wouldn't hold Gabriel's gaze. Gabriel took another step closer to the man and whispered in his ear, "Tell me or I will see that you will not wake from your sleep this night."

The man paled. "I saw him take her by the arm and say something to her, and then she followed him from the ballroom."

"Where did they go?" Gabriel moved aside to let someone pass and jerked his head for the servant to follow him out into the hall.

"I don't know but I have my suspicions."

"Hurry!"

"Below stairs. To the dungeons."

"Why would you think that?"

"There was another woman he held in the dungeons, sir, looked just like her. The duke held her and her husband down there for weeks. I had to bring food to them sometimes. I don't know who they were, but the duke likes women who look like that. He, ah, brings them up to his bedchamber at times."

Gabriel's stomach rolled in dread. "Point me the way."

"Go outside, cross the courtyard, and then enter the old keep. Take the west corridor to the back stairs. Down two flights of stairs are the cells. You should hurry, sir. There is one other thing."

"What is it?"

The man's cheeks flushed red. "I came upon a room one day, a small, out-of-the-way room. I shouldn't have gone inside but I did."

"And?" Impatience hummed along Gabriel's veins.

The man swallowed hard. "There were pictures—paintings and sketches, all over the walls."

"What does this have to do with my wife?"

The man's face jerked up, his gaze meeting Gabriel's. "They were all of her."

Bile rose to Gabriel's throat. He clapped the servant on the shoulder. "Thank you." He turned and ran, pulling the decorative sword from its scabbard of the evening costume provided by Franco.

He hoped the blade would prove strong enough to wield a death blow.

Chapter Twenty-Seven

"Ian, it looks perfect. I can't believe you have managed to make it seem so old." Katherine turned the leather-bound manuscript in her hands and studied it from another view.

"God led me to the right person to help us. Paolo is an extraordinary artist with a scientific mind that is difficult to find in one person."

"We did get lucky."

Ian let the comment pass. Luck had nothing to do with it. Prayers were being answered and he could see how uncomfortable it made Katherine to look at it that way. He continued talking about prayer and God helping them as if she agreed with him, but he never pushed her if she retreated. He could see she was thinking about it more . . . something, many things perhaps, were rising to the surface and he wondered how it would all spill out. He could only pray God had a plan of healing and restoring his wife. He had waited so long that he hardly dared to hope.

For now, he just held her as close as she would let him while she found her way. It had been a tightrope walk these last few days as they had scrambled to come up with a manuscript to pass off as Augusto's original. But he had hope.

Looking at the manuscript, he thought again how it was all coming together. How it just might work. It looked so much like the partial manuscript they had been shown. With Katherine's sharp memory of what had been on those pages and finding Paolo to complete the project, Ian had hope that Franco would believe them. It could at least buy them some time while Franco tried to find someone to unravel the mystery of the invention and possibly try and build it. By then they would have hopefully found Alexandria and be well on their way back to Holy Island—a place far, far away from here.

"I've hired us horses." Katherine brought him back to the plan. "We can be ready to leave within the hour."

Ian looked at their meager belongings mixed in among Augusto's artifacts. There were a couple of paintings still in good shape that he would like to take back to the regent but little else. His books were like sawdust. His clothing—rags. He hadn't left much in the cave when he returned to live in Florence, but what he had left must not have meant much to him. The only exceptions were the paintings, a box full of rusty old metal parts, and an old music box that was broken.

Ian reached inside his pocket for the music box and brought it up into the sunlight to study. A sudden pounding on the door jerked his attention away from the broken pieces.

"Who could that be?" Katherine's eyes were wary as she moved to the window to peer out.

Ian stuffed the music box back in his pocket and edged toward the door. He reached for the sword by the table. "See anyone?"

The pounding came again, louder.

"They're in uniform. And from their uniforms they look . . . Spanish." Her eyes widened. "King Ferdinand. He's found out about the manuscript. You know his sort—ruthless."

The pounding changed to shaking the latch. The door shuddered as someone plowed into it. It was locked and bolted. They always locked and bolted their doors. But that wasn't going to stop the soldiers for long.

"Hurry." Ian motioned Katherine over. "The back window. Grab the manuscript. I'll get our bag."

He rushed to the bed and threw in the most important things—travel documents, some legitimate and others good forgeries, money, clothing. They knew how to travel light with just the bare necessities. It only took moments and they were at the back window. He was about to break the glass when Katherine stopped him.

"Wait. They could hear you and come around. We need a distraction."

She rushed over to a drawer in the room's only desk and pulled out a small hand bomb. She had a knack for explosives, his Katherine, and he couldn't help his half grimace, half grin as she ran to the far side of the house, punched through an upper pane of glass with her gloved fist, lit the fuse with only two strikes of flint, and threw the bomb out onto the side street. It went off with a mighty blast that shook the house and rattled the glass in the panes. Smoke filled the area between the houses.

"Hurry now. We'll have to leave the horses behind."

"Yes, let's run for now. We can always find horses later."

The pounding on the door stopped. They could hear shouts and stomping feet. Ian helped Katherine get her skirts over the edge of the window and sprang through the opening after her. Thank God he was still as quick and nimble as he was at twenty.

There were a few advantages to being world-renowned fortune hunters. Wealth, strength, stealth—he'd become a fair hand at the sword and the travel could be nice. He'd seen most of the civilized world from Asia to America, Salvador to Switzerland, and some not so civilized, places that had changed his perspective forever. As he ran after his quickly fleeing wife, her skirt just visible through the smoke of her bomb, he felt a moment of strangely suspended joy.

He would have never lived such a life without her, and despite being a sheep farmer at heart . . . God help him, sometimes he believed she was worth it.

ALEX JERKED AWAY FROM FRANCO'S hold on her upper arm. "Let me go!"

"Not quite yet," he said through gritted teeth. He rushed them down another flight of stairs to a place so dark, so echoing against the cold stone walls that pure fear leapt to her throat. "What are you doing? What do you want with me?"

Franco stopped and leaned in toward her face. She could just make out his beard and glittering eyes. "I want that manuscript and you are the key to my getting it."

"My parents would never fall for such a trick."

Franco smirked. "Not your mother, perhaps. Cold woman, isn't she? But your father will do anything to free you. And your husband?" He flashed a wicked, leering smile. "That is one secret I didn't discover until more recently." He shrugged. "It doesn't matter. I'm still laughing over the irony, how sublime it is that your new husband saved my life in the street. I'm afraid I won't be returning the favor."

He jerked her farther down a stone corridor lined with cells. Opening one, he pushed her in. "Your father stayed in this one. I thought you might enjoy sharing the same cell." His lips curled into a cruel smile.

"No!" Alex clung to the bars, hearing the sharp clang of the door slamming and the clink of the iron key as he locked the door. "Tell me the truth. Where is my father?"

"Don't worry, my dear. He will be joining you soon."

He turned to go, taking the meager light of his candle with him.

"Wait! Come back."

But he didn't listen, just left her in the darkness.

"Gabriel!" She shouted as loud as she could, the sound of her voice echoing around the cold stones. "Gabriel!"

If only he could hear her. But he must be in the crowded, loud ballroom across the courtyard. How could he possibly hear her? Still, she had to try. She shouted again and again but the hiss of a voice told her she was too buried, too deep in the recesses of this place to ever be heard from again.

HE HEARD HIS NAME! THANK God he could hear her calling! And praise God his hearing was almost as good as normal. Gabriel hurried down the stone stairs, without light but with his sword at the ready. He turned a corner and ran right into the duke. They collided, swayed, and stumbled. Gabriel reached out and shoved him, but Franco had grasped hold of the handrail and only slipped a stair or two.

"Where is she? Where is my wife?"

Franco was breathing hard, even harder when Gabriel's sword came up toward his throat. Franco laughed though, taking out his own sword. "That decoration will do you little good, St. Easton."

His blade shot out, silver light and color, a much better

sword than the paltry ornament that was Gabriel's weapon. Gabriel deflected, more from guidance from the colors sweeping out before the sword than the blade itself. He parried, his sword bending, almost breaking, then turned toward the next flash of color with his shoulder, his free arm shooting out with a punch to Franco's jaw. It was time to fight with everything he had—any advantage. His sword master would be appalled, but this was not a time for honor. It was time to fight dirty.

With a long breath he focused solely on the colors, seeing Franco's next move before the hit, deflecting and leaning to one side or the other to miss the sword's swing. Franco was growing sweaty and furious, heated both inside and out.

Gabriel found an odd state of calm. He was reminded of his fight with Roberé, back in London, that very first time he had seen the colors. But there was a difference now—a big difference. Now he wasn't afraid of them. Now he knew how to use them, how to listen and see where they would guide him.

In a sudden move he had Franco's sword in his hand and swung it around to the Italian duke's throat. Franco panted as Gabriel shoved him against the stone wall of the stairway, the blade piercing his skin. Gabriel wasn't even breathing hard.

"I was mistaken to save your life," Gabriel said it in a quiet way, a reflective way, as if repenting to God for a grave sin.

Franco narrowed his eyes. "You won't kill *me*."

Gabriel quirked one brow. "What makes you think so?"

"Because I think of everything. I knew you would come after us and possibly find us. So I've done something to safeguard my life."

A cold spiral of unease inched its way down Gabriel's back, but he remained outwardly calm. "What have you done?"

"Alexandria's father left her letters. Letters I found." He smiled. "I left them in the cell with her . . . with a few changes."

Gabriel pushed the blade further into Franco's neck, pricking a line of red.

"There is a powder on the papers—poison. If she touches it and touches any part of her eyes or her mouth, it takes little to infest the body. She will die within hours." He shrugged. "Let us just say it is not a pleasant way to go to one's grave. I wouldn't wish it on my worst enemy. Oh, wait. Perhaps I would."

"Take me to her! This instant." Gabriel pulled the sword back.

"I have an antidote." He said it in a singsong voice that made Gabriel breathe even harder and compress his lips.

"Where is it?"

"Ah. That wouldn't be wise of me to say, now, would it?"

"I'll let you live if you save her. I will even go as far as to protect your life in the future."

"Hmmm, a worthy offer. Gabriel, isn't it? You *are* a guardian, aren't you? I believe I will accept." He took a small vial from his pocket and tossed it to Gabriel.

It flew through the air, flew like a tiny beacon of light across the darkened stairs. Gabriel heard the swoosh it made, saw the streak of yellow-white, and opened his hand. He lifted his hand just in time, caught it, and curled his fingers around the life-giving antidote, his heart roaring in his ears.

"Continue down the stairs." Franco held out a key. "You will find her."

Gabriel grasped the key and ran down into the Malaspina dungeons, shouting her name.

When he got there she was standing in a cell, holding a paper, one hand against her mouth, tears pouring from her eyes.

"Alexandra! Drop . . . that . . . letter."

She looked up. "Gabriel!" She rushed to the bars. "You came! Franco, he is near. How did you get past him?"

"I've already dealt with the duke." He took the key from his pocket and unlocked the iron door. "The letter—"

"It's a letter from my father. They were here . . . my father . . . in this cell. There are still his things, some clothes. What do think he's done with them?"

Gabriel took out the vial while she spoke, put his gloves on, and raised it to her lips. "Drink this."

"What?" Her eyes were huge and frightened. "What is it?"

"I don't know how much time I have to explain it. Do you trust me?"

Her lips quivered. "You're frightening me."

"Drink it."

She swallowed hard and nodded, opening her lips around the tiny glass lip of the vial. Gabriel said a silent prayer and poured it down her throat. The thought that the duke would be so sinister as to have him feed his own wife a deathly poison had entered his mind moments ago. But he didn't think so. The duke needed him, his protection, and had played a desperate hand and won. If his wife lived, Gabriel would not kill him nor let him be killed.

Alexandria gasped as it slid down her throat. "It's horrible. Please. What has happened?"

"The letter. It has a kind of poison on it. Did it feel strange?"

She nodded, terror in her eyes. "Like a fine powder coated it, yes."

"You have just taken the antidote, but it is still on your hands. Don't touch anything. We must find water and get your hands and face washed."

"But . . . the letter."

"Leave it. You remember what it said, don't you?"

She nodded as he waved her toward the stairs. "He said to run from this place. To go back home."

"Well, we'll not do that until we've found your parents." He paused on the stairs, longing to take her into his arms but knowing he couldn't touch her. "How do you feel? Any signs of illness?"

She shook her head. "I only feel afraid . . . and angry." Her eyes narrowed. "You promised him something in return for that antidote, didn't you?"

"Yes. I promised to protect his life." There was no use lying to her.

She stared at him for a long moment, breathing hard with disbelief in her eyes. "Well, I didn't promise anything of the kind. I will get the truth from him about my parents and I will seek vengeance."

She brushed past him, her hand stretched out to stop him from grasping her.

"Alexandria, no!" Gabriel hurried after her running feet. Dear God, what would she do?

She flew across the courtyard and charged down the corridor toward the ballroom, burst through the double doors, and stopped, elegant skirt swaying. Gabriel watched, helpless, as her gaze locked on Franco. She walked up to him, purpose in her stride and fire in her eyes.

"Alexandria, stop this. Get back here," Gabriel hissed from behind. He lunged for her waist, thinking to stop her, but she darted away.

She reached Franco, who stood staring at her with grim curiosity. She flung back her hand and slapped him straight across the cheek, her hand pressing hard across his lips. "You'll not steal nor destroy us. We have too much light for your darkness."

He staggered back, brushing the sleeve of his coat against his mouth and spitting profusely.

Alex turned and curtsied to the crowd. A footman stood by with glasses of champagne. She picked up a glass and poured it over her hands and then another, washing the powder with the expensive bubbly liquid, a grim smile across her lips.

Gabriel watched half in horror, half in awe. He wanted to rush her away. He would . . . in a moment. But for these few seconds, he could only stare in wonder at her bravery, her audacious faith that she could defeat such evil.

Then Franco recovered, howled, and charged toward her.

Gabriel grasped her upper arm and pulled her out of the way, running toward the door. A big, common-looking man charged toward them. At first Gabriel thought he meant to stop them, but no, the man put himself between them and the Italian duke.

Gabriel glanced over his shoulder as they ran for the door. Others came forward, looking the same, dressed in simple clothes. They surrounded the duke, stopping him. Gabriel hadn't noticed those men earlier. They didn't belong in this crowd, but they were helping them. They were on their side.

A memory of the men in Calais flashed through his mind. The Carbonari? Could it be those men had not been against them that day but were there to help? He realized the man chasing them had never shot at them while they'd ridden off, only shouted in Italian at them. And the other guards who had been injured . . . that could be explained as self-defense. His guards had fired the first shots.

And one had died.

Dear God, are they friend or foe?

Chapter Twenty-Eight

Carrara, Italy

Something wasn't right.

Katherine ran through the smoke as fast as her skirts would let her, her pulse racing with her feet, but the feeling that something had gone wrong hummed along her nerves, making her look to the right and the left. Maybe it was Ian. Maybe he wasn't right behind her.

She turned her head and slowed, hoping to see him. "Ian?" She said it just loud enough for him to hear if he was close. She turned back and took a few more running steps . . . and slammed into something solid. The impact caused her to reel in a circle and stumble. She would have fallen but for the hands that grasped her and hauled her up.

"Got you," a man said in a thick, Spanish accent.

Katherine balled her hands into a fist and swung at the man's face, kicking out at the same time toward his groin. "Ian! Stay away!"

The man's heavy arms came around her and pinned her flailing arms to her sides. She struggled against him but knew with a sinking feeling that her strength was no match for his. He jerked her around and tied her hands behind her back. "Do not fight me, *señora*. I win with much bigger man. Do you no good."

Katherine turned her head and spit into his face. "Let me go."

The man's thick, black brows came together over furious eyes. He wiped the spittle away with his shirtsleeve and looked to be coming for her with his own blow to her head.

"Ricardo, no," another Spanish voice ordered. They both turned to see a man leading Ian toward them with a pistol pointed at his head. "She will come willingly now."

Katherine moaned as her gaze met her husband's. He gave her a quelling look, asking her to cooperate, she was sure. She took a determined breath. "What do you want with us? Who are you?"

"All in good time, señora." The second man seemed to be in charge. "Back to the house now."

Within moments they were back in the house, the door guarded by Spanish soldiers. The captain directed them to sit in chairs side by side while continuing to point the pistol at them. He pulled up a chair and sat in front of them. "Now." He rubbed his hands against his knees. "I shall ask you some questions and you will tell me what I want to know or you will die."

Katherine couldn't help but admire his matter-of-fact confidence. Her gaze darted to the other man who had taken Ian's bag and was upending it on the table. The manuscript was inside. Should they tell them it was the original?

She quickly calculated the pros and cons of telling the truth that it was a forgery or hoping they would believe it was the authentic manuscript, take it, and let them be on their way. If only she could discuss it with Ian first. She looked over at him and he nodded once. What did that mean? Tell the truth?

"We are here on behalf of His Royal Majesty, King Ferdinand of Spain. My sovereign has been looking for a particular manuscript written by Augusto de Carrara. His patience has grown thin. You were hired to find this book by England's prince regent. Is this not so?"

"That is so." Ian spoke quickly.

Katherine watched in detached horror as the other man lifted the replica of the manuscript from the pile and opened it.

"What's this?" The man named Ricardo closed the book and walked over to them. He held it out to the captain.

"It is the manuscript you seek." Katherine hurried on, thinking Ian wouldn't lie. If they would only believe her this might soon be over. "We were preparing to take it back to England when you started pounding on our door."

A long moment of silence followed as the captain studied every page of the book, sometimes turning it sideways to study the scribbles of scattered words and sketches. He finally looked up and smiled. "It seems authentic but I have a test." He went out and called to someone in Spanish.

A moment later a third man entered the room of their little house and pulled out a packet of papers. He seated himself at the table and placed the papers to one side, the replica to the other, and began comparing them.

Katherine nearly groaned aloud. They were doomed. The pages wouldn't match. King Ferdinand must have also gotten a copy of the partial manuscript. For the first time she wondered if Franco had it too. How many were there? She had only thought England had a copy. She gave Ian an uncomfortable glance. It would have been better to tell the truth.

Her shoulders began to ache from her hands tied together while the man finished his inspection. He abruptly stood and strode over to the captain. With a bow he spoke in swift

Spanish. Katherine didn't have to know what he said . . . it was written on the captain's face—growing redder and angrier by the minute.

The captain waved the man away, stood, and paced. "You lie and try to trick me. The manuscript does not match the copy we have."

"It is what we found. How were we to know that?" Katherine asked, desperate for him to believe her.

"You found no others?" He turned to the two men. "Search the house. Bring anything you find to me." They hurried in either direction to obey.

The captain took a deep breath, as if marshaling his patience, and sat back down across from them. "You found Augusto's cave?"

"Yes." Ian sat forward, shooting Katherine a look that told her to be quiet.

"What was in it?"

Katherine started to speak, but the man flung out his arm toward her. "Let him speak."

She clamped her lips together and sat back. It wasn't the first time men had chosen to speak only to her husband.

"We found some paintings, some ragged cloth that must have been clothing, a few books and papers and manuscripts, but they were so frail. They fell apart in our hands."

"Do you think one of these manuscripts was the one? Where are they now?"

"The remnants are still in the cave. The ink was faded. It was impossible to tell, but we suspected one of them was the manuscript you seek. We made out a few drawings and they appeared the same as the sample we were shown. But they are worthless. You must believe me, why else would we create our own?"

"Why indeed? Did you think to trick your sovereign? Perhaps sell the real manuscript to the French? They have been making inquiries and tempting offers." His dark eyes flashed to Katherine and then back. "The two of you dislike your lives, I think." He seemed angry and genuinely puzzled at the same time.

Katherine squeezed her eyes shut in frustration and despair as Ian explained about Franco and their daughter.

"Now, this is making more sense." The captain nodded and looked pleased. "Of course you would do anything for your daughter." He stood and put his hands on his hips. He stared at them for a long moment and then burst out the words, "I will help you."

Katherine's gaze flew to Ian's.

"*Sí.* We will go back to the cave and you will show me these remnants. My expert lieutenant will study them, and we will take them back to King Ferdinand to assuage his curiosity. Then we will go with you to Malaspina Castle and find your daughter. You see? We can be friends."

Katherine clamped her lips shut so she wouldn't say how deep and certain her mistrust of that statement was. She only knew they had to hurry. The thought of Alexandria being in that castle . . . what that monster might do to her. "We will take you to the caves immediately."

The man smiled with closed lips. "Untie their hands."

"WE ARE BEING FOLLOWED, AREN'T we?" Alex looked over at Gabriel with worry in her voice as they dismounted in front of an inn in Carrara, a city nestled in the foothills of the mountainous marble quarries. It was an elegant little town with an ancient air of grace about it. White Carrara marble with its blue-gray veins were everywhere—inlaid tiles within the street of the square, a glorious cathedral with marble columns and a huge window with a marble rose covering. There were sculptures and life-sized likenesses of mermaids and lions, narrow streets and colorful houses.

The people dressed in muted rose, pretty grays and soft blues with their dark skin and hair, the women beautiful with dark flashing eyes and reddened lips. The older women were softer in a motherly way but still vibrantly beautiful, and the men—classically handsome with open, appreciative smiles when they saw her, whether young or old. It was breathtaking and yet there was another feeling. The feeling that danger lurked here.

"Yes, we are being followed." Gabriel glanced across the Piazza Alberica at the shadowy group of men congregating under a tree. "But I think I recognize one of them as the man who helped us get away at the castle." His voice lowered with a note of wonderment. "I believe that they are on our side."

"How could that be? They don't know us." Alex took Gabriel's arm and they headed for the door of the inn.

"Ah, but they know Franco."

Alex's eyes widened. "An enemy?"

"It is a good possibility. Let's wait and watch them. Be on guard."

They stepped through the doorway and were greeted by an older, plump woman with a large smile. "Such beauty!" she said in English, patting Alexandria's shoulders and then pinching her cheek.

She rattled off several sentences in Italian, all the while leading them to a table and pouring from a nearby bottle of wine. Before Alex could even think to ask for anything, there was unsalted bread and a platter of meats and cheeses, olives, and delicate cucumbers set before them. The woman motioned that they eat. "Bacco, he speak English." She scurried off to fetch him.

A few minutes later a tall, lanky man who must be her husband came in and bowed. "We are honored you have chosen our humble establishment for your needs. How may I serve you?"

Gabriel stood and bowed. "We are enjoying the repast you have so readily provided, but we are here in Carrara in search of someone. A man and woman, actually, who might be going by the name of Featherstone."

Gabriel paused and the man glanced at Alex and then back at Gabriel. Suddenly his gaze swung back to Alex.

"You are their daughter, no?"

He recognized her as so many had. She must have indeed grown into the very image of her mother and not realized it. "Yes. Ian and Katherine Featherstone, sir." They were so close. She could feel it. She leaned forward, tears pricking her eyes. "I have been looking for them for a very long time. People said they were dead, kings have tried to convince me, but I did not believe it. Please . . . do you know where they are?"

Bacco raised his hand and pointed at the window behind them. "They roam the marble caves." He shrugged, his eyes gray-blue and wise. "They search for something of great worth, but they do not know what it is they are looking for." He smiled, his gray mustache curving up, perfectly groomed. "Are they looking for you perhaps?"

"No." Alex shook her head, her mind spinning. They could have abandoned their quest and found her any time they pleased—across Ireland, then Iceland, and now Italy as she had followed their clues. A year she'd spent searching for them . . . a year where so much had happened. She was all grown up now. Married. Would they even know her anymore?

"When did you see them last?"

The man closed his eyes and touched his forehead as if deep in thought. "The house they rent. I saw them carrying things from the mines and taking them into the house."

"Can you take us to this house?"

"But of course."

Gabriel reached into a pocket, pulled out some coins, and laid them on the table. "Let us be on our way then." He grasped his waistcoat and shrugged into it, then held out his arm to Alex. "They are alive," he said softly into her ear.

Her heart raced and then lodged in her throat as they followed Bacco back into the streets.

THE SUN WASHED OVER THE little pale pink house as they approached on foot. Gabriel stopped them before entering, pulled forth his pistol, and loaded it. Alexandria nodded her understanding. The innkeeper quirked a brow, an odd frown that was curious and a little offended, but he waited patiently for him to finish.

Gabriel edged to the door and knocked. When no one came he pressed down the latch, waited for sound from the other side, and then eased the door open. It didn't appear that anyone was home.

They stepped inside but Bacco refused, standing on the step and shaking his head, his face serious. "I leave you now. I wish you peace by your journey's end." He smiled and bowed.

Gabriel closed the door. "Stay alert." He skirted the room, peering behind curtains and in closets and alcoves. Once he was sure the room was safe, he gestured to the kitchen area where a table was loaded with papers, books, and objects. "See what that is all about. I'll check the other room."

There was a bedchamber in the back, small and neat and empty. Gabriel opened drawers and inspected a small armoire.

Nothing and no one. On a sudden impulse he leaned down and looked beneath the bed. There, still visible from the soft light of the curtainless window, was a small, leather-bound book. He fished it out, turned it around in his hands, and opened to the first page.

I hate leaving her this time. It's worse than the others. The way she looks at me . . . I can hardly bear it. But I leave. I want her to be strong. I want her to find her own life like I had to find mine. It's the only way. If I don't allow it to happen, someone will. I would rather it be me.

The next page:

Belfast is a bore, sleepy beauty though. The postmaster was so easy to bend my way. I should have been on the stage.

We'll find it even though my sense is telling me the cost will be great. I even have a strange feeling that this will be our last adventure. How will I survive on that dreary Holy Island as a sheepherder's wife? We've fortune enough to live anywhere, but I know my husband. He will not want to leave Holy Island. I shall have to pick up a new hobby.

A few more pages:

We were accosted by two French men tonight at dinner in Dublin. They promised great riches if we should turn traitor and sell them the manuscript once we find it. I suppose old Louis needs something besides money to hang on to his throne. I can only imagine what he would do with such a weapon. I shudder sometimes, imagining it. Ian told them that our allegiance is to the crown of England. I thought it ill advised to just say it like that, but he always does and we've done well enough thus far.

We are a good match I think sometimes, and at other times, I think we don't match at all. Is that common among marriages?

Gabriel closed the book and closed his eyes. It was Katherine's journal. Should he show it to Alexandria?

"Gabriel, come quick! I think these are Augusto's things!" The object of his thoughts shouted from the other room.

Gabriel put the journal into his inside pocket and hurried to her side. "What have you found?"

"Look! There are a few paintings. He was really very good, wasn't he? And here." She lifted a thin book. "It's falling apart but it has some writings of his."

Gabriel peered over her shoulder at it. The handwriting *did* look familiar. He remembered back in the prince regent's library at St. James Palace when the regent had given him the copy of the partial manuscript to try to decipher. The mechanical drawings had leapt out from the page. Page after page, written over every inch of the pages, squeezed together in corners and boxes, some sideways, some diagonal, running off the page, and then with the slashing lines of a brilliant mind trying to get it on paper as fast as he imagined it, they continued onto the next page. This looked similar and yet different. Perhaps it was for another invention. He turned the page and it crumbled in his hand. Alexandria made a startled sound.

"It's not the manuscript, is it?"

"I don't think so. If it was, they would have never left it here, in plain sight." He set it carefully back on the table. "The question is, where are they?"

Alexandria straightened, got that determined look he now knew so well. "They will come back here. We only have to wait."

Gabriel nodded toward a grouping of chairs. Strange. Two were together and there was one facing them . . . like a standoff . . . or an interrogation. A quiver of unease shot through him. "If they aren't back by nightfall, I fear something bad has happened." He pointed to the chairs. He didn't have to say more, she saw it immediately.

"Do you think they are in trouble?"

"It's possible. But they were recently free and looking for Augusto's cave. Perhaps they went back to search for more clues."

"I wish we knew where it was."

Gabriel sat in one of the chairs and shook his head. "We'll not go into those mines alone. That would be dangerous, especially as it grows dark. We should wait here awhile, see if they show up."

Alexandria sank into the chair opposite him, the sound making a wave of color come from the four legs. He turned his head away and closed his eyes. Tired. They just needed one good night of rest and then, in the morning, if the Featherstones hadn't returned, they would hire miners to take them into the caves.

"How will I ever just sit here and wait? I couldn't possibly sleep." His wife sounded genuinely distressed.

Gabriel paused and then reached into his pocket and pulled out the journal. He handed it to her with a kiss on her forehead. "This should give you something to do."

Alexandria leaned back and held it up in front of her. "What is it?"

"I do believe I found your mother's journal under the bed."

Her eyes widened. She clutched it to her chest, seemingly unable to say a word.

"I'll lock the door and then I'm going to try to get some sleep. Load your pistol and wake me if you hear anything."

She nodded, staring at the little book. She looked to be half listening.

Gabriel made sure the doors were locked, then made his way toward the bedchamber. Her voice stopped him just inside the door.

"Would it be wrong to read it?"

He leaned his hand against the door frame, lowered his head, and closed his eyes. "I don't think so."

When she said nothing, he stepped into the twilight of the bedchamber and knelt on one knee beside the bed. With one hand curled under his forehead, he prayed for his beloved.

Lord God, we all need a mother's love, don't we? Help her find hers.

Chapter Twenty-Nine

The Spanish soldiers followed Ian and Katherine's horses up the steep, winding road into the mountain where the marble quarries were located. There were more soldiers than Ian had first thought, and he couldn't help but wonder if word had reached Franco that a Spanish army was taking over his town of Carrara. What would his reaction be, and would Alexandria be caught in the middle of it? He tried not to worry. The only way out of this was to trust God's guiding light one step at a time.

It felt much like this narrow road with the steep drop on one side and the solid, unforgiving rock on the other. How many had fallen to their deaths on this road? One misstep, the gravel underfoot making the horses slip—it would be easy to make such a fall look like an accident, not that the Spanish wouldn't kill them outright if they wanted to. Still . . . he swallowed hard and turned his gaze away from the sheer drop of jagged rock below. He had never particularly liked heights.

Stay attuned to God's voice. Concentrate on that.

At the mouth of the quarry, the captain gave orders for someone to guard the entrance while a company of six went inside the dark recesses with Katherine and him. The way was easy now that they knew it so well, but one had to be comfortable in tight places during one part of the journey. Ian smiled a little as he squeezed through a tight part of the path, hearing a groan from the captain and some complaints from the soldiers.

"Almost there," he encouraged. A few moments later the space opened up and then they were in Augusto's cave.

Ian lit the lanterns he and Katherine had left there, casting a yellow glow on the beautiful marble that surrounded them. He led the captain to an alcove and held out his hand. "There are some pieces of the manuscript here. We were afraid to move them."

"Very good." The captain motioned his expert over and held the lantern high so they could see in the recess of rock where spiderweb-thin papers were scattered about. "Oh, this is very sad, is it not?" The captain shook his head. "Some great genius was written upon these pages."

"The other manuscripts did have plans for weapons, but they were not as advanced as what we have today. I do not know if Augusto dreamed up something that could be of use in this modern age or not."

"Yes, but the kings think so, so it must be true." The captain touched a cracked leather cover, so old it turned into a dark dustlike substance when he rubbed it. "Can you make anything of it, Enrique?"

The expert shook his head. "No. The light is poor and the ink very faded."

"Very well. Carefully gather up every particle. Put them between the pages of the other manuscript we brought with us." He looked at Ian and then Katherine. "I am satisfied. I believe you tell the truth."

"Thank you." Ian inclined his head.

"We will camp here tonight, and in the morning we journey to Spain."

"But you said you would help us find our daughter." Ian took a step toward the captain.

He shrugged. "An easy convenience."

"You lied," Katherine hissed.

"It ensured your full cooperation." He bowed with mock flair. "You would have done the same in my circumstance, I think?"

It was true. They both knew it. Ian closed his eyes and turned his face away, his heart leaden. Would they really leave Italy and not find Alexandria?

Would they ever see her again?

THEY WOKE THE NEXT MORNING with still no sign of Alex's parents. She had dozed off after hours of reading the journal, her head in her crossed arms at the kitchen table. Gabriel had frowned at that, but they both felt the grim need to hurry, so they headed through Carrara and then up the winding mountain road to the quarries.

"Gabriel, look. There are soldiers guarding the opening to the quarry." Alex crouched back behind a rocky outcropping and moved aside so Gabriel could edge around her to see.

"The Spanish. They've finally caught up with us." Gabriel sighed. "They've set up a camp. Forty men, I'm guessing, horses, well-armed. They even have a cannon."

"And in full uniform. They aren't afraid to let their presence be known, are they?"

"I doubt they fear the Italians. They are not among those known to know about and desire the manuscript."

"King Ferdinand doesn't know Franco very well, does he?" Alex narrowed her eyes. "Do you think my parents are inside? Are the Spanish holding them prisoner?"

Gabriel came back beside her where they huddled close to the ground. "I'm afraid that may be so. It would explain why they didn't come back last night."

"We'll never get past them." Alex shook her head. Fear, anticipation, love, understanding—so many emotions filled her at the thought of seeing them again. After reading her mother's journal, Alex felt she had some understanding of her that had been missing. Her mother wanted her to be strong, independent like her, so she had withheld her love hoping Alex would build a wall around her heart to guard and protect it. She had thought her daughter should have to go through what she went through to be prepared for life.

Alex understood that now. But her mother hadn't counted on Alex's faith, her ability to lean on and believe in God's love, and her steadfast faith that He had a good plan for her life. She hadn't known her daughter was an optimist. Someone who saw the best in people and who people responded to with friendship and love.

But that was going to change.

Alex had decided in the late hours of the night, while Gabriel slept in the bedchamber next door, that she would show her mother the *truth*. That guarding hearts might prevent some pain in life, but it impeded love as well. Especially God's love. She'd been bursting with the image of those walls around her mother's heart and had been reminded of the story of Jericho, the city in the Bible where music and obedient marching had crumbled its walls. At the end of her mother's journal were a few blank pages and she'd been inspired with a message for her mother. Her first poem:

I can feel the walls of Jericho rumble
I can hear the stones begin to fall
I can see the rocks roll and tumble
I shout until my throat is raw

I can see the giants roaring
I can hear the demons scream with rage
All we did was march around this holding
All we did was walk onto this stage

Oh, promised land
I can't allow my eyes to see
These giants waiting to conquer me
I raise my eyes to the Son
Stop this hell-bent, desperate run
And believe in victory

I can feel the walls of my heart shaking
I can hear the wails of my own fear
I want to hide in a life of my own making
The cost to follow is so dear

You back me in my willful corner
You wait for me to seek Your face
You besiege from every quarter
Then You love me with amazing grace

That's what she would do. Love her mother with God's amazing grace. It was amazing because it wasn't hard to forgive her mother for being so shortsighted in her protectiveness. It may take a long time for her mother's walls to crumble, and they might never crumble completely, but Alex felt a deep, abiding patience, a peace that passed understanding, a deep knowing within her, that she would be able to help tear some down. It was a mission she was ready for.

And the Spanish weren't going to ruin it all.

"Perhaps there is another entrance. Shall we sneak around and look for one?"

Gabriel's brows lowered over his green eyes, eyes that glowed in the Tuscan sunlight with intense concentration. "We could get lost in those caves. This entrance must be the one leading to Augusto's cave since it's the one being guarded. Did your mother say anything in the journal about Augusto's cave? Did she mention if they found it and where it might be?"

Alex shook her head. "She hadn't written in it since coming here."

They sat in silence for a moment, thinking. The wind died down and Alex strained to come up with a plan. Suddenly her head shot up. "Gabriel, I hear something."

He turned his ear toward where she pointed and shook his head. "My hearing is still not as good as it used to be. What is it?"

She looked down the mountain, along the road by which they had come up from Carrara. "I think it's horses. Yes, it's getting louder. Someone is coming."

Gabriel grasped her hand. "Quick, let's get behind this shrub."

They crouched down behind the thin bushes and waited as the sound of horses crunching over the gravel road grew louder and closer.

Alex pressed her hand against her mouth, trying to smother her cry of distress when Franco came into view. Riding atop a large horse the color of smoke, he rode with a cavalcade of uniformed men in the duke's white and scarlet colors. Her heart sank. He looked none the worse from her rubbing poison on his mouth. How would they ever get to her parents now?

As soon as they rounded the turn and came upon the entrance to the quarry, the soldiers stopped. She could still see the few taking up the rear so they remained hidden and listened to the shouts.

"What is the meaning of this?" Franco demanded. "Stand down! Who is your commander?"

There was a scuffling sound and then the firing of a musket. Alex grasped hold of Gabriel's arm. "They are going to fight, aren't they?" Perhaps they would kill each other and take care of their problem. But someone would come out victorious. They had to find a way around.

"Franco is a fool. There could be Spanish ships in the harbor of the Ligurian Sea waiting to join these soldiers. Look." The men in the rear of the line were riding forward around the corner in a frenzy to join the fight. The blast of a cannon shook the rock. Smoke filled the air.

"Perhaps we can get through. They might not notice us." Alex begged with her eyes. "We have to try."

Gabriel kissed her on the mouth, a quick, hard kiss, and then took her hand and led her to the ledge where they could peek around and see what was happening. The cannon fired again, clouds of smoke billowing from its round barrel. Shots were being exchanged from men hiding behind outcroppings of rock. A few to one side were engaged in sword fights.

"If we run through on that side"—Gabriel indicated where the cannon sat—"the smoke will hide us. We must pass right in front of it, just after it fires."

"I can do that." She didn't have the Featherstone motto engraved in her heart for nothing. *Valens et Volens*—"Willing and Able."

Gabriel clasped her hand in his strong one. His eyes reflected everything the moment held—longing, determination, courage . . . *love.* "Don't let go."

Alex shook her head, promising that she wouldn't, her heart pounding in her throat.

The cannon went off again, the ball smashing into nearby rock, splaying shards of marble bullets into a mountain that shook and vibrated under her feet.

Gabriel would feel the vibrations.

He would see the colors and they would light their way.

She gripped his hand, her trust complete, and ran with him.

The sting and zip of buckshot flew through the air, shooting out all around them and glancing off rock faces. Men groaned and heaved, fell to the ground among shouts of defeat and victory. The clash of swords and the thrust of bayonets flashed past her like a gruesome play she hadn't paid to see. Smoke wafted through the air, but she kept her head down and her feet flying.

Gabriel veered to the left in a sudden move. His hand loosened in her grip. She didn't turn fast enough. She stumbled, falling on her stomach on the rocky mountain face and hitting her chin against a sharp object. The air whooshed from her lungs, making her unable to move for a moment. When she did look up, it was to see Gabriel fighting another man with a sword. He must have picked it up off the ground.

She curled up and grasped for her little pistol. Before she had time to do anything with it, Gabriel reached down, grasped her hand, and hauled her up. "Run!" He pulled her along behind him.

A soldier spun around and saw them. One of Franco's men, his white uniform coated with musket smoke and marble dust.

He ran after them. Alex screamed as he grasped her shoulder and spun her around.

Gabriel swung around with his sword but Alex was quicker. She lifted her pistol and fired it into the man's chest. She screamed and turned away, running again. They were almost to the mouth of the cave.

Two Spaniards were fighting off the Italians as they neared the entrance. Gabriel pushed Alex through the opening between them. He turned to join the Italians, slashing one of the Spaniards and then nodding to the Italian soldier to help the other one. The soldiers didn't have time to question who they were, and before they knew it, Alex and Gabriel were off, running down the tunnel of the cave.

Their footsteps echoed across the marble rock, but it was soon too dark to see. "Wait. I have to light a candle." Alex dug into her pocket and pulled forth the candle and flint she had brought. They had planned to light some rushes or have another light source before going into the cave, but now they only had one candle. The thought of being deep inside a pitch-black cave, the candle burning out . . . Alex shivered, cold with fear. "I don't think I can do it." She moaned in a small voice. "I'm afraid."

Gabriel took her into his arms. "We will find them before the candle goes out, but if it does, think of it as doing without one of your senses. Many people live their whole lives like that. And besides, these caves are solid rock. There will not be pools or great drops here, just tunnels and places where the miners have been working. I will go first."

Alex nodded and handed Gabriel the candle.

"We still need to hurry but quietly. If your parents are in here, they will not be alone."

They soon came to a fork in the tunnel. One side went smoothly to the left and the other went up, narrowing as it went, to the right.

"Which way should we go?" Alex dropped her head and closed her eyes.

"Might I be of assistance?" A low voice heavy with an Italian accent sounded from the tunnel ahead.

Chapter Thirty

*G*abriel's head jerked around to see more men coming into the light. They were dressed as miners but carried swords with their pickaxes, and one of them, the one who spoke, definitely looked familiar.

It was him. The man who had helped them at Franco's ball.

"Who are you?" Gabriel took the necessary steps to reach them, Alexandria close behind.

"We are the Carbonari. Revolutionists and dedicated to destroying the manuscript, if it exists."

"You know about the manuscript?" Alex came into the light of their lanterns.

"We have learned of it. We have been watching the Featherstones since they came here with their questions."

"What happened to them? Have you seen them? Please, I am their daughter and I have been searching for them for a very long time."

"They disappeared one day and we did not know what had happened to them. We later learned that Franco had captured them and kept them in the dungeons of Malaspina Castle.

Then, not long ago, they came back and picked up their search. We believe the Spanish have them now, here in Augusto's cave. We are waiting to see what they discover."

"You say you want the manuscript destroyed. Do you plan to take it from the Spanish if the Featherstones give it over to them?"

"Yes, of course. No king will have it. We fight for freedom from any monarchy. For liberty!"

Gabriel looked at the man, studying the authenticity of his claims and the passion in his eyes. "If you help us find the Featherstones, free them from the Spaniards . . . then we will help you destroy the manuscript."

Alex gasped. "But shouldn't the regent have it?"

Gabriel shook his head. "I agree with these men that no king should have such knowledge." He shrugged. "If it even exists."

The man held out his hand, his dark eyes steady and sure. They shook, sealing the bargain.

"Come, they are this way."

With the light of the Carbonari's many lanterns, they made quick time through the winding marble tunnels. Deeper and deeper into the mountain they went, the air thinning and the lanterns sputtering. Gabriel hadn't seen a single color since entering this fortress. He didn't know if he was happy about that or not.

Something strange was happening.

He shook his head against the clogged feeling in his ears as they ascended. Altitude, the doctor had said. That and atmospheric pressure. His body didn't adjust well to these.

But why? He'd never had problems before. He'd always been the picture of health—stamina, strength, intelligence. He'd always learned things easily—connected the dots of thought before the instructor said it, or the book explained it, or . . . sometimes even . . . perhaps before anyone else had ever thought it. He could relate to Augusto in that. After hearing his story that the old man in Iceland had read to them about him . . . the story of his life . . . Gabriel had felt a certain connection with the genius.

He'd had his conversion too—to Christ—to salvation, but when he heard Augusto's simple story and how radically it had changed his life . . . well, Gabriel's conversion still felt more like a struggle—sometimes in his head and sometimes in his heart. Not quite that, but not so overwhelming as Augusto's.

He wanted that.

Was he too stubborn? Hadn't God broken him enough with his affliction? Did he just want too much?

A female scream pierced the air.

"It's my mother!"

Alexandria pressed past Gabriel and the other men, shoving them with her hand, the look of an avenging angel on her face. "Let me by! My parents are just through there!"

They ran after her, hearing cries and scuffling. Would they be too late? What were the Spanish doing to them?

Gabriel pushed the questions away and clawed behind her through the narrowing tunnel of stone toward the sounds. Alexandria burst through first. His heart stopped, clenched, hoping she wasn't running into a trap or worse, the scene of her parents' murder. He heard her gasp and cry out. Then he came through the opening himself.

He saw a faint streak of blue and then a sword flashed toward his face. He deflected it, more out of a long-standing habit against his sword master than anything, but it saved his neck. He parried, glanced about to see what had become of his wife, and then swung a death blow. It happened so fast.

He whirled around to another attacker, the Carbonari at his side, slashing and hacking like he; his wife gone to ground, cowering in a corner with others who looked like her.

With her family.

They'd found them!

The knowledge ran like wildfire through his veins, making the sword flash and fly through the air. The colors danced—pale and reliable with a cadence he knew to follow. He tuned into them, felt them fully. Parry, riposte, thrust, stab, and slash—his feet moved forward and then backward. Another one down.

There were six of them against their nine, and it didn't take long before the Spanish soldiers were lying on the cold marble, bleeding lines of red to intermingle with the smoke blue lines that made Carrara marble world renowned.

His breath came hard and fast from his nose as the last Spaniard fell. Gabriel turned, saw his wife, and went to her. He threw down the sword, heard the deep clatter, and saw spirals of green, like a sorcerer's smoke. It floated above the sound and then disappeared into nothing.

He smiled.

He was *glad* they were back.

"Alexandria." He hauled her up and into his arms.

She buried her face into the nook of his shoulder. "We did it. Oh, Gabriel, my dearest." She pulled back and stared into his eyes, reaching out and touching his cheek. "We found my parents."

THE CARBONARI PULLED THE DEAD and wounded back toward the entrance where they planned to discover who had been victorious between Franco and the Spanish army. Gabriel spoke to the leader before Alex could pull him toward her parents.

"If we find the manuscript I will find you." He said it in a soft voice that Alex could just make out, but she was too relieved to worry about what might happen to this manuscript that had caused so much trouble. She just wanted her parents out of here and safe.

Alex turned to see her parents getting up off the stone floor. Her father rushed to her and gathered her in his arms. "Your mother said you would come, but I still can't believe it. Are you really safe?" He buried his face in her hair. "The Duke of Massa? How did you get beyond his reach? I have so many questions, but I just want to hold you and know you are really here."

"I'm really here." She pressed the side of her face into his neck. She looked over at her mother and had to blink away a fresh pool of tears. She was standing in silent elegance, but there was something new, something dear in her eyes. A look filled with quiet pride, a calm assuredness that Alex had done exactly as she had expected and hoped for.

And love. A deep, abiding love that had been there all along but was closer to the surface now. As if Alex was ready for it . . . or perhaps it was Katherine who was ready, she didn't know. But it was new and it was welcome.

Alex held out her arm and beckoned her mother into their circle.

Her mother came toward her and drew her into her arms. "I knew you would come." She held Alex away and looked deep into her eyes again. Her mother smiled a slow, gentle smile. "You have grown up, haven't you?"

Alex nodded. "More than you know."

"I saw that it would happen this way. Do you have many stories to tell us?"

Alex laughed with a glow of happiness bursting through her. "Oh, yes. Many stories. And people you must meet."

Her mother's gaze slid to Gabriel. "Is he one of them?"

"Yes." Alex pulled free of their embrace and went to her husband. "Come and meet my parents."

She took his hand and led him over to her parents, her heart beating loud enough it must be heard through the room.

"Gabriel, these are Katherine and Ian Featherstone."

Gabriel bowed his head.

"Mother, Father . . . this is Gabriel Ravenwood, the Duke of St. Easton and . . . my husband."

Her parents stared at him for one, two, three heartbeats, and then Katherine swept into a low curtsy. "Your Grace." There was a note of triumph in her voice.

Her father did not bow. He lifted his chin toward her taller husband, dark brows coming over his gray eyes, and said in a most serious tone, "Married? She's too young . . . and—" He shook his head as if unable to go on for the moment. "I demand to know how this happened!"

Alex stifled a giggle, and then when her father's eyes met hers, she completely sobered. "It's a long story but he is a most excellent husband."

Gabriel bowed again to her father. "Sir, I would be honored to answer all of your questions at another time, but I fear Alexandria is correct that it is a long story and"—he looked over his shoulder—"we may not have much time. The Spanish are in a battle right now with the Duke of Massa and his men. Neither are friends of ours, so I am assuming not friends of yours?"

"Franco can rot in—" Katherine started to say.

"And the Spanish double-crossed us," Ian added in a terse voice.

"Yes, well, I have a similar sentiment toward both of them." Gabriel gave her parents that half-cocked smile that seemed the stuff of magical qualities. "The manuscript. Quickly tell us. Have you found it?"

Her father shook his head and her mother hurried the explanation. "We found nothing in Florence but a great deal here. This is Augusto's cave. You know of Augusto de Carrara?"

"Yes, I found Enoch in Iceland. He read me the story."

Her mother smiled, tilting her head. "I knew you would. Wasn't he wonderful?" Her lips pressed together for a moment. "So much to talk about." She glanced at Gabriel. "But not now. We found what might have been the original manuscript, but it was too old." She shook her head. "It wasn't legible, just turned to dust when we touched it."

"I am not certain that it was even it, but it had some similar markings." Her father shrugged. "It looked the closest to the partial we had been shown. Have you seen that?"

Gabriel only nodded. There wasn't time to tell them about the secret room in St. James Palace and the half-built machine he had found.

"So . . . there is nothing to give any who want it." Her husband's piercing green eyes focused on something, and then with a shake of his head, he looked away. "The question is, can we convince all who want it that it doesn't exist?"

The fact that powerful rulers—kings, dukes, groups of vigilantes like the Carbonari, possibly the pope—might not believe them, might think they would keep it for themselves, took root in each of their hearts.

"We think we convinced the Spanish captain, but I'm not sure Ferdinand will believe it." Her father's mouth turned down in a grim line. "We have to flee, pray God we escape with our lives."

Gabriel drew his sword. "If the Spanish have won, we must fight. If Franco has won, we can bargain. With the Carbonari on our side, he will have to listen to reason."

Alex hoped the duke had won.

But then, thinking of the last time she had seen him, perhaps a Spanish army was the lesser evil.

Chapter Thirty-One

W ait." They were just leaving the cave when Gabriel
called out. He held out his hand and closed his eyes.
The colors began again and they were strong. He opened his
hands, seeing a soft glow of green on them and then glanced
around the cave. Colors, like a reflection from a deep, dark
pool. Blues and greens flickered against one of the cave walls.
He looked to Alexandria.

"What is it?"

He gestured to the curved marble wall and pressed his
fingers against his forehead. He didn't want to appear a freak
of nature to her parents—he had yet to tell them how much
he loved their daughter—but the colors were growing stronger,
the hues deepening. He couldn't resist them. It was as if they
were calling his attention in a demanding way, like the most
lilting, hauntingly beautiful piece of music.

"Are you seeing them?"

"Seeing what?" Ian demanded, but Katherine put her
hand on his arm with a stilling look.

"Yes. There is something here."

"Then you must discover what it is." Alexandria gazed up at him with confidence in her eyes. "Show us."

He took a deep breath. No one said anything as Gabriel walked toward the undulating colors. They changed as they turned, like ribbons with different shaded sides. He couldn't help but smile. His new relatives might think him mad, but these colors, these particular hues of blue and green . . . purple . . . they beckoned him like heaven's lights . . . they filled him with pure *joy*.

God in heaven, don't let me mistake this. Don't let me fail You.

He saw it then. The way he had wanted Augusto's conversion, Augusto's revelation for his own. Gabriel's conversion was different but nothing less, no less great or powerful or even satisfying. They just had different paths. They were created for different purposes. A laugh escaped him. He touched the cave wall and the colors changed, came together toward a source and swirled.

There is a key.

The thought came, unbidden. His fingers felt around the edges of the marble. It was somewhere . . . he could feel it . . . see it. There.

A groove gave way to a tiny indention. When his hands met it, a spark of pure white shot from the place—like heat but it wasn't hot. "Here."

He placed his fingers in the groove and felt around the indention. He pressed on it. He tried to pry his fingernail into it. Nothing happened.

"A key," he muttered.

"A key?" Alexandria's voice was pure color.

He nodded and closed his eyes. "Augusto's inventions. Was there a key mentioned?"

Alexandria paused. "Enoch. Remember when Enoch showed me the book? Oswald's story of Augusto? He pointed to the book and said the key was in the book." Her gaze flew from Gabriel to her mother. "You left that clue for me. That book. Do you know what the key is?"

Katherine shook her head. "I told Enoch that the book was the key so he would show it to you. You were the key, my dear. I knew with the right clues you would follow us."

"It must have something to do with the story about Augusto. There is a clue in the story. We all heard it. Think . . ." A long moment of silence followed.

Gabriel felt the indention with his finger. "It has to be something small." He glanced around the cave. Nothing. Except some faint green light about Ian . . . around his coat. The same green that was on his palms.

"Lord Featherstone—"

"Ian, please."

Gabriel pointed at his chest. "Is there anything on your person?"

He patted his pockets and then paused . . . put his hand in the inside pocket of his coat, and pulled out a small pile of metal and marble pieces. "We found this in the cave. I think it was a music box."

Color shot from his palm where the pieces lay, clinking together as Ian moved them. Gabriel went closer and leaned over the pieces of the broken music box. "Light, please."

Katherine brought the lantern around and held it high. Alexandria looked anxiously at Gabriel and then at her father's palm.

Gabriel dug with his forefinger through the parts. When his fingertip touched one of the pieces and it rattled against another, a burst of bluish purple shot out of Ian's hand. "I think we've found it."

"Of course," Alexandria and Katherine said together. "It

was his mother's, the only thing he had left of her. He must have treasured it," Alexandria finished the thought.

Gabriel picked up the piece of grooved metal and held it up to the light. It was long, indented, in a kind of metal, silver perhaps, that had not rusted. Delicate and small. He took it over to the indention in the wall, reached around, and carefully inserted it into the small opening.

Color shot from the space so brilliantly that he cried out, fell halfway to his knees.

"Gabriel!" Alexandria rushed toward him, but he held out his other arm to stay her.

"It's so bright." The words escaped his throat. He couldn't look and yet couldn't look away. It was as if the veil that separated mortal from immortal had ripped, and in that tear he saw a glimpse of heaven's light, heaven's colors.

He staggered back. A mighty shaking began all around them. A grinding sound vibrated the marble walls. Alexandria cried out. He took another step back, gathered his wife to his side, and with this new part of his family, they watched as the marble wall rolled away.

A shaft of pure sunlight streamed from the roof of the cave, revealing an enormous hidden room. They took a step forward, standing side by side as the sun moved to midday. The angle of the light changed, the beam casting its glow in the middle of the room where Augusto's masterpiece sat, over ten feet high and six feet wide, a beautifully carved machine with a marble base, the top made of crystal so clear it appeared to be glass. The light hit the crystal and then bounced in all directions, cascades of colors in every shade of the rainbow shooting across the room.

"I can see the colors." Alexandria started to take a step forward, but Gabriel held her back. "Wait."

The sun inched another degree, the colors bending, hues deepening, and then the beginnings of movement from the machine. A crank of marble turned, creaking with a groaning sound of rock on crystal.

Before anyone could move another step, a soft sound emanated from the music machine. And then another . . . and another. The shaft of light moved again, opened up and took up the full space of the crack in the ceiling, shooting rays of pure sunlight directly on the entire top of the crystal. Another groaning and then . . . *music*.

Alexandria reached for Gabriel's hand. "Oh, Gabriel."

The song began like a lullaby, sweet and tender, bringing them to tears, but it soon turned to something else . . . something deeper, richer, the colors coming from the machine overwhelming in their beauty and clarity—each note pulsing with *love*. The tone was like one might imagine angels would sound like, the purity, the crystal clear resonance—*oh, God*—something inside Gabriel began to shake and quiver. Something hard, deep within him began to give way.

Alexandria openly cried. Her mother stood staring, tears streaming down her cheeks, and her father—he looked ready to kneel. And then he did, which made Alexandria go to him and cling to him, both of them staring at the machine with tears rolling down their cheeks. Gabriel glanced at Katherine, who would not look at anyone—only stood softly crying, her mouth a little open as if she couldn't breathe—her whole being trembling.

Healing music.

Gabriel stepped closer, the colors undulating in a way that made him laugh and cry at the same time. Unmatched joy flooded him. Peace, like he'd never felt, made him wonder so many things at once—how had they ever questioned God and His love?

How had he ever questioned so many things in his life?

God was omnipresent, omnipotent, omniscient, sovereign. He hadn't left them nor forsaken them—not ever. Not from the moment He made Adam from clay and all of mankind to the moment when they would see Him face to face and be reawakened, reborn, made eternal . . . to live with Him forever and always feel this peace, this joy.

This *love*.

His breath shuddered out with a laughing cry. He stepped closer and looked up. He could see it. The sunlight was playing the song. There were etchings on the crystal, lines and points and tiny rectangles, like a strange language or map—the key. The engravings would regulate the intensity of the light rays that passed through the double-refracting crystal. Each etching produced a different sound, a different tone. Augusto had taken the idea of the music box and made his mother an astounding gift, hadn't he? Sunlight that played etchings of crystal.

Augusto's love song.

Gabriel watched in growing astonishment. The images of the part of the manuscript he had seen in the prince regent's library in St. James Palace so many months ago came alive in his mind. The mathematical equations from Augusto's pages leapt to life. He shook his head slowly back and forth in wonderment. He could see them in the colors. The colors had value, like equations, like the rays of light held weight and measure, like music and math combined in a perfect symphony of sound.

In a sudden shock of insight, he saw that the plans to make this machine were not in a manuscript, they were written in the music, on these etchings.

This machine, this music box, *was* the plan and it was more . . . so much more.

Oh, God, my God. He fell to one knee looking up at the swirling colors, his chest shaking with silent sobs. These weren't just plans for a musical instrument played by sunlight . . . this knowledge, this leap in scientific thought, would open scientific doors no man had opened. This machine could lead to hundreds of inventions . . . thousands. The kings had been right. It *could* lead to the world's most powerful weapon, and so much more . . . God help them all if men could harness the power of light? Color?

Was the world ready for Augusto de Carrara's genius?

Could they let anyone find this? What would the world they lived in do with such knowledge?

It could destroy them all.

A sudden commotion from behind them, a clattering against the beauty, drew his attention toward the entrance of the cave. The Duke of Massa stood there, draped in his costume of white and scarlet, blood accenting the red and making the red of his eyes crazed with victory.

He looked from Gabriel to the invention. He walked toward it, stared, and then cried out, the ethereal music still filling the room. His hands rose as if to worship it.

Gabriel moved to Alexandria and pulled her back, took her into the protective circle of his arms. They all watched, suspended and in wonderment, as the power of the music fell over Franco and his men.

ALEX MARVELED AT THE POWER of God's presence in the room. Some of the soldiers knelt, looking up at the shaft of light. The wonder in their faces transformed them, as if their heaven-born persons rose to the surface and their earthly-clad selves fell away. Others shielded their eyes and raised their arms against the light, against the beauty of the heavenly sound, against Him.

"Many are called, but few are chosen."

Alex heard the Scripture and a sob escaped her chest. *Turn, turn, turn to the Light . . . please.* Her whole being cried out the prayer, but she was not afraid. Perfect peace filled her. She was not afraid they might turn and kill her, kill her beloved, her parents . . . She was not afraid of anything.

I have seen the glory of God. She wept with the music and knew, whether dead or alive to this world, she would live in the knowledge and grace of that place for the rest of her life. It was a gift that would never be taken from her.

Franco looked around at them all—stolid, unmovable, his hate-filled gaze met hers.

Days ago, *yesterday,* she would have lifted her chin and met that gaze with an equal challenge, but now she wept for him. She saw him lost and tortured forever. Her heart echoed Jesus' words. *Forgive him, Lord. He knows not what he does.*

The duke turned from her tear-streaked face as if he couldn't stand to look at her compassion-filled gaze any longer. He turned back to the machine and narrowed his eyes. He stepped toward the giant music box and laid his hands on the Icelandic crystal.

Gabriel took a step as if to stop him but Alex clung to his arm.

The sun shifted . . . colors burst through the room, through Franco. He screamed as if burned. He let go, sprang back, and fell to the floor.

Alex gripped her chest with one hand. *No! Please. Humble yourself before Him, before you die . . . so that you might live!*

He writhed on the floor, trembling and shuddering on the cold marble, foam coming from his mouth. He shuddered again and stopped. They all backed away in horror and awe.

The light changed again. The music faded to soft sounds and then nothing but the silence of a cave.

A hue and cry came from the duke's soldiers. They rushed to his body, but no one would touch him. Gabriel came over to Alex and led her out of the secret room.

The others followed. Gabriel nodded toward two of the duke's soldiers. "Drag him out."

They both shook their heads, eyes wide with terror.

"Do it or I will see that you remain in there with him."

They jumped to pull him out.

Alex huddled with her parents as Gabriel went to the indentation in the wall and paused. He turned and looked at each of them.

Her mother nodded.

Her father nodded.

Alex smiled, feeling it light up her whole face. It was the right thing to do. She nodded.

Gabriel took the key from his pocket, inserted it, and turned it the other way.

THEY WATCHED AS THE WALL moved back into place. Gabriel looked at each of them by turns—Ian, Katherine, Alexandria . . . *his family*. He looked down at the Carrara marble floor, rough stone but with the potential of creative genius. Only God could have made such a thing, knowing all they would do with it. Made everything . . . knowing all they would create with His creation.

He gave each of them a joy-filled smile. They would forever share this. They would know each other more fully and better in the future for this adventure together.

Perhaps Katherine had been right all along.

Perhaps they had needed this journey, this adventure, to bind them.

It was in her eyes that she had seen glimpses of it. He nodded toward her and she nodded back.

He looked at the four soldiers that had come in with Franco. He looked each of them in the eye, one by one, and one by one they told him with their eyes that they would never, ever tell of this place, this machine, this glimpse of heaven's music. They were too afraid. Too curious to ponder it themselves, in a quiet place where they could sit in old age and contemplate, wonder with astonishment and some disbelief that they had seen something so extraordinary.

It was their shared, silent promise.

Epilogue

Holy Island—1879

"Great-grandmamma, tell us a story! *Please!* A new story!"

Little five-year-old Alessandria ran to Alexandria's lap and climbed upon her frail knees to nestle against her chest. Her legs shook with the child's squirming weight, but Alex didn't mind. She loved her five children, twelve grandchildren, and seven great-grandchildren the way she had loved her whole life—with everything she had.

The other little ones gathered around and some of the adults too, taking seats around her to hear the story.

She turned to Gabriel with a twinkle in her eye.

Should she finally tell the story? The secret they had been keeping for a lifetime?

They wouldn't know it was real—that it had really happened. They would think it was just one of the many made-up tales Alex had told over the years. Tales of an admiral named Montague and his many high-seas adventures, tales of an Irish giant named Baylor who could take a man down with a single blow but wept when his wife sang an Irish tune sounding like the *sidhe*—the fairy creatures—and quivered at the very thought of her temper.

She had told tales of Irish castles and Spanish kings, volcanoes with pools of blue and bubbling mud pots. Tales of treasure seekers and ancient maps and lands that her parents had seen. There had been so many stories, finally shared over the years by her parents, for her to pass down.

But there was one story. One book that had found its way into her hands, by fate or predestination, or promise, *by God's grace*. And that was Augusto's tale. It was so close to the truth that she'd not brought it out, but now, on their sixtieth wedding anniversary, and so close to seeing heaven's gates for both of them, she reached over and squeezed her beloved's thin hand.

"It does feel like time."

ALEXANDRIA SMILED AT HIM, HER lips thin and quivering. He looked back at her and knew, knew everything about her, knew what she was thinking, knew the moment, ripe and full, in her eyes, when she had decided to tell the story.

An old man at ninety-three years, his face wrinkled with time's tracks but his eyes, his emerald eyes still glowed with a panther's stealth. He turned them on her with that knowing look and nodded his agreement.

She laughed and his aged lips turned up in that one-sided smile he knew always . . . still . . . turned her knees to mush. He chuckled and turned away before she could see the sheen of tears in his eyes.

My God, how I love her.

She would tell the story of Augusto and his marble cave. Of the magical machine that made heaven's music. They wouldn't know it was true. She would tell them to inspire dreams of the life to come, but she wouldn't tell them it was true, to protect their own journey . . . just like her mother had.

They would have to find God's path for themselves.

It was the only way.

"All right, everyone. Gather around and I will tell you a story I have never told anyone, except your great-grandfather. He knows it." She smiled at each of them. "Because he was there."

She winked at the children as they gathered closer to her skirts and pulled out an ancient-looking book with colored ink and the monastic Lindisfarne script that was so beautiful. Just to see it made a person wonder at the beauty of the story. Gabriel leaned back in his rocking chair and watched her, bursting with pride.

His wife. Alexandria Ravenwood, the famed Duchess of St. Easton—famed for her charity, for her kindness, her loving spirit—still a Featherstone at heart—*Valens et Volens*—always "Willing and Able"—but now a Ravenwood too. A St. Easton duchess with another motto that she had always lived by so easily—*Foy Pour Devoir*—"Faith for Duty"—and a woman who knew how to choose both, balance both throughout all their lives. He smiled and then looked down to hide it as she opened Augusto's story and began to read.

Gabriel leaned back in his rocking chair and closed his eyes, listening to the sound of his wife's voice. It sounded just as it did when he first heard it—on board that ferry to Calais. He dozed, time coming back in waves of memories across his mind. He saw her running down the marble-floored hall of his number 31 town house on St. James Square, that beast of hers, Latimere, in tow and taking down some of his prized possessions.

Prized possessions.

There wasn't anything—not one thing—from that old life that meant anything to him now. Not the music room at Bradley House, not swordplay or horseflesh, not politics or the glitz and glamour of society, not the *opera* even. Not his knowledge, nor his wealth, not even the refurbished grandeur of Lindisfarne Castle on Holy Island, where they had lived most of their lives.

No, other than God, to whom he felt as close as Augusto had ever come, Gabriel really only had the energy left to care about twenty-five things in his life—twenty-five people—and they were all here with them tonight.

He opened his eyes and looked at their enraptured faces, all of them listening to his wife's story of Augusto and the cave pool and the manuscript. He looked down at his lap and laughed quietly.

Some of them believed it.

His beloved finished the story and then also dozed while the rest of the family had cake. He nodded off again too and then came awake when his great-grandson tugged on his trousers.

"Read me the comic, grandpa-great."

Robert had always gotten the title backward. Gabriel smiled and pulled him up onto his lap. He took the newspaper into his hands, shook it out, and folded it into one long page.

"There now, which one?"

"There. That'n."

Gabriel nodded, reached for his spectacles, and glanced at the boxed comic. "That one." He automatically corrected in a soft voice. His gaze strayed though. The paper crinkled like the rustling of leaves.

A streak of color, his favorite shade of blue—like an Icelandic pool, like the Tuscan sky on the clearest day, like Alexandria's eyes—flashed across the page.

He blinked, exhaled with a smile. He hadn't seen the colors in so long.

His eyes caught an advertisement beside the comic:

Elektrotechnische Fabrik J. Einstein & Cie., Munich, Germany.

A new company has opened its doors to the excitement of the scientific community by Hermann Einstein for the study of direct current and the manufacturing of electrical equipment. The company will begin production within the year, and there is hope that new discoveries will be made. Einstein resides with his wife, Pauline, and their newly born son, Albert.

Another flash of color streaked across the paper, swirling around the last name. A jolt of excitement filled his chest. He gasped.

"Gabriel? What is it?"

"Alexandria." His beloved was beside him, leaning over him, grasping his face between her hands.

"The colors." He lifted his hand to her cheek, his heart bright with happiness.

"They're back?" She gripped his hand, tears in her eyes.

He nodded. "I can see heaven. I can hear it. Do you remember?"

She bent over his hand. "Oh!" A cry came from her chest but her eyes . . . her eyes looked down into his, full of the promise of eternity together. "I remember."

GABRIEL TAPPED THE PAPER STILL in his hand, Robert having run to his mother. Gabriel smiled up at her, only forever her. His voice was thin, so thin and weak, but full of joy. "There is something about this Einstein fellow, mark my words." He chuckled and then closed his eyes.

Perhaps this Albert Einstein would spend some time in Italy, Lord? He must hear the story.

The colors flashed around him and surrounded them all—he saw his mother and father, so long ago gone from them. He saw Ian and Katherine, beckoning with the sounds of angel song behind them. He grinned. Montague, oh, and there was Baylor and his lovely Irish wife they'd all visited so often over the years.

And Jane . . . they'd lost his sister two years ago, just a few years after dear Meade had passed into heaven. And then there, beyond Jane, stood two men—a monk and a large man in a long brown cloak. He had a round, glowing face. He was smiling at Gabriel and nodding.

Augusto.

So many loved ones . . . so many colors . . . hues that even he had never seen. They didn't hurt his eyes. He didn't have to look away.

They encompassed him, filled him to overflowing, floating, calling, perfect peace.

But Gabriel didn't join them yet. He took a sudden breath, his spirit returning, hearing God whisper that it wasn't quite time. He and Alexandria had one last thing to do before seeing God face-to-face.

One last story to tell.

Scientific Note

During the writing of this series, I was honored to consult with experts of science and history. One interesting finding was concerning Icelandic crystal and its role in the development of many scientific fields. Leo Kristjánsson, a geophysicist at the University of Iceland, writes this about Icelandic spar:

> Iceland(ic) crystal was a name used c. 1690–1780 for transparent, colorless crystals brought to Europe from a site at the Helgustaðir farm in Eastern Iceland. They turned out to be composed of very pure calcium carbonate (calcite, trigonal $CaCO_3$). The expression "water-clear" sometimes appears in descriptions of the best specimens. Since 1780, Iceland spar has been the most common designation for such crystals. They were quarried commercially for export at Helgustaðir at intervals between 1850 and 1924, the major effort in 1863–72 yielding a few hundred tons in all. At other times crystals were picked at the site by occasional visitors. They frequently reached 15–20 cm in dimensions; an exceptional one of about 60 cm is in the British Museum.

These crystals had a property called double refraction or birefringence: a narrow ray of ordinary white light (coming, say, directly from the sun or a lamp) incident perpendicularly on a spar crystal with parallel sides is split into two on its way through it. On exit, these two rays both continue in the same direction as the incident ray, but they are now separated by about 1/10 of the thickness of Iceland spar traversed. One of these rays has been to some extent dispersed into the colors of the spectrum. Their total energy is less than that of the incident light by about 10 percent, due to reflections at the two surfaces. However, these two rays turn out to be significantly different in character from ordinary light, caused by a phenomenon called polarization. The ordinary light in the incident ray is a wave where vibrations are taking place at random in all directions transverse to the beam. In each of the two emergent rays, the light vibrations occur strictly in a plane, these two planes being at right angles to each other.

The pronounced birefringence property made the Iceland spar crystals very valuable for use in science. By letting polarized light from one crystal interact with a material (by refraction, transmission, absorption, etc.) and analyzing with help of another crystal what happened to the light in this process, much information could be gathered about the internal structure of that material. Light from hot objects or from the sky, reflected light, fluorescence, light in rainbows, could also be analyzed by these crystals.

Regarding the weapons referred to in *A Duke's Promise,* research using polarized light has indeed

advanced many branches of physics, chemistry, crystal-
lography, mineralogy, materials science, engineering,
etcetera by up to several decades compared to the
estimated progress of science without Iceland spar in
the nineteenth and early twentieth centuries. It is suf-
ficient here to mention the electromagnetic theory of
J. C. Maxwell (c. 1865): its conception depended to
a significant degree on experiments by himself and
others with polarized light. It is therefore certain that
these crystals indirectly aided in the development
of modern weaponry, such as high-energy lasers and
nuclear bombs.

Reading this and discovering that Einstein used Icelandic
crystal in his work, which contributed to his monumental
discoveries in the field of theoretical physics (especially for his
discovery of the law of the photoelectric effect), and the contri-
bution he made toward the making of the atom bomb, makes
the possibility of him finding Augusto's invention interesting
indeed. When I started this series, I had no idea the connections would come together so beautifully. Of course, God did,
and He gets full credit for that.

Leo Kristjánsson said it best to me when he said, "The
description of colors and music is a bit difficult to imagine, but
it could well be made to look credible in an animated scene of
a movie."

I agree.

A little science, a little imagination, and an invention
that gives us a peek into heaven. Perhaps someday we will see
Augusto's music machine on the silver screen.

Or something like it past heaven's glorious gates.

Discussion Questions

1. When Gabriel finds out that Alexandria has kept her fear that John violated her from him, he is upset and wonders if he really knows his wife. Has your spouse or someone close to you ever done something so shocking (good or bad) that you wondered if you really knew that person? Or was it you? What happened and how did you handle it?

2. Alexandria is struggling with adapting to communicating with Gabriel with his hearing problems and being newly married. If you are married, what was that first year like for you? Anything you would go back and tell yourself if you could? If not married, what do you imagine the first year is like? Any advice you would give yourself beforehand?

3. When Gabriel's hearing comes back on the ferry, he is joyful, hopeful, and yet fearful that it won't last. Have you or someone close to you had an "affliction" that kept you on edge and having to day by day trust God to get through the roller coaster emotions of it? What happened? Any Scriptures that really helped during that time?

4. Along the same theme as the last question: When things get tough in life and you're going through a valley or trial, what are some of your immediate reactions? Do you:

- Call on friends?
- Submerse yourself in the Bible and prayer?
- Muddle through with a depressed/bitter/sad attitude?
- Seek counseling from church/books/other resources?
- Cling to your spouse and/or loved ones?
- Pull yourself up by the bootstraps and plow through alone?
- Other?

5. As they better adjust to being married, Gabriel and Alexandria learn to work together and allow each other to bring their individual strengths to the adventure they are on. If you were on a quest, what would your greatest strengths be? Weaknesses?

6. Gabriel and Alexandria hire impersonators to fool the regent's guards, and anyone else who might be spying on them, that they are still honeymooning in Paris while they escape to Italy. How are your skills at impersonating others? Can you mimic anyone? Who would you like to impersonate for a day if you could?

7. Gabriel and Alexandria take a big risk and journey by hydrogen balloon to reach Italy faster. What's the biggest risk you've ever taken? How did it turn out?

8. Have you ever been on a hot air balloon or something similar (parasailing, bungee jumping, skydiving, extreme sport or ride, etc.)? If not, would you like to? Which one?

9. Gabriel is in distress while on the balloon and vacillates between coping with the fear/anxiety and trusting God that He is in control and has it all planned for Gabriel's good. Have you ever tried hard to trust God but kept falling back when the pressure was too great? The Bible has a lot to say about trials:

- 1 Peter 1:7 (KJV): "That the trial of your faith, being much more precious than of gold that perisheth, though it be tried with fire, might be found unto praise and honour and glory at the appearing of Jesus Christ."
- 1 Peter 4:12–13 (NIV): "Dear friends, do not be surprised at the fiery ordeal that has come on you to test you, as though something strange were happening to you. But rejoice inasmuch as you participate in the sufferings of Christ, so that you may be overjoyed when his glory is revealed."
- James 1:12 (NIV): "Blessed is the one who perseveres under trial because, having stood the test, that person will receive the crown of life that the Lord has promised to those who love him."

How do you deal with the trials in your life?

10. Alexandria's parents have been captured and thrown into the dungeon. Have you ever had a "prison" experience? What happened?

11. Sometimes, right before a big breakthrough, people endure trials and suffering to the point where they want to give up. Have you ever experienced this? What happened?

12. The machine at the end turns out to be so much more than they thought. What did you think of what it turned out to be? Did you have a guess beforehand?